UNRAVELED
THE HENRY BROTHERS

AMY KNUPP

CHAPTER 1

There was a reason I hadn't been back to my hometown in sixteen years.

Sixteen life-changing years. Yet as I approached the town limits of Dragonfly Lake on this brisk, drizzly March morning, there it was. That familiar feeling slid into my gut like an acid bath, sucking my self-confidence out of me and threatening to turn me back into an insecure girl from the wrong side of the tracks.

The ancient wooden sign that read "Welcome to Picturesque Dragonfly Lake, Population: More than a Couple Dozen"—hand-carved by Anna Delfico's grandfather long before the population had grown to more than a few thousand on a good summer weekend—came into view. I sat up straighter and steeled myself.

I glanced down at my armor—high-dollar, designer-label, tailored black pants, silky cream-colored blouse, the trench coat that'd cost more than my monthly rent, and especially the red-soled, black ankle boots—and muttered out loud, "You're not that girl anymore."

My silver Lexus ES 350 was further proof, considering my ride out of Dragonfly Lake all those years ago had been in the passenger seat of my friend Holden Henry's beat-up old puke-green Chevy Impala.

But as soon as I reached the downtown area—the highway becoming Main Street and the speed limit plummeting—I bit down on the inside of my lip, taking in the sight of everything that had once been so familiar. The elementary school, where I'd been the janitor's daughter. The high school, where I'd been the geeky straight-A student with no social life to speak of. The Dragonfly Diner, where all the kids hung out for fries and shakes—except me.

I turned the radio on and cranked up a rock music station, as if that could drown out the world outside my windows. When I was almost to the lake itself, its grayness blending in with the colorless sky, I took a right turn on Honeysuckle Road and forced my mind to the mission at hand.

My boss, Angelica Marks, had summoned me to a construction site meeting with no concern for my Monday schedule or my to-do list that never seemed to get any shorter. I was fine with the to-do list and the schedule and was used to doing whatever Angelica required. It was part of my job as the executive vice president of development for Marks International Hotels, a job I mostly loved.

My relationship with Angelica was not so clear-cut. On the one hand, she was a difficult person. Demanding, a perfectionist, with a cold edge to her personality that didn't encourage close personal ties. She expected the utmost from her employees, but I couldn't fault her for that. Those expectations were why she led a billion-dollar boutique hotel development company with sixty-two exclusive properties around the globe. She'd built up Marks International from nothing, and despite her less-than-warm personality, she inspired loyalty and hard work from her minions. My assistant, Bethany, was holding down the fort for me in the

Nashville office, as curious as I was about why Angelica needed to talk in person.

All that aside, I owed Angelica for everything I had. Which was why, when she'd texted me at six forty-nine a.m., asking me to make the hour-plus drive to the jobsite at Dragonfly Lake, I'd told her I'd be there by eight thirty.

The clock on the dash read 8:23, but the hotel site, just a mile or so down the road from the town I'd grown up in, was only three minutes away. Closer than I liked to cut it, but traffic in Nashville had been particularly shit show-ish.

I hung a left onto the construction site and couldn't deny the little spark of excitement at laying my eyes on Marks International's latest endeavor. It wasn't quite finished, but the exterior was getting there, and it was impressive. It made my blood pump to see it in person, something I didn't normally get to do until a property was finished.

As the VP of development, I was involved in demographic analysis, site selection, and the preliminary details for each new property. Scouting was a big part of my job. With this particular property, though, Angelica had seen the real estate listing on the shore of Dragonfly Lake and decided she wanted a property close to home. That had essentially taken me out of the equation, which was ideal, since I'd been avoiding going back for so long.

Scanning the muddy lot, I located the trailer that had been Angelica's temporary home office for the past several months, parked my car, headed up the three steps, and went inside.

I expected to find my boss rattling off orders to her assistant, Sabrina, or with a phone to her ear, giving someone a silent glare that somehow transmitted over the line. Instead, she sat at the desk, alone, staring off into the distance, rubbing her chin pensively with one hand.

Weird.

Angelica was a lot of things, but pensive wasn't one of

them. She was all about action. Getting shit done and done right. Yesterday.

"Good morning," I said.

She jerked toward me, as if she hadn't heard me come in. Also out of character.

"Good morning, Chloe. Have a seat." She offered what I'd almost call a smile. It didn't really reach her eyes, but still, usually she didn't even try, and I tilted my head, thinking, *What the hell is going on?*

"Where's Sabrina?"

"She's handling a meeting with the landscape architect's team. Would you like some tea?" she asked, leaning her thin frame forward and nodding at her mug. "I've got cinnamon goji berry matcha."

I was a coffee girl through and through, and Angelica always had been too. It was one thing we bonded over—as much as a girl could bond with her cold, strict boss—the coffee in the office had to be high-quality Jamaican blend, or sometimes we got ahold of some top-notch Hawaiian. Angelica insisted on it even though she was onsite at the latest property eighty-five percent of the time.

Even if I were a tea lover, that blend sounded like some kind of health potion. "I'm good," I told her as I sat in one of the hard, uninviting chairs opposite her. I took out my electronic tablet, ready to jot down whatever I needed to act on, as I always did.

"No notes," Angelica said, sounding… restrained. Serious. She was always serious as a heart attack, but today she was… morose.

My heart pumped harder as adrenaline shot through me. What crisis had cropped up? What obstacle did we need to overcome? Trouble-shooting and thinking on our feet were big parts of our jobs, but something in her tone in those two short words told me this one was going to be a doozy.

"What's going on?" I prompted when she didn't immediately speak up.

She opened her mouth as if to answer, then closed it, and my imagination went wild. Was there an issue with the latest inspection? Had someone screwed up majorly enough to make us miss our deadline for opening? Had there been a construction accident and the foreman had landed in the hospital? That was the kind of vibe I was getting from her.

Instead of filling me in, she pushed her chair back and stood, crossed her arms, paced a few steps, and stopped with her back to me.

"Angelica?"

She pivoted, the move efficient and precise. I heard her inhale, then she said, "On Friday, I was diagnosed with an aggressive type of brain cancer."

My heart stopped. My brows shot up, and my mouth gaped open as that sank in. I tried to swallow my fear on her behalf and watched her, waiting for her to tell me it wasn't so, but of course, if it wasn't, those words would never have crossed her lips. She wasn't one to joke around. Her face gave no hint of emotion.

"I'm… God, Angelica. I'm so sorry to hear that."

She walked back to her desk, then past it, as if she couldn't bear to sit down, and I watched her for a cue. I'd learned to read her pretty well in the twelve years I'd worked for her, but she wasn't making eye contact and had her walls up high. Now that I looked harder, I noted she looked tired, worn down, a little thinner than usual, with dark shadows under her eyes.

As I was trying to come up with something else to say—what the actual hell was the right thing to say in this situation?—she lowered herself to her chair. There was a millisecond when her defenses failed her, and her chin succumbed to a minute quiver, then she clenched her jaw against it.

"I'm taking this week to organize, and I'll be out indefinitely starting next Monday." I was still playing catch-up in my head when she continued, "I want you to take over the Dragonfly Lake project, effective as soon as you can get your team prepped to cover for you."

"Of course," I said on autopilot. Her wish, my command. Never mind that it was a giant honor to step in as the leader of this project—of any project—in her stead. I'd process that later, after the whole cancer bombshell took hold.

I wanted to ask her what her prognosis was. That seemed like pertinent info whether it was your boss or your family member, but...

Hell. What would happen to Marks International if she wasn't here to run it?

Would I even have a job in a year's time?

Congrats on being the most self-centered girl on the planet.

"I don't request that of you lightly," Angelica said, all business. "I know this town makes you uncomfortable."

"It's okay," I assured her.

Uncomfortable wasn't the right word. *Regressive* was more spot-on. Dragonfly Lake had the power to make me regress to that insecure teenage version of me in a heartbeat. It wasn't logical, but I'd experienced it first-hand not fifteen minutes ago.

But regressing seemed like nothing compared to what Angelica was dealing with. I would big-girl-panty my way through it and count my blessings. Bethany was a top-notch assistant, and between us, we'd figure out how to conquer the upcoming challenges.

Questions zipped through my mind so fast I couldn't decide what to ask first. Before I could say another word, she continued.

"The more you can sit in on this week, the better. I'd like a smooth transition. With three months till opening, we don't have time for delays or bumps. We can't push back any of the future projects."

At the word *future*, Angelica's brow furrowed slightly, which was saying something, because I was ninety-eight percent sure she Botoxed regularly.

"You'll be back in time for the Hallstatt project," I said supportively.

At Marks, we generally had one project in construction stages at a time. Hallstatt, Switzerland, was directly after Dragonfly Lake, and we were scheduled to break ground in July.

She laughed hollowly, then sobered up in an instant. "I don't think so." She pressed her lips together. "If the doctors can be believed—and I'm seeing some of the most reputable in the country—I'll be lucky to be alive in a year."

"You're a fighter, Angelica—"

"Oh, I'm going to fight. But I'm also a realist." She swallowed and blinked, and once again, she looked... human. Vulnerable. Scared.

I'd never in my life seen Angelica Marks look scared. Not for a single second.

I wanted to contradict what she said, throw out some positive something, but I knew that wouldn't help.

"I never thought I'd have to consider what to do with my life's endeavor at age forty-eight," Angelica continued. "I've always planned to work until I'm eighty."

I nodded. I'd heard her say she had no intention of ever retiring. She thrived on her work, lived for it. Put everything she had into it. She was an inspiration to me, regardless of her less-than-warm personality.

"I spent the weekend thinking." She let out another humorless laugh. "So much damn thinking, and none of it happy thoughts. Let me tell you, Chloe, it sucks to look at your own life from a new perspective and realize how much you've screwed up."

"I don't think you've screw—"

"I've lived my life all wrong," she insisted in that tone that brooked no arguments.

I bit down on anything I was going to say and sat back to listen. Because clearly she was going somewhere with this or needed to get something off her chest, and that was the one thing I could offer her.

"I've put every last drop of my focus into this company. I've loved it more than any man in my life, nurtured it the way most women nurture a child, put all my hopes and dreams into it."

"You know I've always admired your dedication," I said.

She was shaking her head, still looking off into the distance. "It was all wrong. I was wrong. I should've made time for a family, should've let myself fall in love, get married, have children. Because as it stands, I have no heirs to leave my life's work to. This is my legacy"—she spread her arms to encompass the portable office, but I knew she meant the whole company—"and... who cares?"

It was on the tip of my tongue to assure her that I cared, but she went on, picking up steam.

"I'm worth nearly a billion dollars, a billion fucking dollars, Chloe, and I've got no one to share that with. My company is worth even more, and I have no family to will it to. No children to carry on my endeavors. All these years, I knew what I was giving up. There were moments when I was lonely, when I would've liked to have someone there for me, with me, but instead I chose to give everything I have to this company. But guess what? This company won't be there to hold my hand when my hair falls out. No flesh and blood of mine will be there to see that my life's work goes anywhere. And all of a sudden, with that doctor's words on Friday..." She shook her head, and her voice went quieter. "All of sudden, that matters to me, Chloe."

I sucked in a shaky breath, stunned by what she said and,

I could admit, a little twitchy at the fact that I had a similar take on work. But this wasn't about me, and I was only thirty-four anyway.

"I have never felt such regret as I did over the weekend," Angelica continued. "Heart-deep regret that I have no one. No built-in support system when I need it. No Marks offspring to take over when I'm gone."

"I'm sorry," I said, knowing full well how lame that response was. I searched for something better to say. Anything. Came up blank as a brand-new whiteboard.

My boss shook her head and sat up straighter, finally looking directly at me, as if coming out of a fugue. "After deliberating for the past forty-eight hours, I've decided to leave Marks International to one of two people. Either Gloria or you."

I fought not to let any reaction show on my face.

Eighty percent of business is keeping your emotions out of it. You can have them, just don't show them and don't make decisions based on them.

How many dozens of times had Angelica hammered that into my head? I grasped on to that tenet now. But I'll be honest—my initial reaction was…Gloria fucking Herrera?

She, too, was an executive VP—there were five of us in the company. She, too, had been handpicked in college by Angelica to be mentored and eventually to enter the fast track within the company.

"I'll be straight with you, though, Chloe… I'm leaning hard toward Gloria."

I bit down on my lip, literally to keep from saying the first thing that came to mind. Another habit honed by my boss.

I tilted my head and waited for her to say more.

Angelica shot a half grin my way and said, "I can hear your thoughts, Ms. Abrams. You're wondering why. What Gloria has that you don't."

Pretty much. I nodded succinctly.

"You're my best worker," she said. "There's no question. You're my workhorse, my go-to, my office mate on the weekends. But to give you this company would guarantee you'd continue to make the same mistakes I've made. All work, nothing else worthwhile in your life. And yes, you have the right to make those decisions for yourself, but I don't have to be an accomplice anymore. I won't be."

I frowned. What part of *you're my go-to* equaled *not entrusting my company to you*? It made about as much sense as building a luxury hotel in the slums.

"Gloria leaves by six o'clock every night," I pointed out, beyond biting down on my lip now.

"To go home to her family. She has balance in her life, like you and I have never had. She works her butt off for ten hours a day and then she goes home to recharge."

"You're punishing me for being hardworking?"

"Not punishing. Trying to help you in my possibly misguided way. But I'm the boss. I can do that." Her tone was closer to her usual pre-cancer-diagnosis one. "When was the last time you had a relationship with a man, Chloe?"

I didn't bother to reply because she knew the answer. I didn't do relationships. I did flings, hookups, and a lot of solo nights. By choice. But it was my choice, dammit, and it should be considered a positive attribute, not a weakness.

"When was the last time you even went on a date?"

Holden, my friend from childhood, came to mind, because two weeks ago, he'd taken me to his dad's wedding as his plus-one. We were just friends, regardless of the fact that I'd had a thing for him since high school, but...

As long as it's not hurting anyone, sometimes it's best to tell people what they want to hear and make it true afterward.

"The guy I went to the wedding with a couple of weeks ago? We've been... seeing each other."

If you called texting back and forth like we always had *seeing each other*. But this wasn't hurting anyone. In fact,

Holden never needed to know. Probably. And if he did, well, I'd figure that out when I needed to, but he was a good guy, and he'd likely play along if necessary.

Angelica narrowed her eyes at me, and it made me want to squirm. Luckily I was also well versed in resisting the squirm urge.

"What's the name of this man?"

"Holden Henry. He lives here in Dragonfly Lake. I've known him since grade school, and something just… clicked at the wedding."

Not exactly a lie, if clicking could be one-sided and if you overlooked the fact that it'd been years since my initial one-sided "clicking" with Holden.

She studied me silently for several seconds that stretched out tautly. "Is it serious?"

"I've never felt like this about anyone else." That was completely true, pathetic or not, but in this moment, it served me well.

Angelica brought her steepled hands to her face and pressed her index fingers to her lower lip thoughtfully. Assessing. My gaze didn't waver.

"You can bring him to the anniversary dinner Friday night." She frowned. "Likely my last. I'd like to meet this gentleman."

Her tone didn't give me an opening to argue or hedge.

Holden had said he owed me one for being his wedding date. I hadn't taken him seriously at the time, but now… it looked like I might take him up on it. I just hoped he was free.

Telling him about my little mistruth to my boss would be embarrassing, but if I knew him, he'd laugh it off, give me a hard time, then play along if at all possible.

Please let it be possible.

Because as much as I'd wanted Holden over the years, I'd always wanted even more to one day take over for Angelica. I'd never once imagined it could be this soon, but I was capable and ready when needed; there wasn't a doubt in my mind. Contrary to Angelica's belief, I did care as much as any heir or offspring could. In fact, I cared more. Like she'd said, I lived exactly like her, giving this company my all.

And since it wasn't hurting anyone, I would happily pretend Holden and I had a serious relationship if it gave me a better chance of being the one Angelica chose to take her life's work into the future.

I just needed to find a way to break it to him.

CHAPTER 2

"Last thing on my list," my brother Seth said as my other brother, Cash, checked his watch.

I already knew it was ten till eleven and that Cash was itching to get back into the kitchen to make sure everything was under control for lunch. I also knew without checking that it was. His kitchen staff was on top of things. They had to be, otherwise Chef Cash could morph into a stereotypical temperamental tyrant right before their very eyes.

I raised my brows at Seth to encourage him to get on with it. We all had shit to do.

As Seth met my gaze, there was a flash of something in his eyes that put me on alert. Told me I wasn't going to like whatever his "last thing" was.

"Spit it out," I said, leaning my elbows on table nineteen of Henry's Restaurant.

This was our meeting spot every Monday at ten a.m., strategically located to avoid pissing matches over whose office we met in, Seth's or Cash's. My office was the bar, but when we'd tried meeting there, they'd accused me of paying more attention to the behind-the-bar tasks than the agenda.

"The Bergman lot," Seth said, tapping the eraser of his mechanical pencil on his handy-dandy notebook.

My jaw clenched before I could check that reaction.

"It's time to do something with it," Seth continued as my body tensed. "I'm going to call Darius Weber this week to get his take on what we might be able to get out of it."

Cash's response was a single nod.

I was just opening my mouth to give my opinion on calling the real estate agent when Seth jumped back in.

"It's not good business to let a lakefront lot sit there and do nothing for us. You know that."

I did know that, but it did nothing to lower my frustration.

"Another month," I bit out. "Give Kemp and me another month to reorganize, see what our next move is."

"We're not putting it on the market yet. Just gathering info," Seth said in that tone intended to make peace and reassure. Shocking to no one who met the three of us, Seth was the middle brother and was often a buffer between Cash and me—and Hayden, our little sister, and me as well.

"We've held on to it for years for this brewery pipe dream," Cash said. "That's not paying the bills."

I snapped, "You got your pipe dream with your oversized kitchen for your oversized ego—"

"Guys, reel it in," Seth broke in. "You can beat the hell out of each other later, but this is a business meeting. Quit provoking him," he said to Cash. "Stop taking his fucking bait," he directed at me.

"Can't have a restaurant without a functional kitchen," Cash said.

"Dammit, Cash. No one's debating that," Seth said, his voice entirely under control even though my oldest brother and I knocked skulls regularly and aggravated the hell out of him.

There was a good possibility Cash and I knocked skulls more than necessary for just that reason. It was amusing to get a rise out of the most even-tempered of all of us.

This time was for real though. Cash was being a grade-A asshole, which wasn't at all out of character for him.

"We have eight minutes until Riley unlocks the doors, and you know Sergio and Marty will be right in for the Monday COMs meeting. Can we finish?" Seth said.

The Curmudgeonly Old Men convened here every Monday and Friday to discuss books, argue politics, and grump at each other. The two seniors Seth mentioned were always early.

Cash gestured for him to get on with it while I nodded tightly.

"Holden, we agreed to give you to the end of last year to see where you and Kemp could get on finding acceptable investors for the brewery idea. It's been almost three months since then. Last week's news wasn't what any of us hoped for, but we can't sit on the land forever."

"I know that," I said in a low voice. I shook my head, because I really didn't have much of a leg to stand on when it came to more time.

We'd been so sure we'd finally found an investor who didn't insist on gaining too much control over our business. When they'd decided to fund a different project, we'd been devastated.

The "brewery idea," as Seth called it, was my dream, not my brothers'. Mine and Kemp Essex's, who I'd been friends with for years. We'd always loved beer and had gotten into our share of trouble long before we were legal, in part due to that love of malt and hops. A dozen or so years ago, I'd delved into home brewing, and Kemp had been immediately intrigued. So intrigued that he'd eventually gone to school specifically to become a brewmaster. I'd taken some classes as well, plus had a shit ton of experience home brewing. Between the two of us, we'd be able to run one hell of a brewery, and we hoped to do it in conjunction with the restaurant that had been in my family since the sixties—Henry's.

There was just the small matter of start-up money, which, in fact, was anything but small.

Because we'd taken out a big loan three years ago to remodel and add on to the restaurant, Henry's was already deep in the hole. We were climbing our way out steadily, maintaining profitability, but banks weren't lining up to add to our debt.

Kemp and I had been trying to find private investors, but there were lines we weren't willing to cross as far as how much control we were willing to give up.

I'd dreamed of capitalizing on my family's double lot with over two hundred feet of frontage on Dragonfly Lake. Until the past couple of years, though, my focus hadn't been spectacular. I'd had my hands full with managing the front of house for Henry's plus my social life. Yeah, it sounds shallow and stupid now, but I was busy enjoying my twenties. It wasn't until my grandmother died, leaving the restaurant to my brothers and me—and Hayden if she'd wanted it—that we went all in on the remodeling, revamping, re-everything of Henry's.

I still had a lot going on socially, but I liked to think I'd stepped it up and taken on a lot more responsibility as well. I just wasn't sure I'd convinced my business partner brothers of that. Maybe I never would.

"I'll keep you two apprised of everything I learn from Darius," Seth said, as if that could appease me.

I wasn't appeased, but I was out of arguments for the day.

"Anything else?" I asked.

"That's all I've got," Seth said.

"I've got a chowder to check on," Cash said as he shoved back from the table and stood, then sauntered off.

I headed toward the bar, which I'd had my back to during the meeting, facing, instead, the view of the lake. When I went from the dining area to the bar, the scowl on my face eased as I did a double take of the woman sitting at the bar on the far stool, closest to the main door.

Her profile was to me, her head buried in her phone, hair cascading down to block her face, but I'd know those glossy coffee-brown locks anywhere.

I went toward her. "Chloe?"

Sure enough, her head popped up and she shot me a half-hearted smile as she sat up straighter. She was dressed in tailored business clothes and looked like the badass competent woman she was, except... there was something *off*. Like she was nervous maybe. She glanced my way but not *at* me.

Whenever Chloe was uneasy, it made me wary and ready to handle whatever had her off-kilter. Small towns didn't tend to be kind to the janitor's daughter, and she'd taken more than her share of shunning and bullying and being treated as less than. I'd gotten into more than one fistfight in high school on her behalf, and eventually the guys got the message that she was off-limits. A few of the girls, though... High school girls could be something else.

I glanced around for the source of her uneasiness, but there was no one else in the bar.

Once I was behind the counter, facing her directly, I raised my brows in question, unable to tamp down on a big, welcoming grin.

"Hey, EVP," I said, my nickname for her ever since she'd been promoted to executive vice president.

"Hi," she said simply. No explanation for why she was suddenly back in Dragonfly Lake.

"What the hell are you doing here? Don't get me wrong; I'm happy, but...?"

"Hoping to get some lunch at what I've heard is the best place in town." She looked from side to side, sizing up the bar and the adjacent dining area, one of three. "It's incredible what you guys have done to it."

"Which you would know if you'd ever been back in the past however many years. Why now?"

"I was summoned to meet with my boss at the worksite this morning."

"Good ol' Madame Dictator. She treating you okay?"

"She treats me well and you know it," Chloe said, and I could swear her uneasiness increased as she fidgeted.

"She *pays* you well," I corrected. "Not the same. Can I get you a drink?"

"Got any coffee?"

"Got something better." I opened the under-the-counter fridge and took out the growler I'd brought from home. I grabbed a beer-tasting glass and held it up in question.

"One of your concoctions?" she asked. Of course, if she'd ever come around these parts, she'd know. When I had a good batch of home brew, I didn't chintz on sharing with friends.

"It's a strawberry-lemonade pale ale. Better for summer, but I never know how long it'll take to get it right."

Chloe eyed it with less enthusiasm than I'd hoped.

"I see how you are," I said. "You stop in town for a history-making visit, come into my restaurant for the first time since my brothers and I have owned it, but you only want to go halfway." Teasing dripped from my tone, and I gave her my butt-hurt act.

"Stop," she said with a laugh. "If your ego needs me to try it, then pour me a taste. A small taste," she tacked on as I lifted the growler victoriously to pour. "I have to drive back to the office after lunch. The Nashville office," she clarified.

With respect to that, I kept it to half the sampler glass. This was stronger than the average beer.

After sliding the glass to her, I pulled out a menu and set it in front of her.

She ignored the menu, taking the small glass—a rounded bowl with a short stem—in her hand. With a tilt of her head, she studied the light blond liquid.

"Try it already," I said. "You're killing me."

"Didn't want to get a-*head* of myself." She grinned and waited for me to acknowledge her pun.

"How much *lager* are you going to make me wait?" I tossed back.

With a laugh, she said, "Whatever it takes to make you *hoppy.*"

With that, she tipped the glass up and took a dainty, tentative swallow.

As she lowered the glass and let the liquid roll over her taste buds, her eyes widened. I was suitably gratified when she took another, bigger swig, her reluctance gone.

"Holden, this is really good."

Comments like that never got old. "See what you've been missing?"

"I'm impressed. If I didn't have to work, I'd order the whole bottle."

"You would not, lightweight."

As Chloe raised her glass again, Seth came behind the bar and helped himself to a cola from the fountain.

"Chloe," he said, showing some of the same surprise I had. "It's good to see you."

"You too," she said. "What would you recommend for lunch?"

"Smoked pork sandwich is popular," Seth said. "Or if you want a salad, the walleye niçoise is my favorite."

"Thanks."

While she continued to peruse the menu, Seth said in a quieter voice directed at me, "You okay?"

"Fine," I said, managing to keep emotions out of it. I

wasn't fine, but I also wasn't a four-year-old. And I didn't really blame my brothers for not having a brewery underway. I blamed Cash for being an asshole but nothing more.

With a nod, Seth left the area and went to do what he did best—hide away in his office.

"I'm going to take the pork advice," Chloe said. She studied the menu another few seconds. "A salad for my side, please."

As I went to the register to enter her order, she said, "Why'd he ask if you're okay?"

Once I input the order, I sauntered back in front of her, taking in the rest of the place with a quick glance. A forty-something couple I didn't know had just come in the door and were being greeted by Elijah, the weekday lunch host. Sarai, one of the servers, was at table seventeen rolling silverware in napkins. Sergio and Marty were making their way from the parking lot to the door.

I let my gaze skim over Chloe sitting there in my bar, with her pretty brown eyes, soft-looking skin, and uncharacteristic unsureness. She was watching me not-so-patiently, so I blew out my breath and filled her in. "That possible investor I told you about at the wedding? Fell through a few days ago. My brothers are ready to sell off the Bergman lot."

Her lashes lowered in disappointment that I knew was real—Chloe was always real with me. "That sucks, Holden. I'm sorry."

My friendship with Chloe was weird. We'd been friends since grade school, when her mom had been a server at this very restaurant, which was then owned and run by my grandmother. On the nights when both of Chloe's parents had to work late, my mom let her stay at our house, which was several evenings a week.

We'd been in the same grade, reluctant buddies at first. She liked to read and I liked to raise hell. The thing that eventually broke the ice, though, was a school library book I brought home one week. It was a book of puns for kids. I liked it because it made me laugh, and she probably liked it because it was a book. We'd spent hours reading them aloud, a section at a time, laughing and making up our own. Puns had been our thing ever since.

Now I talked to her every few weeks, or more often if a punny mood struck one of us. We'd been known to message back and forth for a stretch of days, exchanging puns. We'd also been known to go weeks without seeing each other, since she lived an hour away in the city, and she refused to set foot back here. Yet whenever we saw each other, usually lunch or dinner when I was in Nashville for something, it was as if we'd talked just yesterday. It was why I'd taken her to my dad's wedding. I'd wanted to take a plus-one, but I hadn't wanted a *date* date because I'd still been a little weird about my dad remarrying. Chloe had been exactly what I needed—supportive and comfortable.

"What's another setback at this point?" I said as if it didn't matter. It mattered, but it wasn't going to defeat us. We just needed time to reorganize.

"It sounded like it was a done deal," she said. "Which makes it suck double, huh?"

"We've got some colder leads to double back on."

"Take a sample of this stuff when you meet with them." She set her empty glass down. "Truly, if everything you brew is as good as that, people will be lining up to invest." Her eyes narrowed. "It's potent too. May I... have another half glass?"

Maybe it would help her relax. The longer she sat there, the more wound up she seemed. Once Sarai brought her lunch out, I went to the walk-in to grab some stock that had gotten low over the weekend, busied myself prepping the bar for the week, and stepped in to seat Loretta Lawson and Dotty Jaworski while Elijah was seating another group.

When I got back behind the bar, Chloe had drained the second beer and pushed her half-eaten lunch away.

"It's not good?" I asked. "I can get you something else."

"What? Oh. No, it's good. Really good. I'm not that hungry."

"What's bugging you, EVP Chloe?"

She threw her head back and closed her eyes. I heard her take in a breath. Then she came forward and thumped both hands on the bar, not quite looking at me.

"I… did a dumb thing."

"That doesn't sound like you."

Without acknowledging my comment, she told me about her meeting with her boss. I straightened as she explained the woman's diagnosis and impending absence. The more Chloe explained about taking over the Dragonfly Lake project, the more I considered taking back all the bad things I'd said about Madame Dictator over the years. It sounded like she was finally giving Chloe the responsibility, recognition, and opportunity she deserved.

And then she got to the part about her coworker being favored because she was married and settled.

"What the hell? That's counterintuitive," I said.

"That's my opinion as well," Chloe said. "She went on about balance and how she's lived wrong and doesn't want me to make the same mistakes."

I scowled and maybe growled a little, because once again, the world was throwing Chloe a roadblock. This girl could not catch a damn break. She'd tell you meeting Angelica in the business mentoring program at her college was a break, but I maintained it was the beginning of a long, punishing sentence. And here was more proof.

"I'm having trouble summoning sympathy for that woman," I muttered.

"I don't plan to lie down and let Gloria have it without a fight."

"Thatta girl." I nodded resolutely.

Chloe pressed her lips together, her face scrunched into an expression of doubt. "I told Angelica I'm in a relationship. With you."

A grin crept across my face. Of course she had. "You're brilliant. Take that, Madame Dictator."

She didn't smile. Still didn't look at ease.

"What aren't you telling me?" I asked.

"I'm getting there," she snapped. "She asked if it was serious, and I said it was. So she insisted I bring you to the company's anniversary dinner this Friday."

"Okay." I nodded as that sank in. "Okay, we can do that. So an evening of acting 'serious.'"

It might be a little awkward, because there'd never been anything romantic between Chloe and me, but I could give that power-trip woman one hell of a show.

"Really? You aren't pissed?"

"I'm pissed as hell that she's throwing out this bullshit excuse to keep you from what you deserve. Trust me, we're going to give her a show. At the end of the evening, she'll have zero reasons not to leave you her company."

While her shoulders relaxed a little, her eyes still searched me, as if there was more to my reaction. There wasn't. I was in. One night of my life to help my deserving friend was nothing.

Chloe's lips switched from a frown to a slow grin. "You are my favorite human in the whole wide world, Holden Henry."

I went around the bar to stand next to her stool. She pivoted to face me. I took both of her hands in mine, lacing our fingers together in what I would call more than a friendly touch. On purpose. If we were going to be convincing, we needed to cross a couple of boundaries we'd never crossed before.

I pulled her to a stand, dragged her closer, and pressed a

brief kiss to her lips. It wasn't passionate, but it was the first time our lips had ever met. Hers were soft, warm, alluring. As I pulled her into a hug to reassure her, because I didn't miss the shock in her eyes when I'd kissed her, I got a whiff of her sweet, slightly floral scent like I never had before.

"That needed to happen before our show Friday night," I whispered in her ear. I could feel her head craning, looking to see if anyone had seen us kiss. I didn't care if they did, as it was nobody's business but ours.

"Probably true," she said. "You could've warned me." Though the words scolded, I could hear a smile in her tone.

"Friday night, be ready for anything, Chlo. We got this."

CHAPTER 3

CHLOE

thought I was ready for Friday night. It turned out I was wrong.

I was *so* not prepared for Holden and all of his attention, even though I'd spent four days psyching myself up for it, four nights losing sleep over it, and the two hours before he picked me up at my apartment coaching myself to be indifferent to him and his touch.

When I'd rushed out of Henry's on Monday about three minutes after that kiss and after losing a battle with Holden over paying my lunch tab, I'd sat in my car for a hundred and twenty seconds—as long as I thought I could get away with without Holden noticing and concluding I was a big mess after a platonic, two-second press of his lips to mine.

I'd driven to the town square, parked my car, and walked to the gazebo, umbrella in tow. Because of the weather, the square had been deserted, allowing me to stand there under the gazebo roof, suck in air, and try to regain my composure.

If anyone had asked, I would've told them I was getting the alcohol effect from that strong beer out of my system. But

Holden's effect on me was more potent than any alcohol I'd ever tried. After a half hour, I'd forced myself to get back in my car and drive to the Nashville office just in time for my meeting with my staff.

Tonight's annual company anniversary dinner was at Sin's in the Wentworth Hotel, which was close to downtown Nashville, on Hale Street. This was where it'd been for a few years, as it was Angelica's all-time favorite, and I couldn't argue that John Sinclair, the executive chef, always prepared fantastic food.

As Holden turned his Mustang into the parking garage, I hoped I could get the food down this year with my stomach such a mess of nerves.

He pulled into a spot and turned off the engine, then grabbed my hand.

"Wait a second," he said.

I would've replied, but my mouth was so dry I could hardly move my tongue.

Still holding my hand, he turned slightly toward me, as much as he could with the steering wheel in the way. I was studying our hands, my heart pounding. His was large, so strong, not smooth like the guys I tended to hook up with on the rare occasion I was moved to do so.

"I'm kissing you for real before we go in there," he said.

"For real?" Like, he meant it?

"Tongues and all. We're going to get this over with now, so we're at ease and as natural as possible in front of the dictator."

So not actually for real. *Get this over with* left no question about whether this meant anything to him. Though that's what I knew and expected, there'd been a little spark of hope for those two seconds before he dashed them.

This man had me so far off my game it wasn't funny. I needed to snap the hell out of it, or Angelica would see through the ruse in a New York minute. That wouldn't only be detrimental to my cause but super embarrassing. It was embarrassing enough I'd needed to stoop to this level, this dishonesty, in order to have a chance at my dreams.

Believe me, I'd questioned my own ethics numerous times over the past few days. However, coming clean at this point would be even more humiliating. Also, ultimately, I was confident that I would be better to lead this company than Gloria Herrera.

And there was the not-at-all-small matter that I loved Marks International nearly as much as Angelica did, and regardless of her dysfunctional personality, I still wanted to take her business to the top, continue to build its portfolio and status in the hotel industry. I'd put everything I had into it for more than twelve years, and I'd always envisioned being a part of this company until the day I retired.

I was jolted out of my thoughts when Holden cupped my chin and turned my head toward him in the nearly dark front seat. Without giving me another second to prepare, his lips landed on mine.

I tried not to get sucked in—figuratively speaking. I told myself, *Business. It's business. He's doing this as a favor.*

Holden's clean, woodsy scent and the rough, masculine texture of his jaw in my hand—no idea how my hand even got to his cheek—were too much. *Business* flew out the window by my second heartbeat.

I closed my eyes and breathed him in as I felt his tongue slide over my lips. I didn't hesitate to open to him, and swear to God, it was like a switch was flipped inside my body. Like all my little eggs in my needy ovaries had woken up at once and were screaming, *This one! Mate with this one!*

Pressure and need built deep in my core as our tongues met and tangled. My hand slid to the back of his head, and I clung to him, wishing I could arch my suddenly aching breasts into him.

Had I been more in my mind, I would've been mortified when a needy little moan came out of me.

When Holden replied with a growl, still kissing the hell out of me, I only slipped further under his spell.

He ran his fingers through my hair, catching them up in the long strands and keeping hold of me in a sort of caveman-like possessive move, and… oh, holy hell, I liked it.

I liked it to an embarrassing degree.

This was a game to him, I reminded myself, and that was enough to pull me back. Rein in my desire for him. I ended the kiss, took my hands back, and grabbed my purse from the floor. Breathing. Practically panting. Trying to catch my breath and reset my equilibrium.

God have mercy, Holden Henry kissed like a dream. A passionate, attentive, sexy-as-hell dream.

This was the absolute last thing I wanted to learn at that exact moment.

I had to go face a few dozen of my colleagues and fellow employees, and worse, Angelica "Madame Dictator" Marks.

Holden let out a breath that sounded like *whew*, and I wasn't sure what that meant. I couldn't let myself think about it right now. I hopped out and heard Holden's door open too, but not until I'd closed mine.

Somehow I had to figure out how to convince my boss Holden and I were serious, convince Holden I was unaffected by that kiss, and convince myself to not think too hard about any of it. Self-protection was vital—for both my pride and my heart.

And wasn't that just as easy as falling off a log?

Yeah, and knocking your head along the way, landing in a deep lake, and drowning.

Before I'd gotten enough oxygen to my brain to start thinking straight, Holden was at my side, taking my hand as if it was the most natural thing in the world.

"Like I said the other day, we've got this, EVP Chloe."

As we walked toward the nearest hotel entrance, I said, "You probably better come up with a better nickname for your *serious girlfriend* than EVP Chloe."

"You're right." He opened the door for me, and once we were making our way across the marble floor of the beautiful, classy lobby, he put his arm around me. It was a toss-up which I liked the feel of better—his hand on my waist or his fingers entwined with mine.

Bottom line, I liked them both too much.

But that would work in my favor for the next couple of hours, I reminded myself.

And then I would do a brain wash and try to forget all of the charade.

———

HOLDEN

"You take the lead, darlin'," I whispered into Chloe's ear as we walked into Sin's.

I loved the feminine smell of her hair. And while I was confessing, I'd just add that that kiss out there in my car? Jesus. It'd caught me off guard and turned me inside out. Chloe's response had been like throwing jet fuel on top of a bonfire.

Stand the fuck back.

I'd already known how badly she wanted Angelica to pick her to take the helm of the company, but the way she'd kissed me had thrown about three exclamation points on that fact.

People had been letting Chloe down since she was a little girl, and I was *not* about to be added to that list. We were going to convince her boss we were in love tonight, and we were going to win her the company in the end.

There were probably three dozen people in the upscale dining room, standing around, mingling, most of them with a cocktail in their hand. It had apparently been closed to the public for the evening, so this group had it to themselves. Right away, Chloe's assistant, Bethany, came up to us, and Chloe introduced us, then Bethany hurried off to greet others who'd just arrived.

All it took was a quick scan of the room for me to figure out which one was Chloe's boss. She was at least a few years older than most, but that wasn't what gave it away. The slender redhead had an air about her as if this was her kingdom and these were her worker bees. She held herself regally, her posture perfect, her business suit undoubtedly more expensive than my car. At her side was a brunette maybe a couple of years older than we were who I guessed was her unlucky assistant.

Though Angelica was smiling at the people she spoke to, there was a distance between her and everyone but her assistant, and I didn't just mean a physical distance. It was sad, actually, especially knowing what she was facing health-wise.

Chloe introduced me to a few people who were nearby, and I went to get her a cocktail and me a root beer. Alcohol was for relaxation and fun. Tonight was business, and I had a job to do.

When I returned to Chloe's side, I noticed Angelica and her sidekick making their way toward us. I slid my free arm around Chloe, resting my hand at her waist. She wore ankle-length tailored pants, a silky top with thin straps, and a cropped jacket. My hand found its way beneath the jacket, so there was only a thin fabric between me and her flesh. I felt her hip bone and the way her body dipped inward at her waist, and even though I was supposed to be prepping for the dictator lady, my mind took a side trip. Something about the intimate touch rattled me. I knew Chloe well, probably as well as anyone, save for her friend Presley and maybe her mom and dad, but I didn't know the female side of her. The sexual side. I hadn't given it any thought, because we'd always been buddies.

That hip bone though…

The feminine, intriguing curve inward of her torso…

With a mental head shake at myself, I turned my attention back to the women who were almost to us. This close, I could see the boss lady's eyes better, and there were shadows there, fatigue. And an astuteness that kicked my heart rate up as her gaze dipped down to my hand on Chloe's waist, as if she was assessing us. Looking for the truth.

I felt Chloe's body tense, and I gave her side a little squeeze, unsure whose benefit it was for—Chloe's, the dictator's, or my own.

"Good evening, Angelica," Chloe said. "Sabrina."

I wasn't sure if she was aware she huddled into me a little closer, but it worked for the charade.

"Chloe. I've been anticipating this." Chloe's boss gave me an obvious once-over, as if she hadn't been assessing the shit out of me from the moment we'd walked into the room.

"Angelica Marks, Sabrina Wilkes, this is my boyfriend, Holden Henry."

She didn't stutter over the word *boyfriend*. Of course she didn't. Chloe was a pro at business.

I had to remove my hand from her side in order to shake Angelica's hand. The woman's shake was everything I'd expect from a shark. Sabrina merely smiled warmly and said hello.

"I've been curious about the man who's lured Chloe into something besides work," Angelica said. "You're not at all what I expected."

The look on her face left no doubt that she'd expected *more*. Probably some douche in a suit with a seven-figure salary, a Porsche, and an Ivy League education. I was man enough to admit that kind of guy would be more suitable for

Chloe, at least on paper. But what she had was me. Tonight was about Chloe's needs, not my ego or issues.

A server approached Sabrina and consulted with her, and she excused herself to follow him to address whatever he needed.

I returned my attention to the dictator. "I know she's devoted to your company, so I'm flattered she chooses to spend her extra time with me. A lot of her extra time lately." I poured it on thick, smiling down at Chloe.

The boss lady raised a brow at me in challenge. "And this all just came on suddenly?"

"I like to think of it more as we've spent two and a half decades building our relationship and it's only deepened recently. Finally."

"And yet Chloe didn't mention it until this week."

"It's been…" Chloe spoke up at last, but she hesitated, and I silently encouraged her to keep going, whatever she was going to say. "It's felt a little too good to be true. I was afraid to jinx it."

"But now suddenly you're more sure?" the dictator asked, that damn brow going up again in doubt.

It pissed me off that this woman had so much power over Chloe. I was determined to set her straight once and for all. If this was my one chance to sell us, I was going all the hell in.

"Seems that way, since she agreed to marry me not two hours ago," I said, looking Angelica Marks straight in the eye. I wasn't proud of my skills at little lies, but let's just say growing up as the Henry troublemaker, I'd had some practice. Unlike all those times, this was for a damn good cause. One that was of the utmost importance to Chloe.

With my arm back around her, I felt a little jolt from her, and I hoped her boss had missed it.

I looked at my "intended" with a sheepish grin and said, "Was I not supposed to say anything? I'm sorry, darlin'." I pressed a quick kiss to her lips. "I'm dying to yell it from the rooftops."

As Chloe gazed up at me, her eyes spoke volumes. Chapter one was that she was going to kill me later.

"The ring will just have to be that much bigger," she joked, and not for the first time, I thought she was a genius.

"You don't have a ring?" the dictator asked, still looking skeptical.

"Spur-of-the-moment, from-the-heart thing. If you'd told me a month ago I'd have the chance to make Chloe mine forever, I would've told you it wasn't possible, as much as I've always wanted it. Tonight, the moment was just… right."

"It was perfect," Chloe managed, and the girl definitely had some acting chops I hadn't been aware of. The way she gazed into my eyes, even I was almost convinced she meant it.

Angelica studied us for a couple more seconds, then said, "Let me be the first to congratulate you." Her eyes narrowed an almost indiscernible amount, and though she said the right words, I could still feel her doubt. "I wish you a lifetime of happiness."

"What?" A man who'd been nearby apparently overheard our "news" and joined our huddle to get the details. The man he was with, who I was guessing to be his significant other, joined in, and both of them hugged Chloe and shook my hand.

Word spread faster than a rumor in a small town, and before dinner was served, champagne was flowing in our honor. People seemed genuinely happy for Chloe, which told me she was respected and liked among her colleagues. No surprise to me.

It started to make sense why she hadn't come back to Dragonfly Lake, where she'd never been treated right or as an equal, let alone as an executive vice president.

The influx of people congratulating us and wanting to

meet Chloe's "lucky guy" kept us busy and allowed me to avoid any private conversation with her. She'd likely save her scolding for later, in private, anyway.

I'd decided to enjoy the celebration while it lasted. With the whole company believing our engagement, it seemed like a win to me. I'd just have to remind Chloe of that.

CHAPTER 4

HOLDEN

The drive from the Wentworth Hotel to Chloe's apartment was only about three minutes, but it was the longest three minutes in recent history.

She hadn't said a word beyond short answers and a thanks here and there since we'd left the restaurant and walked back through that fancy lobby. Since there'd been no audience out there, we hadn't needed to act engaged or in love, and based on the tension pulsing through her, she very much was *not* in love. Pretty safe to say, at that moment, she didn't even like me.

I fully expected her to unleash on me any second. I'd known that was coming since about three seconds after I'd told her boss we were engaged, and I'd give her, we had some details to work out about how we'd handle this.

I'll be honest, as we'd sat there eating our prime rib and the dude to my right had gone on and on about his favorite spots to fish on Dragonfly Lake, I'd nodded and faked interest while my brain was catching up with what I'd gotten us into.

So I couldn't blame Chloe for being a little upset, but we'd figure out a game plan.

Any second now.

Instead of dropping her off in front of her high-rise building, I pulled into a visitor parking place, killed the engine, and got out. Before I could open her door for her, Chloe burst out of the passenger side, not meeting my gaze.

We walked side by side to the apartment lobby, got in the elevator, rode to the sixteenth floor, still in silence. Once she let us into her apartment, I braced myself, but there was no explosion.

I should've known better. Chloe wasn't one to lose her shit even when she was really upset. But still, it caught me off guard when she turned to face me and her eyes were about to overflow with tears.

"Chlo," I said, stepping toward her, but she put her hand up, shook her head.

There'd been plenty of times over the years when something had upset her nearly to the point of tears, but I was not used to being the cause of it.

I didn't like it.

"Go ahead and yell at me," I said. "Get it out."

She let out a frustrated, aggravated grunt. "I can't even really be mad at you because I know you did it to help me," she growled out. "But what in the name of God were you thinking, Holden?" She pressed her lips together and went on before I could answer. "Engaged? To be married? Do you realize the epic clusterfuck you've caused?"

Okay, that was closer to a rant than a cry, and I'd take that any day.

"Clusterfuck is a little strong."

"Are you serious? Have you thought this through?"

We'd been in the entryway, and she stepped into the kitchen now, opened a cabinet, took out... Twizzlers. Of course. Some people coped with alcohol, some with vaping, but Chloe's go-to was red licorice ropes.

She bought them by the jar, and she popped the top now and pulled one out.

As she took a bite, I said, "We'll figure it out, Chloe. The main thing is we convinced your boss that we're in a serious relationship."

With a loud exhale, Chloe turned away but didn't let go of her plastic tub of rope candy. I waited while she chewed, bit off another chunk, and chewed some more with her back to me.

"She's skeptical, to put it mildly," she finally said.

"We sprung it on her. We'll convince her in the end."

As she helped herself to another rope, she turned toward me again, giving me a look like I was dumb as dirt. "The way I see it," she said between bites, "we have three options. One, we break up in the next week. Call off the engagement. Two, we run away to Europe and live our separate, un-engaged lives and no one knows the difference. Three"—she scoffed— "we try to find a way to convince people we're really engaged for the next few months and deal with the breakup later."

I couldn't help it. I laughed at the Europe option. "They do have good beer in Europe, but that commute would be a killer. We're not backing down now. That would defeat the purpose. So I guess we're planning a wedding."

I acted nonchalant, but there was an uneasiness in my gut at the thought of anything to do with weddings and marriage. Until those words had popped out of my mouth earlier tonight, none of it was on my radar. Not for me, not any time soon. I hadn't had a girlfriend for... I didn't even know how long it'd been. A couple of years at least.

Now I was engaged. Sort of.

But not going back on my word, my scheme, or one of my longest friendships.

Okay. We could pull this off. Like she'd said, for a few months. I liked spending time with Chloe, so we'd just spend a lot more time together. And based on that test in the car tonight, kissing her sure as hell didn't suck. She was turned back toward the counter, still shoving candy in her mouth like Bugs Bunny chomping on carrots, and I looked at her in a new light, letting my eyes roam over her body like I hadn't before.

She was slender, tall, and though she dressed more business-badass than sexy, she had a body underneath that I suspected might be surprising in a good way, particularly if you found yourself suddenly engaged to her. I'd already felt the way her waist dipped in and her hips curved out, and I couldn't lie—now that I was thinking about her that way, I was curious. I wouldn't mind knowing more of her body.

I know. Typical horndog man. It *had* been a while since I'd gotten laid.

I shook myself out of that line of thought, back to the problem at hand. Because so far, sex was not on the table…

"It's going to be okay, Chloe."

"It's not going to be okay."

I shrugged. "We'll be convincing."

She whipped around, fire in her eyes. "Are you listening to yourself, Holden? Why would you want to put yourself through this charade? I'm going to be working in Dragonfly for the next few months, so it's not like we can claim to be too busy and hardly ever see each other."

I studied her face, with so much outrage in it, so much worry clouding her pretty eyes, and it tugged at something inside of me. That same something that was fed up with the world for making her fight extra hard for everything for so many years. Her parents were decent people and undeniably loved her, but even they had never really fought for her, probably because they'd always been so busy working multiple jobs to make ends meet.

I'd been accused of being a sucker for a damsel in distress

a time or two, but Chloe was no damsel in distress. Far from it. She'd always carried on, no matter what the world and its assholes threw at her, and now would be no different even if I begged off.

I wasn't going to beg off though.

I'd gotten her into this jam, and she and I would get her out.

"You need to move in with me," I said.

She laughed. Actually laughed, though I didn't think there was much humor in it. More like an *Are you fucking crazy?*

"You can come home to me, your fiancé, every night after work. We'll eat together, be seen around town together. People will get so used to seeing us together that they'll think nothing of it—"

"There's one big, fat flaw in your plan," she said.

Narrowing my eyes, I asked, "And that is…?"

"Who in their right mind from Dragonfly Lake would ever believe that you, Mr. Social, Mr. Popularity, would ever want to be with the outcast trailer trash girl?"

"Why wouldn't I? We've been friends for close to thirty years. You're pretty and smart and a master of puns. Why the hell wouldn't I see you as more than just a friend?"

A question I might need to ponder later, when I was alone.

"The real question," I went on, "is why you'd settle for me, a guy with no education who works at a restaurant."

"Owns a restaurant," she corrected. "Everyone loves you. Why wouldn't I?" Her cheeks pinkened slightly. "Think about this for a minute, Holden. Really think. You'd have a roommate, for starters. You haven't had one for a long time. You'd have to spend so much time being seen out and about with me that you'd get sick of it in a week. And you wouldn't be able to date other people. For months."

I might've flinched internally at that, just for a second, but realistically, I hadn't been on a date for a while. It wasn't easy to find someone new in a small town when you were in your thirties, and I didn't have time or energy to put toward meeting someone outside of Dragonfly Lake. I'd been working too much and spending my spare time with Kemp, trying to make our brewery dream viable.

"I'm fine with it. We'll have fun," I said.

"Holden—"

I didn't put a lot of thought into what I did next; I was just tired of arguing, tired of her coming up with reasons this wouldn't work when I was sure we could make it work. I closed the space between us, trapped her between my arms as I rested my hands on the countertop on either side of her, and kissed her.

Within seconds, I brought my hands to her back, because I wanted to feel her in my arms. The kiss that was supposed to be either for show or to shut her up turned into more as Chloe let out a sexy little whimper, wound her hands around my neck, and arched her body into mine.

As soon as I felt my body start to respond to her, I ended the kiss. I wasn't supposed to be into it for real, just convincing, and I didn't want to freak her out or make her think I had any motive for going through with a fake engagement other than getting her what she wanted for her career.

With a goofy grin to cover my reaction, I said, "Together we could be *pun*-stoppable."

She pressed her lips together, something close to a grin tugging at her mouth. "You really are a glutton for *pun*-ishment."

"On the contrary. I think you're *pun* in a million."

That got an eye roll and a head shake.

"Chloe," I said, going serious. "Do you want the dictator to rule you out as her predecessor or do you want to get what you want and deserve?"

"You know the answer to that," she said quietly, eyeing the red candy again.

I picked up the jar, took out a rope, and handed it to her,

not in the least bit tempted by it, as I thought red licorice was disgusting.

"You're the best person for the job, right? Better than Gloria?"

"By a long shot. Objectively speaking." The corners of her lips tilted upward.

"Then let's do this," I said. "We can get you moved in this weekend. Pack some clothes and we'll worry about your lease later."

She grabbed the jar and the candy from me as if her life depended on it, stuck one end in her mouth, and bit down with a vengeance. I couldn't completely keep the grin off my face, because this tough-as-nails girl seemed to think she needed artificial red dye and sugar to get through tricky decisions, hard times, and stress. Sometimes I swear she lost sight of what a badass she really was.

Once she swallowed, she said, "Let's sleep on it. You might be impulsive, but I like to think things through. This way, you can decide whether you're really up for such a sacrifice."

"Deal. I work until eight tomorrow night but let's talk after that."

"If either of us has doubts, we call it off. Stage a breakup," she insisted.

I nodded once, leaned in, pressed a platonic kiss to her candy-sweet lips, and turned to go.

Fact was, I wasn't sure if I was willing for that to be the last time I kissed Chloe. There was too much I didn't know about her, that I'd never thought to wonder about her, but now... I was starting to wonder.

CHAPTER 5

CHLOE

Once Holden was out the door, I leaned my back against it, still hugging my Twizzlers jar, thinking even if I consumed all three jars in my possession tonight, it wouldn't put a dent on the shaky stress fest inside of me.

I reached into the pocket of my jacket and took out my phone.

Are you home yet? I typed to Presley, my best friend, who lived two floors up in the same building. She'd been out of town all week, and I hadn't had a chance to fill her in on anything. None of my week was suitable for a text convo; it was an in-person wine and Twizzlers convo.

For a couple of hours now. Tonight was your work thing, right? Boring as always?

She didn't even know Angelica was sick, let alone all the Holden drama.

Can I come up? I typed, biting my lip till it hurt.

Of course.

That was all I needed. I slipped out of my apartment,

phone, keys, and candy in hand, and speed-walked to the stairwell at the end of the hall.

Presley whipped the door open as soon as I knocked, and I made a beeline into her apartment.

"What in the blazes of hell is going on?" she asked, closing the door behind me.

Her apartment layout was identical to mine, and I went past the kitchen, into the living room, kicked my shoes off, and plunked my butt in one corner of her plush dark gray sectional that felt like a warm hug.

Presley stepped into the kitchen, which was open to the living room, and gave my candy jar a look. "Rosé then?"

Presley was a wine snob and had long ago proclaimed that a lighter one like rosé paired best with my beloved red candy ropes.

"Or vodka," I muttered, knowing full well she didn't stock it.

A cork popped off, glasses clinked, and soon enough, she was carrying two full glasses into the room. She set mine on the coffee table and snuggled into the opposite corner from me.

"Bad week?" she said, then took a swallow.

I held out my jar, and she dutifully took a rope. What were friends for if not sharing in one's vices, or at least indulging one in them?

"Angelica announced she's terminally ill," I told her, because we didn't have time to beat around the bush here. I had a major problem I needed to solve. Not that I wasn't sympathetic to Angelica's much-bigger-than-my problem, but I couldn't solve hers.

The jury was still out on whether I could solve mine.

I filled Presley in on the main points, including the ridiculous reason my boss was leaning toward Gloria over me to leave in charge of the company.

Presley squinted at me like that was the dumbest thing

she'd heard. "She's off her rocker. Has she already started treatment? Maybe it affected her brain?"

I shook my head. "She starts next week, so this is all her."

"I know a person's perspective can do a one-eighty if they're faced with life-or-death news, but that seems like an altogether different person. So what are you going to do about it?"

"Already did it," I said, chewing another bite.

"Of course you did." Presley raised her brows and looked as if she was bracing herself.

"I might have told her I'm in a serious relationship."

Presley took that in, nodded slowly, as if thinking that wasn't as bad as she'd expected. So I continued.

"To Holden."

Presley's mouth opened wide, eyes went huge, then she pressed her lips together as if to stifle a grin.

"I know," I said, my eyes fluttering closed. When I opened them, I went for the wine.

Before she could ask me when I'd gone so stupid, I spit out the rest of the story—about breaking the news to Holden, about the party, about his big, spontaneous "upgrade" in the lie.

Presley popped up off the couch, pacing to the other side of the living room, taking a drink of wine, then pivoting to face me.

"I've only been gone for five days, Chloe," she exclaimed. There really wasn't a better word than *exclaimed*, and I couldn't blame her. My life had become exclaimable. An exclamation?

Shit show would suffice just fine.

Her gaze veered to my bare ring finger, and I told her how Holden had handled that part of the tale before she could ask.

She swigged half her wine and stood there, as if she couldn't quite wrap her head around it all.

I was pretty much in the same boat.

Presley went to the kitchen, picked up the bottle, brought it back to the coffee table. "We're going to need this."

"I can't argue with that."

"So. You're fake engaged to the guy you've had the hots for for years."

"Fact." I'd confessed my crush one night after too much wine—red wine. That stuff was from the devil.

"What are you going to do?"

"Eat my candy. Drink your wine."

Presley didn't even laugh. "And then what?"

"That's why I'm here, Presley. What *am* I going to do? I can't let Holden do this, can I?"

"Do you think Angelica believes your story?"

"I'm pretty sure she doesn't. He insists we can bring her around."

"Let's go through options," Presley said, and this was why we were friends. Our brains worked similarly. Not surprising, since I'd met her in the business school at college. We'd had multiple classes together our first year, had hit it off, and then roomed together. While I'd gone into hospitality and tourism management, she'd focused on finance. Now, she was my financial adviser as well as my BFF.

I swigged some wine, washed it down with more candy, then sat up straighter, feeling like we could figure this out if we put our brains together.

I counted the possibilities on my fingers as I listed them. "One, we could break up this weekend. Two, we could fake it until after Angelica makes her decision. Three, we could run away to Europe—"

"Shut up," Presley said, waving off that last one. "Four, you could fake it at first and end up making the guy of your dreams fall in love with you."

"*You* shut up," I said, scowling and ignoring how very much I wanted to dwell on that one for a minute—or a week. "Let's at least be realistic."

"Totally realistic. But if you want to ignore that one for now… Basically you can take the story back and give up on your dream job or go all in, start planning a wedding, and do what's not only best for you but best for Angelica's company."

"Basically."

"The Chloe Abrams I know doesn't usually roll over and give up."

"The Chloe you know also doesn't usually perpetuate giant lies to get ahead."

"Well, if you actually get engaged, it's not a lie, right?"

I narrowed my eyes at her, because it was starting to sound like she had a valid point.

"Right?" Presley repeated. "Engaged is engaged. And that is a relationship, even if it's not based on undying love."

The world is full of gray areas. Position them to your advantage.

There was Angelica's voice in my head, repeating something she'd beaten into it dozens of times over the years. I'd never had a problem with it before, because it was all about positioning and marketing, not lying.

"I suppose we could go with that," I said, overcoming only one of my many qualms.

"But? What else is holding you back?"

After half the jar of Twizzlers, I was finally sugared out. I set the whole thing on the coffee table, leaned back, hugged a throw pillow to my chest. It'd taken a long time for me to open up completely to Presley back in college, a long time to trust, and now she was the one person I knew I could tell anything. Even when I was still working it all out in my head.

"It's super sweet that Holden sprung this on Angelica for me, but"—I shook my head—"it's too big of a sacrifice."

"For him."

"Of course for him."

"What if you let him decide that?"

"He already thinks he did. He invited me to move in with him."

Presley's eyes widened and she mouthed, *Woooow.*

I mouthed back, *I knooooow.*

"I can think of a way you could make it worth his while." Presley's grin and the naughty spark in her eye made it clear exactly what she meant.

"Wouldn't that be one step short of prostitution?" I asked, rolling my eyes.

"No money exchanged," she said without hesitation, still grinning.

I shook my head. "I'm not sleeping with him."

The grin dropped off her face and she asked, "What's important to Holden? Is there anything you could offer up to make it more even? Because I totally see what you mean. He's being awesome, but how's he going to feel in three months?"

I popped up off the sectional, pressing my lips together, my mind sparking thanks to her questions.

I knew exactly what Holden wanted, and it was as high stakes to him as my career was to me.

"What would it take to get about a quarter million of my money for an investment?" I asked her.

A loud exhale burst out of my friend. "Whoa. Slow your roll, my friend. What is this crazy talk?" Presley asked.

"If I wanted to invest in a business—"

"What business?"

"Any business," I said impatiently.

"Chloe," she started, but I didn't let her continue.

"We've switched from friends to business for a minute. I'm asking you, as my financial manager, if I could access two hundred fifty thousand dollars of my money within, say, a few weeks."

"Give me a few minutes." Presley stood and went to a carry-on bag that was sitting on the floor outside of her home office. She took out her laptop, went back to her place, and sat down.

While she tapped on the keyboard, presumably accessing my financial info, I finished my glass of wine and helped myself to another. I didn't know exactly how much seed money Holden and Kemp needed, but the investor who'd fallen through most recently had been throwing around two hundred fifty K. I had it and then some. Between my money insecurity from growing up dirt poor, my generous—and well-deserved—salary, and my wiz of a financial manager who had a knack for making my money work hard for me, my net worth would likely shock anyone who'd known me growing up. It was seven figures, closing in on eight. It was how I slept at night.

I didn't spend a lot of money, probably to an extreme. It'd taken me a few years to be able to buy expensive clothing. I didn't have multiple closets full, only one, but the pieces I did have were high-quality designer pieces. My rent wasn't cheap, but this also wasn't a luxury building. My main indulgence was my Lexus, but even that was on the practical end of luxury. I also treated my parents to anything I could get them to let me buy them, but I had to be creative about it because they didn't want handouts.

Mostly, I saved and invested my paychecks. I'd never taken a cent out to invest in a business before. It could be risky, I knew, and my financial risk tolerance was normally middle-of-the-road.

But I did have the money. The question was, how much I could get my hands on? And was I willing to take that risk to make an engagement worth Holden's while?

By the time Presley had answers for me, I'd made my decision.

CHAPTER 6

Saturday night at Henry's turned out to be a madhouse.

It was Kona Powers's sixtieth birthday, and Abraham, her husband, had invited half the town for her birthday dinner. We had that rambunctious group in the dining area closest to the kitchen, farthest from the bar, the most out of the way, and we'd dedicated two servers entirely to their needs. Alcohol was flowing, so while I oversaw the entire front of house, I also pitched in and delivered cocktails to the birthday party as needed. Dakota Dawson was working the bar tonight and doing her usual efficient job of mixing drinks and meeting demands, and the servers were keeping more than busy. It'd be a good tip night for our employees.

The dinner rush was starting to slow down when I made my way to the bar to put in Kona's order for a mai tai. As I entered the bar area, I spotted Chloe at the counter with a dinner plate in front of her—a recently plated serving of venison medallions with butter bourbon sauce. I glanced at my watch and saw it was after seven thirty, which meant it was nearing time for me to head out. With Chloe. The thought didn't suck.

We'd been so busy that I'd barely had time to think about her, about us, about our situation since I'd come in at ten thirty this morning, but I'd done more than my share before that.

When I'd woken up today, doubts had plagued me. Would we be able to pull off a fake engagement? Living together? Would I drive her nuts? Annoy her with my work hours, habits, dedication to my brewing dream? Would such a grand effort sway Angelica in the end and get Chloe what she wanted?

But as I approached her from the side, after conveying Kona's order to Dakota, those doubts dissipated. When Chloe spotted me and sent me a warm smile, my worries faded and seemed unrealistic. Just looking at her, I wanted to make it work.

"Hey," I said, momentarily resting my ass on the stool next to her, one of only two free ones in the place at the moment. As the dining rooms emptied out, the bar would get busier, even though we were a restaurant first and foremost. We kept the bar open until eleven on weekends, so we did some extra beverage and appetizer business.

I wasn't sure where we stood or what she was thinking after having twenty-four hours to consider our next move, so I didn't lean in to kiss her. I could admit to being a little nervous about her decision. It didn't make sense, as it was *her* future at stake, not mine, but if she'd decided it wasn't worth it, if she said she didn't want to move in with me and be my fake fiancé, it was going to sting the ego.

"Hi," she said, pausing with a forkful of venison halfway to her mouth. "Have you been this busy all evening?"

"It's been nuts all day," I told her, moving my lips close to her ear because it was also loud in here and difficult to hear. "We had a group in the bar to watch the Predators this afternoon, plus Kona Powers's birthday celebration tonight."

A smile crept across her face. "I haven't seen Kona for ages."

Kona was the school librarian, first for the grade school, then later she'd moved to the high school. It made sense that Chloe had a soft spot for the kind, book-pushing woman.

"You could wish her a happy birthday," I said.

Chloe glanced around and shook her head, and my guess was that she was worried about who she might run into. It was a fair enough worry, as half our clientele were people we'd known all our lives, and some of those were on Chloe's list of people she thought didn't like her. I was confident that most of the people who'd given her trouble over the years had matured and would treat her fairly now, but that would take time for her to believe.

While my head was still close to hers, she caught my arm and said, so no one else could hear, "Should we act engaged?"

"You tell me," I said.

Instead of telling me, she kissed me, a quick hello kiss that ended up lingering for a couple of extra seconds. I was pretty sure that was her doing, not mine, and it had that curiosity from last night rearing its head again.

I didn't have time to ruminate on it, because Dakota hollered out, "Bossy Boss," irreverently, as she often did, and nodded to Kona's drink, which she'd put in the servers' area at the other end.

As I nodded at the bartender, I noticed Lucy Whitmore at one of the high-top tables, eyeing me—*us*—speculatively. Let the rumor mill begin.

"Duty calls," I told Chloe as I stood. "I'll be done in half an hour or so. Take your time and enjoy your food."

"Impossible not to," she said, her cheeks slightly flushed, maybe from the kiss, maybe from all the bodies and the warmth of the room and the top-notch food.

Cash might have asshole tendencies, but he produced magic in the kitchen on a daily basis. I was man enough to acknowledge that he was the reason Henry's was becoming a destination restaurant. Seth was our business manager, our eight-to-fiver, in charge of operations, paying the bills, keeping the lights on, that kind of thing, and that was his strength. The marketing that helped spread the word about Cash's high-caliber food was also thanks to our cerebral middle brother.

The three of us had strengths to complement each other, or so that's what everyone said. With Cash and Seth, I could see it. All I did was hire, fire, schedule staff, make sure things ran smoothly outside of the kitchen. I didn't consider it a particular skill set, though Seth insisted it was, that my social skills were invaluable. To me, that sounded like bullshit to make the youngest brother want to keep contributing and not feel like a loser.

I was all about contributing, but I wanted to do more. I believed I could help continue to build Henry's reputation as being worth the drive from miles around with the addition of a brewery. Someday. I was tired of being the guy who didn't add anything unique, didn't pull his weight in running the place.

The Powers party had finished their desserts, and a few of them were nursing final cocktails. The middle section was down to three occupied tables, and the area closest to the bar had only one couple left. Things were winding down for the evening. Both Cash and I were off at eight and would leave the restaurant in the hands of Riley O'Brien, one of our assistant managers, and Zinnia York, the sous chef.

I loved Henry's, loved working here, loved the nonstop energy and the people who came and went, but tonight, I was more than ready to resolve some things with Chloe. I took care of the last of my managerial duties, checked in with Riley, then sidled up close to Chloe's barstool, where it appeared she'd just finished the hummingbird cake and pushed her plate away. Her flash of a smile, when she saw me, was less than convincing and a lot less genuine than when I'd first seen her tonight.

"You okay?" I asked as she buried her head and dug in her purse, presumably to pay for her dinner.

"Ready to get out of here."

"Was something wrong?" I sat on the next stool, puzzled. Concerned. "If your food wasn't right—"

"Food was outstanding, especially the cake." She didn't glance up at me, and then she darted her gaze past me, to the end of the bar.

A trio of guys I didn't recognize were on my other side. Farther down, at the last stool on this side and the one at a right angle to it, on the corner, were Anna Delfico and Olivia London, both of whom we'd gone to school with. They came in at least once a week, either together or with other people.

"Chloe?" I looked back at her.

She pulled out a wad of cash, stuffed it in the bill folder, and as Dakota came back by, she slid it forward with an over-friendly smile. "Thank you," Chloe said, and then she stood on the side opposite from me, pulled her purse strap up on her shoulder, and raised impatient brows at me. "Are you coming with me?"

Confused, I glanced back at the guys at the bar, who were wrapped up in their drinks and the game on the TV behind the bar. Anna and Olivia didn't appear to notice anyone else in the room either as they were deep in a private discussion.

I caught up to Chloe, as she was already in the entry foyer, nearly to the front door.

"Have a good evening," Natalie, Kemp's little sister and also the host on duty for another half hour, said. "Bye, Holden."

"Night, Nat. You work tomorrow?" I asked.

"I've got the day off. I have a physics test Monday."

"You'll ace it. Have a good night."

By this time, Chloe was out the door, on the walkway in front of the building. She'd finally stopped to wait for me.

"Hey." I took her hand when I reached her, squeezed it. "Did somebody back there upset you?"

She frowned, averted her gaze, then shook her head. "It was an ingrained reaction. My bad."

"To Anna and Olivia?"

"You know we were never friends."

"You weren't enemies either."

Anna and Olivia had been two of the most popular girls in our class, but unlike some, to my knowledge, they'd never been mean girls.

"You're right." Chloe blew out a breath and a self-deprecating laugh. "This place makes me wrong in the head."

"Henry's?" I frowned, struggling not to be offended.

"This town," she said, shaking her head again. "It puts me on defense. It's illogical, I know. I saw Anna and I was instantly *that* girl, the janitor's daughter."

"I always liked the janitor's daughter. I'm a sucker for good, *clean* fun."

She nudged my side with her shoulder as if to push away my pun. "You're the opposite and you know it."

"You're an executive vice president of a global business now, Chloe. You're intelligent and successful, and you probably make more in a month than a lot of people in this town make in a year."

She nodded halfheartedly, distracted. "Speaking of that…" She nodded to the old Bergman building on the adjacent lot. "I'd like to see inside. Your plan calls for keeping the building but gutting it, right?"

"Right." It took half a second for me to catch up with the subject change and wonder where she was going with this. "The building is solid and would work perfectly for what we have in mind." It didn't take much to switch me into brewery mode.

The Bergman building had originally been a hardware store but had been empty for years. My grandmother had gotten it for a steal back in the seventies when the Bergmans moved their store to a bigger building two blocks away on the corner of Main and Hummingbird Road. She had never done anything except maintain it minimally. Like Seth had said, it was a waste to let it sit there, and our grandmother had held on to it, waiting for the "right" time to sell it or do something with it, but had never run into an opportunity she'd deemed worthy, in spite of multiple offers over the years. More recently, the value of the lot itself was so high, being lakefront, that the feasible offers had slowed down a lot, and any that had come in, I'd convinced my brothers to hold off on.

We walked across Henry's parking lot to the old building, and I dug out my keys. I'd been carrying the spare around with me for a couple of years now, holding out hope that Kemp and I could realize our dreams.

When I unlocked the door by the loading ramp and pushed it open, then flipped on the lights, the same thrill zinged through me that did every time I was in the space. It might be an old, dusty two-story former hardware store right now, but when I looked at it, I imagined big, beautiful silver fermenters, floor-to-ceiling windows to the two-story brewing room, rich wood accents, gleaming concrete floors, the smell of yeast…

"Tell me what you have in mind," Chloe said, her expression neutral, which was better than some people who walked in and frowned at the current state of the place.

I took her hand and pulled her gently forward, section by section, inadvertently giving her a mini education on our needs and plans and how a brewery worked.

Deep into a description of the fermenting stage, I caught

myself and shook my head. "Sorry. I can get carried away. I'm sure that's more than you ever wanted to know."

"I want to know everything, actually," she said, and something in her voice grabbed my attention. "Maybe not tonight but this is kind of fascinating."

"This? Brewing beer? You barely even like beer," I said lightly.

"I usually choose other drinks, but the samples you've given me… Those were different."

"Better," I said, confident. "Thanks for indulging me. I want this so bad I can taste it—"

"Is it strawberry-lemonade?" she asked grinning. "Or caramel and malty?"

"Both and more. I'm working on an orange wheat I think you'll like. Are you ready to go—" I almost said *home* but realized that sounded presumptuous.

"We need to talk. Where should we talk?" She'd gone serious, and for some reason, my pulse kicked up.

I reminded myself this was her deal. Her stakes. She was driving the bus here, and if I could help her, so be it. If she chose a different route, that was her right.

"Come on." I guided her back to the door with my hand at her waist, killed the lights, and locked up.

Instead of heading to the Henry's parking lot, which was down to a handful of cars, I took her hand and walked toward the shore. There were several benches along the water, on either side of the long dock where people could park their boat while they ate at Henry's, and one of those benches was hidden by a storage shed between the restaurant's lot and Bergman's. I led her there.

The night air was fresh and mild and smelled of lake water and spring and hope.

"Will this work?" I asked as we reached the most private bench. There was no one out here tonight, but give it a month and a half and it'd be teeming with people.

Chloe nodded and crossed her arms over her chest as if she was chilly. She wore skinny jeans, ankle boots, and a lightweight black sweater. I took off the jacket I'd worn all day for work and held it out so she could slip it on.

"Might smell like the restaurant," I said in apology.

"Thank you." She slid her arms in, pulled the sides together in front, ducked her face, and sniffed. "Smells like you."

I laughed. "Hope that's a good thing. So…" I waited while she sat, then I lowered myself next to her on the bench, keeping several inches between us. No charades here, and I didn't know where we'd come out on the other side—fake engaged or broken up or something else.

Before I could fully exhale, Chloe popped up off the bench and paced a couple of steps away. "I have a proposition for you." She pivoted toward me but kept her eyes to the ground, and I waited.

After a little more pacing, during which I fought the urge to remind her this was me and she could say pretty much anything, she seemed to gather her courage, faced me, and sat on the edge of the bench beside me. Pulling one leg up underneath herself, she sat sideways and her eyes drilled into me. I straightened, raised my brows.

"I want to up the ante." She clung tightly to the cuff of her jeans above the ankle boot, her knuckles white in the light from the lampposts along the length of the dock. "Instead of being fake engaged, we make it real—but temporary," she said in a rush. "We can discuss how long the marriage is, but that way we're not lying. I'm thinking a year or so, and I know that's an eternity, but before you say no, hear me out." She paused, sucked in a big breath. "I want to invest in your brewery. I've got a quarter of a million freed up, or it will be in the next couple weeks. Is that a suitable amount?"

Whoa.

I wondered if I needed to clean out my ears, but there was

no debating what she'd just said. My eyes popped wide open and words failed me.

With a glance back at Chloe, I confirmed she was looking at me expectantly, and then I noticed something more in her eyes.

This beautiful girl who'd just offered me everything I'd ever wanted actually looked at me with a hint of insecurity, as if afraid it wasn't enough. Maybe afraid *she* wasn't enough. I hated that that was so ingrained in her.

I studied her, giving her a chance to take it all back or tell me she was only kidding, but her brown eyes were as unwavering and sincere as I'd ever seen them. I leaned forward, lodged my elbows on my thighs, ran a hand over my mouth. My brows popped up as I searched for words. Any words. It was so much to take in…

"It was just an idea," she said, sounding embarrassed, apologetic as she swiveled her body to face the lake, lowered her foot to the ground.

I whipped my hand out and caught her arm, alarmed that she'd concluded so quickly that my silence was dissatisfaction.

"I fucking love the idea," I said, still reeling, trying to sort out all the things spinning through my head. "How do you have a quarter mil just sitting around?"

I knew Chloe was paid well, but she and I didn't discuss the specifics. Money was a sore subject for her.

"Presley's an investment guru," Chloe said humbly. "The girl can work wonders."

For the first time, I wondered just how much of a nest egg she'd hoarded away. Her financial status had never mattered to me, not when she'd lived in a worn-down trailer just outside of town with her mom and dad and not now, when she drove a Lexus and paid hundreds for a pair of shoes. Clearly, I'd had my head up my ass while she was making a fortune. I couldn't be happier for her, investment offer aside.

The investment offer though…

I launched to my feet, as if that would help things sink in.

A quarter million was doable. We'd been shooting for four to five hundred thousand, knowing that was our pie-in-the-sky, but we could work with less.

I let out a jubilant howl, pulled Chloe off the bench, wrapped my arms around her, lifted her, and swung her around in two full circles. The only reason I let her feet touch the ground again was because I was in danger of toppling both of us over. I settled for hugging her to me.

"Holden," she said, sounding serious, not like the over-the-moon son of a bitch who'd nearly knocked her to the ground.

I pulled away, told myself to calm the fuck down, and turned my attention to her.

"You heard the part about us getting married for real, right? Not just acting like we're engaged? I mean, it wouldn't be a real marriage, more of a business deal. We both get what we want. But I know that's a lot." She blew out her breath. "A lot."

"I'm in," I said.

"It's still a marriage though. A sacrifice," she said, narrowing her eyes. "I want you to think hard about it, Holden."

I stepped closer, nudged her chin up with my finger so she'd look at me and *hear* me. "I'm the one who sprung an engagement on you. To help you."

"True," she said, one side of her mouth twitching toward a half grin. "But there's a difference between a fake engagement and actually getting married."

"I was okay with it before, Chlo," I said, "and with the possibility of you investing in my dream…" I shook my head, overwhelmed that she would do this, still slightly stunned that she had the means, and blown away that she'd do it for *me*. "Quit trying to talk me out of it. We've got a deal. We have a lot of details to work out, but…" I glanced around, noted that we were still alone out there, with no one visible on the shore in either direction, no boats nearby on the lake. What the hell. Actions… louder than words…

I went down on one knee, grasping her hand in both of mine. "Chloe Abrams, will you marry me?"

CHAPTER 7

CHLOE

"Eighteen months," Holden said as we drove from Nashville to Dragonfly Lake Sunday evening.

"A year is plenty," I told him.

We might have slept on this whole plan of ours, but I still didn't believe he'd truly thought it through. One year was a long time to have a roommate. To have a wife. To be monogamous… and didn't *that* just bring all kinds of uncomfortable thoughts to mind?

Today had started with a seven a.m. text plea from Angelica for me to meet her at the construction site. Knowing it was the last one of those less-than-reasonable asks for a while—maybe forever—I'd jumped in the shower, thrown my hair up still wet, and made the trek south without hesitation.

Looking like she hadn't slept all weekend, Angelica had handed over the keys to everything, taken me through the worksite without any workers around, pointing out expectations, potential trouble spots, and a zillion other tidbits I might or might not remember. She'd also broken the news that Sabrina, her assistant, was shifting from Angelica's work assistant to her personal one.

Sabrina had been a layer of reassurance for me, some crossover between everything Angelica had in her mind and everything I needed to pick up. While I could still consult with Sabrina if necessary, I'd need to have good reason. I couldn't deny that I was relieved Angelica would have *someone* who was at her side during what would certainly be some ugly times.

After our meeting, I'd picked up Holden, and we'd headed back to Nashville to pack my clothes, toiletries, and other necessities—my coffee stash and three plastic tubs of Twizzlers, for example—to move in with him, plus some other eventful stuff, like lunch, and oh…

Holden Henry had bought me an engagement ring today.

Sitting there in the passenger seat of my car—Holden had insisted on driving since I was beyond exhausted—my heart caught again as I glanced down at the round-cut diamond on my ring finger.

Once more, I reminded myself it was just for show. That he'd insisted on buying it instead of letting me pay for it didn't mean a thing other than it appeared more "normal" and probably assuaged his male pride, and those were the reasons I'd eventually given in. I'd figure out how to repay him later, after we ended the marriage. He wasn't made of money, and the financial ramifications for him would probably last longer than our marriage of convenience itself. I wasn't okay with that.

"Eighteen months is more realistic," he insisted now. "Neither one of us is the type who would give up on something we wanted after only a year. Besides, didn't the doctors give Angelica up to twelve months to live?"

"They did."

Angelica had said it previously, and based on how she'd looked this morning, I had to agree that that might be overly optimistic. Emotion balled up in my throat even though she and I weren't *personally* close. It was still going to be a giant loss, and I hated to think about it.

"If we're going to do this, we need to do it all the way in order to get the desired result," Holden said.

He glanced over at me when I didn't say more, too bowled over by this wave of sadness. Keeping one hand on the wheel, he reached across the console and took my hand in his other one and just held it. He caressed his thumb over my fingers as we drove by farmland, trees, hills, and a stunning number of country churches.

"Does all of this make me a bad person?" I asked quietly, finally letting out the thought that'd been jabbing at me for more than a little while. "We're deceiving a dying woman to get what I want."

"Angelica has a brain tumor," he said soberly. "She's likely not long for this earth whether you try to convince her you're the better option to take over her life's work or not. I don't get the impression it's money you're after."

I shook my head. "I have money."

It had taken me a long time to grow into the shoes of someone who had money. Like, years. My very first paycheck from Marks International, though a fraction of what I now made, was damn good money for a new college grad, but I'd had the mindset of a destitute girl for a long time after it.

Now, even after the investment in Holden's brewery, I had enough smartly invested that I could live for years, decades probably, without another paycheck.

"I love the company," I said, my voice thick. "I know you don't understand my relationship with Angelica, my dedication to her business, but I don't think I could love it more if my own parents had birthed it and built it up."

"I don't question that at all."

Working for her had changed my life. She'd never treated me like a poor girl, had only seen my potential, my smarts, my determination. Not only that, she'd sparked in me a true passion for the hospitality industry.

"She's all about giving people top-notch service and unforgettable experiences—a stunning water view from a private balcony, a supremely satisfying four-star dinner, a peaceful day of pampering in a lush spa," I told him. "I fell in love with it too. I thrive on creating resorts that specialize in these."

I'd learned long ago that life could be relentless, and it was the little moments of good that made it fulfilling. Holden's family had been responsible for my first travel experience ever, taking me on a weekend trip to Dollywood. I'd never even been in a hotel room before, and the lodge we'd stayed in had seemed so luxurious. That trip had made an impression and stayed with me over the years. This kind of feeling—but on a grander scale—was what we endeavored to offer at Marks International.

When I glanced over at him, he'd tilted his head and was nodding thoughtfully. "I actually get that. For me, a brewery is sort of similar. Sitting and enjoying a damn good beer is a quality experience, just on a smaller scale. I want to do that for people."

I hadn't seen it before, but there really was a similarity in what we were each driven to do. "Maybe someday we'll offer your hand-crafted beers at Marks properties all over the world," I said enthusiastically. I dropped the smile instantly. "But not if Gloria Herrera is in charge."

"All the more reason we do this," Holden said.

"Gloria's good at what she does," I acknowledged, "but she's a lawyer at heart, not a leader, and I honestly believe she'd never be up for the amount of travel the job requires."

"It's, like, seventy-five percent of the time, right?"

"Closer to eighty-five or ninety," I said. "The only time Angelica is home is between projects. I don't think Gloria, with her happy family, could handle it."

"It's why you've never wanted to get married," Holden said, removing his hand from mine as the speed limit decreased and he slowed the car.

I absently ran my index finger over the stone in the ring. "Angelica's job isn't compatible with a husband or a family. Which is another reason for you and me to split up sooner rather than later."

He exhaled loudly, pensively. "If you really think a year is long enough to be believable and to show the dictator we're serious, then we'll do a year."

I couldn't help laughing a little. "Like a prison sentence?"

He glanced at me then returned his gaze to the road. "Never."

His response was so intense, emphatic, but I couldn't help worrying about what Holden was getting himself into. However, he was a big boy—I glanced at his hands on the wheel at that thought and, yep, big—and I *was* exchanging a quarter-of-a-million-dollar investment for the privilege of his time and…

"A year then," I said, biting down on my insecurities, some of which had to do with those large hands and… I could *not* let my mind go down that road.

I turned my attention out the window as we drove past the old-fashioned white church on the right, some scattered houses on both sides, the Barn Bar on the left that meant we were at the outskirts of town. The town where I'd be living again for the next twelve months.

"Chloe," he said, expelling a noisy breath, "do you understand that you've offered me the world? Marrying you is not a hardship. We're friends. We'll be roommates. We'll be business partners. To me, being able to open a brewery is worth everything. We might even have fun with it." He sobered up instantly. "Unless you're thinking it's going to be torture to be with me and you're wanting out for your sake."

It was going to be torture, but not for the reasons he thought. Not for any reasons he would ever know.

Surely it would get easier to spend time with Holden, though, without giving in to the attraction I'd always felt. Right?

I forced my tone to be light and nonchalant and said, "There's nothing torturous about a *stout* business deal."

He shook his head, grinning, and I expected him to volley back a pun. Instead, he reached across the console again and this time gave my thigh a squeeze. "It's more than business, and everything will work out. There's one more thing for us to discuss," he said as he signaled to turn into Tripz, the convenience store a couple of blocks from the heart of town. "When can we tell Kemp the good news?"

"Which good news are you referring to?" I asked with a laugh, knowing full well he meant the investment bit and not the wedded bliss bit.

"I think he'll be more excited about the money, but only by a little." He winked at me, and that shouldn't have had an effect on me, but naturally it did. Holden and I shared a secret, at least for now, and the intimacy of that fact and that wink and the handsomeness of that face and the alluring sparkle in those eyes...

Stop thinking like that.

"You said he was out of town this week?" I asked.

Last night, we'd agreed not to tell anyone anything about either our planned courthouse wedding or our business deal until we worked out details together. Presley was the only other person who knew the truth.

"Ironically, he's in South Carolina for a brewers' conference until Thursday." Holden steered close to the pumps and stopped the car. "I'd rather tell him in person, but keeping it to myself is killing me."

"I don't think we should make my name as the investor

public," I said, giving voice to one of the thoughts that had circled in my mind last night.

"Why not?"

"It's… suspicious. We get married at the same time I invest in your business."

"You're probably right," he said. "But Kemp needs to know."

"It's your call how much you tell him. I already told you Presley's in on it."

"I'll level with him. But no one else."

"Agree," I said easily. "The more people who know, the higher the chance of it somehow getting back to Angelica."

"And we're not telling anyone here in town that we're getting married until after we're officially hitched."

"Except our families. Right. Which we're doing this week. As soon as I can get into my new office and figure out when I can take a couple of hours off."

With that in mind, I slipped the ring off my finger and stuffed it down deep into the front pocket of my jeans, which, yes, did happen to be an expensive brand. I wanted to run in and grab a twelve-pack of cola for my office, as well as some snacks and breakfast bars. I didn't have it in me to hit the Country Market for groceries yet tonight, and engaged or not, I wasn't yet comfortable eating Holden's food stash, if he had one. I suspected he grabbed most of his meals at Henry's anyway.

I met Holden at the gas tank and slid my card in before he could. Once the transaction was done and he'd begun filling the tank for me, I headed inside. It wasn't until I was walking through the door that it occurred to me I should've asked if he wanted anything. I wasn't in the habit of having someone with me at the gas station, let alone having someone intricately involved in my life.

As I went down the snack aisle, focused on finding some

edible breakfast bars, I registered a woman's voice down the way from me saying, "Well, well, well."

I whipped my head up and felt like I'd walked right into a brick wall.

Magnolia James was the last person I wanted to reconnect with, *ever*, and there she was, looking prissy and judgmental and as put-together and beautiful as always.

Her long strawberry-blond hair hung in model-perfect waves nearly down to her elbows. Her creamy skin was flawless and tinted with blush, her eyes heavily but effectively made up, and her lips colored with bright red lipstick. On her arm, perched at an angle so everyone could see the signature H of the Hermes logo, was her handbag that had likely set her back five figures. She was the kind of person you always hoped got fat and ugly after high school, but nope. That's not how it had worked out for mean-hearted Magnolia. Her waist was tiny, her legs were slender and toned in her short skirt, and her boobs were noticeably bigger than I remembered.

"Magnolia," I acknowledged without a smile. She didn't deserve one of my smiles.

"I never thought we'd see you back in town, Chloe Abrams," she purred.

If I'd had my way, she wouldn't have, but instead of responding, I picked up a bag of chips, as if I'd barely noticed her.

"Dressed to impress, and on a Sunday, no less." She made a little sound in her throat. "It's good to see you've made some *external* changes."

I shouldn't have dignified her bitchy comment with any kind of response, but I made the mistake of looking at her. Her judgy gaze was roving over me, from my Jimmy Choo chunky heels to my jeans to my designer black blazer and tee. Overdressed for a Sunday? Some might say so, but at the moment, I was relieved that I never left home without looking my best, hair done and full but light makeup.

Heat crawled up my neck, my outer armor seeming to fail when faced with my biggest childhood nemesis. Magnolia was the one who'd taught me what a mean girl was, back when we were six years old. She was spoiled, born with a silver spoon and a sharp tongue in her mouth, and the only child of the family with the biggest house in Dragonfly Heights.

She'd tormented me throughout our childhood, calling attention to my shortcomings and my family's economic status at every turn, with disdain and mockery. One of the first run-ins I remembered was in first grade. My mom had made a lot of my clothes back then, and usually they were simple and plain, as dictated by cost. So when she'd presented me with a pink T-shirt that she'd appliquéd a teddy bear onto, I'd felt like a princess.

Today was an awesome day. I could barely wait to get into Ms. Tanney's classroom so everyone could see my brand-new teddy bear shirt.

I put my jacket on the peg with my name, hung up my school bag, and practically bounced to my desk.

As soon as the bell rang, kicking the school day off, Ms. Tanney greeted us and asked us all to stand to recite the Pledge. Normally I was a quiet kid, the shy one who didn't raise her hand often to participate, even though I usually knew most of the answers to the teacher's questions. Today, though, when Ms. Tanney asked for a volunteer to lead the Pledge of Allegiance, I raised my hand.

When she saw me, she was quick to call my name and didn't hide her surprise. I held my head up high as I went to the front of the classroom, hoping she would notice how cute my shirt was. She gave me a warm smile and nodded encouragingly.

Magnolia raised her hand to volunteer every single day, but Ms. Tanney was the nicest teacher and made sure everyone got a turn. Magnolia sat in the front row, and today I could hear her voice reciting louder than everyone, as if she couldn't stand for anyone other than her to be the leader. I didn't let it sway me from my job though. I knew the Pledge like a pro and even knew what all the words meant. And I wasn't about to let anything darken my new-shirt mood.

After the Pledge, Ms. Tanney read us the announcements, then said, "Okay, class. It's time for reading circle. Everyone find a place on the rug."

While we all made our way to the back of the classroom, where there was a rug with a bunch of colorful circles on it, the teacher went to her desk. I was heading to my favorite circle, a bright yellow one on the right side, near the windows, when Magnolia came up beside me.

"New shirt, Chloe?" she asked loudly enough that all the kids around her could hear.

I turned to her, grabbing the bottom hem and glancing down at my teddy bear. "Mm-hmm," I said proudly.

As soon as my gaze switched to her face, my smile faded because her expression was… not friendly. Not at all.

With a sneer, she said, "It looks like your mom sewed it out of scraps." She drew the word scraps out, as if that was as gross as dog poop, and then she glanced at the gang of pretty girls around her. They all laughed.

Shame burned hot inside of me, even though I didn't under-stand, not really, why the shirt I'd been so excited about was some-thing to laugh at. I did understand that the laughs were not in a nice way.

Shattered, embarrassed, I diverted my path and sat on the circle closest to me, a stupid, ugly gray one. I didn't care about my stupid circle anyway.

I hadn't known the word *derisive* by definition, but I learned it through Magnolia's tone and the other kids' reactions that day. I'd never worn my teddy bear shirt to school again, saving it for weekends so my mom wouldn't catch on that I'd been made ashamed of it.

Standing there in Tripz as a thirty-four-year-old woman who'd made millions, staring back at an insecure bitch who'd probably earned exactly none of her own bajillions, it was as if we'd slipped back to grade school, and all my six-year-old self-doubt and embarrassment flooded me.

Magnolia's over-made-up face looked less pretty in that instant. Like I'd been doing for so many years, I straightened my back, dug myself out of my go-to feelings of being less than, and replied to her *external changes* comment as nonchalantly as possible, with a glance at her chest, "And I did it without paying for surgery even."

With the phoniest of phony smiles, I lifted my chin slightly and walked away. Heart racing, I snagged the twelve-pack I'd come in for from an end-cap display, strode to the checkout counter as if I didn't have a care in the world, paid for my items with minimal small talk with the teenaged clerk, and walked out the door. It wasn't until it closed behind me that I let out a shaky breath.

Holden was back in the driver's seat, so I ambled to the passenger side, aiming for unbothered, and lowered myself to the seat.

There must've been something in my expression that said I was bothered, because he said, "Are you okay, darlin'?"

With a deep inhale and a brief bit of self-talk where I reminded myself Magnolia was a cockroach and it would suck to be her, I nodded and forced another smile. "Yeah. I'm good."

As we drove out of the parking lot, I congratulated myself for zinging Magnolia back for once and for getting through that run-in with only a brief slide back into my former unsure self.

I really was okay.

Until we turned into Holden's driveway and I remembered I'd be sleeping in his house tonight.

CHAPTER 8

t'd been about twenty-four hours since Chloe had offered up seed money for our brewery, and I was still fucking giddy about it. We had a boatload of details to iron out and get in writing, including settling on a company name, but that would come.

I couldn't tell a soul yet, and that only added to the whole feeling of being about to explode with the news, like a lidded bottle of home brew that had been vigorously shaken up.

I pulled Chloe's car up to my garage and hopped out. Seeing the light on next door, I walked around to the passenger side of the car and opened the door before Chloe could. The look on her face was one of confusion.

"Loretta's still up," I said in a whisper with a nod in the sixty-something woman's direction.

When Chloe narrowed her eyes as if racking her brain, it struck me she didn't know the owner of the yarn shop or that the woman kept track of everybody's business and then some.

"Busybody," I said quietly, keeping my body between my

fiancée and the older woman's house. "A sweet lady, but let's just say we need her to believe we're in love."

"She gossips," Chloe said with a nod and a frown.

"Not mean-heartedly, but she prides herself on knowing what's going on in this town, and she has the means to spread it. She owns the Fat Cat Yarn Shop." I gestured with my head toward the backside of the Main Street stores that were visible from the other side of Loretta's garage, then extended my hand, practically feeling my neighbor's eyes on my back.

Without blinking, Chloe took my hand and allowed me to pull her out of the car. "Supposed to be a big moment," I said, then wrapped both my arms around her, lifted her off the ground to kiss her, and did a half spin with her to set her on the driveway.

She held on to my upper arms to steady herself, avoided my gaze, then let out a quiet, self-conscious laugh.

"Going to take me a bit to get used to this," she whispered. "Thanks for thinking on your feet."

I offered my arm for her to take and accompanied her to the trunk, getting caught up in the charade.

It only took the two of us three trips to unload everything she'd brought, which admittedly wasn't much. I had all the furniture we needed, and she'd said she'd sort through that later, when she decided what to do with her apartment.

We stacked her boxes against the wall in the dining area for now, her suitcases alongside them.

"It's not a big place," I told her, thinking how strange it was that she'd never been here before and now she was moving in. "Master is there"—I pointed to the interior door by the back entry where we'd come in—"and everything else is pretty much right here."

Half of the house was one big open area from front to back that included the living and dining areas and the kitchen. The second bath and bedroom, which I'd set up as my office, were up front next to the living room.

"I'll unpack my food," she said. "Where should I put everything?"

I picked up the box marked kitchen and carried it to the counter. "Anywhere it fits. Shouldn't be a problem. I'm low on groceries right now."

My phone vibrated, indicating a message, so I pulled it out and saw Seth's name. I tapped it to read the text he'd sent to both me and Cash.

I heard back from the real estate guy on the Bergman lot today. Value has skyrocketed. He said the new hotel will make lakefront property even more in demand. He has a couple of people who might be interested. I'll fill you in at our meeting tomorrow.

My heart took off at a sprint and my fingers flew over the screen as I replied. *Do not do anything with the lot. I've got a line on an investor. Give me a few days and I'll have more info.*

I'd promised Chloe I wouldn't tell anyone about her involvement yet, but it was killing me not to tell my brother everything so he'd know this time it was going to happen. There'd been more than a couple of leads that hadn't panned out in the past. Nervous energy propelled me to pace toward the front of the house and back.

Seth's reply came quickly. *Time's running out, Holden. Lots of money at stake.*

You said a month. I'll have the investment in hand before then. Slow your roll.

"Impatient fucker," I muttered to myself as I paced back toward the living room, waiting for more, but the dots didn't come immediately.

Finally, they did, and then his reply appeared.

We'll talk tomorrow.

I could tell in those three little words he didn't believe anything would come through, and since I couldn't say anything more specific to convince him right now—and didn't want to jinx anything before Chloe, Kemp, and I had paperwork signed anyway—I shoved my phone back in my pocket.

I looked up to find Chloe walking by me, toward the front of the house where my office was. Caught up in my thoughts, I didn't think anything of it until she came back right away, looking puzzled and maybe a little bothered.

"Everything okay?" I asked.

"It's a nice place," she said, but there was something to her tone that said otherwise.

"It's small but it works. At least it always has for one person."

"There's only one bedroom," she said, her forehead furrowed.

"I use the front one for my office." I stated the obvious, starting to suspect what her hang-up was.

"It makes perfect sense," she said, seeming to snap back to herself a little.

She went over to the living area and sat on the couch. Pulling her legs up under her, she nibbled on the tip of her thumb, obviously preoccupied to the extent that she barely noticed when I strode over and sat down at the opposite end from her.

I knew running into Magnolia James at the gas station had messed with Chloe, but I didn't know if that was still bothering her or if moving into my house was the problem. My house with only one bed. Suddenly there was tension in the air between us, an awkwardness. Nothing like the easy friendship we'd had for so many years.

Probably not Magnolia, I decided. That snobby, holier-than-thou bitch could be unpleasant on a good day, but Chloe could hold her own.

It had to be the sleeping arrangements.

We hadn't discussed them. I hadn't thought about it that much because I'd been so wrapped up in thoughts about the brewery.

"Chloe, what's bothering you?"

She flashed me a smile, but it wasn't a genuine one. It was a tired one or maybe a stressed-out one. To be fair, she was also, for all intents and purposes, starting a new job in the morning.

"Talk to me."

"I'm just really tired," she finally said. "It's been a long day. A big day. It's not every day I move in with a boy."

"It's not every day I give a girl an engagement ring," I said.

"A fake engagement ring," she corrected.

"I'd say that rock is as real as they get. At least it better be or we got ripped off." I was teasing, but Chloe didn't smile.

"I'm paying you back eventually."

"We're not going to talk about that."

The ring hadn't been cheap, and I wasn't made of money, but I wasn't worried about that. Both Chloe and I were giving up some things, but more importantly, we were each getting the chance to make our dreams come true. You couldn't put a price tag on that.

She hopped up off the couch nervously. Without another word, she went to the coat closet, opened it and glanced around, closed it, went to the hall bathroom next to my office, walked into it, came back out.

"What are you looking for?" I asked, getting to my feet to help her with whatever she needed.

"Extra blankets."

"Are you cold?"

"Going to sleep on the couch."

"You don't need to sleep on the couch," I told her, stepping closer to her.

"I can't sleep in your bed."

I let out a laugh at the scandal in her voice before realizing that was the wrong thing to do. Her back stiffened.

"Chloe, we're engaged. We're going to be married. Married people sleep together."

"I don't want to invade your bed."

I didn't answer right away because I really hadn't thought this far, not in detail. Sure, it had occurred to me we'd be living together and sharing everything, but as I looked at her now, standing only a couple of feet away from me, her chest rising and falling with every breath and my attention getting caught up on it, I couldn't help thinking about how it'd felt to kiss her.

Sharing a bed could be uncomfortable at first, no two ways about it. But it wasn't like she was a complete stranger or someone I didn't hold a great deal of affection for. "We used to have sleepovers when we were kids all the time," I finally said. "Remember when we got in trouble for scaring the crap out of Hayden by making creepy noises outside of her window?"

Chloe let out a half-hearted laugh. "There's a big difference between eight-year-old friends and"—she bit her lower lip—"us. Now." She waved a hand toward me and then to herself, drawing my attention to the soft-looking skin that peeked out above the modest neckline of her shirt.

It was different, I had to admit. Eight-year-old Chloe had been a little kid, not a woman with a body that, not going to lie, I had definitely taken notice of in the last week thanks to our new situation.

"You're not sleeping on the couch for a year," I said. "What would Loretta think?"

"Screw Loretta."

I'd rather screw you, in the best possible way.

The thought filled my mind before I could rein it in, and then, naturally, I couldn't *not* imagine Chloe in my arms, in my bed, naked…

There was the truth, staring me in the face: I wouldn't

mind a physical relationship with Chloe for the duration of our marriage.

Could I go for a year without getting laid? I probably could if I had to. When I was married to Chloe, though, I wasn't going to sleep with somebody else.

There was no denying that a friends-with-benefits relationship, or rather a marriage-with-benefits relationship, was appealing. But what would that do to our friendship when it was time for us to go our separate ways?

I didn't even want to think about that right now. And I sure as hell wasn't going to bring up the possibility of sex. Chloe was on edge enough as it was. It was more important to put her at ease and convince her that she was welcome to share the master bedroom with me. Without benefits.

"We'll get used to it," I said. "I have a king-sized bed. I'll stay on my side. I promise."

She let out a nervous half laugh. "I trust you. Of course I trust you. It's just awkward."

"It'll only be awkward for a minute," I said, hoping I was right.

No, I *was* right. This was Chloe. I'd known her for nearly thirty years. We'd make it be okay. For everything we both stood to gain with this agreement, we could figure it out. Our friendship was too important not to.

"If you can't handle it," I said, "we can get a bed for the office." The last thing I wanted to do was make her uncomfortable.

She straightened, looking as if I'd thrown out some kind of a challenge. Her chin went up a degree.

"What would Loretta say?" she threw back at me, and I couldn't help laughing.

"We might need to invest in some black-out drapes just for her side of the house." Naturally, the bedroom and my office were both facing Loretta's place.

"It'll be fine," she said. "Like you said, we'll get used to it.

I'm going to get my pajamas on and then work for a bit. I need to get some things figured out for work tomorrow."

"Help yourself to whatever you need. Feel free to unpack your stuff. We're getting married this week, Chloe. We might as well start acting like it."

As soon as those words were out of my mouth, I realized they could be taken to mean more. That wasn't my intention. So I just shut my mouth and went to the kitchen for a beer. Chloe rolled one of her suitcases into the master bedroom, and I realized I needed to make room for her stuff in the closet and the dresser.

I followed her into the bedroom, where she had her suitcase opened up on the floor. "I can empty a couple of drawers for you," I told her, going into my closet, "and there's plenty of room for you to hang things. If we need to, we can buy you a separate dresser. Just let me know what you need to be comfortable. This is your home now."

She didn't say anything. But she did follow me into the closet and nodded when I pointed to the extra space for her to hang her clothing.

"Don't worry about emptying drawers tonight," she said. "It's late and we've had a crazy-long day. I just want to get my pajamas on and collapse."

"Let me know if you need something."

I walked out of the bedroom, got myself a home-brewed lager from the fridge, sauntered to the front of the house, looked out the window on the front door at nothing but darkness. Then I went into the office and surveyed it as if I was actually thinking of getting Chloe a guest bed.

Only if she pressed the issue would I take that step. What would we tell people who came over and saw that she had a separate bed? Without one, there was no doubt we were in this. We were together. We were going to be husband and wife in almost every way.

As I took several gulps of beer, my mind went to

analyzing the flavor. I'd been thinking this one to death, but something was off. As I stood there avoiding thoughts of the lightning-speed changes going on in my life, it hit me what the lager recipe needed.

I set the beer on my desk, pulled out my phone, and typed in a note about the change. I took another swig and let the beer roll over my tongue, then nodded. It didn't suck as it was, but that one little change would get it to what I'd originally imagined.

There was nothing like the feeling of nailing a flavor, and though I had to mix up a new batch and wait weeks before I'd know for sure the change was the right one, my step was lighter as I exited the office and went toward the kitchen to deliver my empty glass. Even though I didn't have the recipe quite right, it'd gone down easily.

When I was almost to the kitchen, Chloe came out of the bedroom, and I froze in my tracks and swallowed hard.

Apparently she'd done exactly as promised and put on her pajamas. I just hadn't had a visual of what that meant until now. It wasn't something I'd forget anytime soon.

Did she have on a sexy little slip of a nightie? No. No, she did not. If you saw her pj's in an online ad, you'd think *meh*. But seeing the very small black-with-white-heart boxers and the plain white cropped tee on Chloe, particularly as she had both arms above her head to pull her hair up, which made that little tee climb upward and reveal her bare belly, I was not thinking *meh*.

I was thinking it was going to be a very long night.

CHLOE

It was nearing midnight and I was still curled up, sitting on the couch with a blanket and my laptop in front of me, pretending to work.

Curled up sounded so cozy, but what I was really doing was cowering. Avoiding. Procrastinating.

I did not want to walk into Holden's room and climb into his bed, because I knew I'd never get to sleep.

I was as ready as I was going to get for work tomorrow. There wasn't a thing I could do to prepare myself any better. Most of the adventure was going to be handling whatever came up, diving into whatever needed to be done, acquainting myself with every facet of the property, and I was up for that. I thrived on the challenge. However, if I was sleep-deprived, my first day could be a disaster.

My eyelids were heavy, my vision was blurry, and I was just being stubborn and stupid by sitting here for so long.

The truth was, I wasn't sure I would have given in to sharing the master bedroom with Holden had he not presented it as a challenge.

I couldn't back down from a challenge and he knew it, so there was nothing left to do but buck up, get my ass in there, and try to get some sleep for my first day on my newish job. Staying up any later was sabotaging myself for a very important day.

The lights in the bedroom had been off for over an hour, and there was nothing but silence throughout Holden's small house that, in any other situation, I would have referred to as cute and cozy. But living here, with him, made it seem smaller and not so comfortable.

I'd get used to it eventually. I had to.

I put my laptop away, packed up my work bag, and bit the bullet. After turning out the living room lamp, I used the light on my phone to find my way to Holden's bedroom. I couldn't see how it would ever feel like *my* room.

In the moonlight coming through the cracks around the blinds, I could just barely make out Holden in the bed. He lay on the side closest to the door, facing away from me right now, but once I crawled under the covers, he'd be facing me full on.

With a silent but deep inhale, I made my way to the far side of the bed, pulled back the covers minimally so as not to disturb him, and eased my way onto the edge of the mattress. I lay on my back, staring up at the ceiling, my heart on overdrive.

When he didn't stir, I let out my breath and thought belatedly that I needed to find something to help me sleep. Melatonin? A meditation app on my phone? A home-brewed beer? I was open to anything.

"I was beginning to think you were avoiding me."

Holden's voice was low but it still startled me. God, that half-asleep voice was sexy.

Not helping.

"Lots of work," I whispered. "Go back to sleep."

He let out a sleepy cross between a growl and a sigh.

So not helping, I thought to myself.

He rolled onto his back, and within seconds, I could hear the even breathing that told me he'd fallen back to sleep.

My foolish traitorous brain couldn't help but wonder what he was wearing to sleep in. Boxers? Pajama pants? Nothing?

God above, if he slept in the nude…

Surely he wouldn't sleep in the nude with me next to him. Not on our first night as roommates, right? As much as I was trying to block out every thought about Holden's big, tempting body and the fact that I was a couple feet away from him, my body wasn't getting the memo. My brain was on full what-would-it-be-like-to-be-in-his-arms mode.

There was an ache beginning deep in my core, and my

breasts tingled with need. No matter how much I lied to myself during the day, there was no hiding from what I really wanted here in the middle of the night, in the dark, in Holden's bed.

I wanted him. I wanted him so much it literally hurt.

What if I just rolled over toward him and seduced him?

I had to stifle a laugh at myself because that would be the dumbest move I could make.

Holden was, first and foremost, my friend. One my best friends. Our friendship was real. Unlike the engagement and the marriage, the friendship was the thing that needed to last longer than a year. Crossing that line into naked times with him would be short-sighted and a mistake that would be impossible to come back from. No-brainer.

Feeling the weight of the world on my shoulders and the needy ache in my womb, I rolled to my side away from Holden and squeezed my eyes shut.

Somehow, I was going to have to figure out how to sleep next to this man.

CHAPTER 9

CHLOE

The past twenty-four hours had been... not the average day in the life of Chloe Abrams.

After spending my first restless night in Holden's bed, I'd had my first day in charge of a stunning under-construction hotel. I mean, the contractor was in charge of the details, but I was in charge of everything including the contractor. What it came down to was a very stressful day, where several major problems had occurred, all while I sorted through the dozens of applications that had come in for the general manager position.

As it turned out, I thrived on all of it.

It was just after seven p.m. when I left my trailer office, thinking how ironic it was that the top-tier job I'd always wanted had me back in a trailer after all these years. For so long, I'd wanted nothing more than to get out of the one I'd grown up in.

I climbed into the passenger seat of Holden's car, exhaled, and wilted.

"Hey, fiancée." Holden's voice had warmth and humor in

it that made up for that particular *F* word that threw me off. Then he leaned across the front seat, squeezed my hand, and kissed me. It was short, sweet, and enough to un-wilt me and send my heart hammering.

"Hey," I managed, trying to sound as if that kiss was the benign peck he'd intended. I could just imagine how fast he would retreat if he ever found out how much I liked every moment of contact between us. "Thanks for picking me up. I'm not looking forward to this."

We'd decided via text message today that we'd visit my parents as soon as possible, before they heard our news from someone else. Though word was likely starting to get around, there was a good chance my mom and dad had not heard the news yet since they'd never been very social. Just like me, they'd always been on the fringes of Dragonfly Lake life.

Holden had told his brothers we were engaged this morning at their weekly meeting at the restaurant, leaving out all the parts about our deal and the fake bit. Apparently Seth had stared at him for a few seconds, then said, *That actually makes sense.* I wasn't sure how to take that.

Cash's response was less surprising. The chef had questioned what the hell Holden was thinking with the suddenness.

Their sister, Hayden, had gotten wind of the news, likely from Seth, and she'd sent Holden congrats via text message and demanded we all get together soon to celebrate and, no doubt, so she could get all the details.

Holden drove along the undeveloped stretch between the hotel and town. Instead of continuing along Honeysuckle Road, which would take us through a residential area, then to Henry's and back to Main Street and the heart of town, he turned off to the west.

I leaned my head back and closed my eyes, needing a few moments of escape from the crazy train my life had morphed into. I'd worn my engagement ring all day, but even though I hadn't had much time to think about it at work, my thumb wouldn't stop stretching over to it and fiddling with it, running the pad over the diamond, back and forth, like it was some kind of growth instead of a happy promise.

My eyes popped open when Holden took my hand in his and ended my fidgeting.

"Are you nervous?" he asked.

"Of course."

It wasn't just that we were telling them we were getting married. It was also that it'd been sixteen years since I'd been to the house where I'd grown up.

"How do you think they'll react?" he asked.

"Surprised," I said. "But they've always liked you and your family. I think they'll be happy."

Their potential reaction wasn't the reason I felt like throwing up the microwave popcorn and Twizzlers I'd had an hour ago for a working dinner. It was twofold—not only was going back home a big, uneasy deal but this would be Holden's first time ever in my childhood home. Though he'd frequently given me a ride home from school, I'd never once invited him inside.

My parents' lives hadn't been easy, and that showed in the trailer where they'd lived since before I was born. They'd grown up in Kentucky, been high school sweethearts, and wound up pregnant with me before they'd graduated. My mom's parents had kicked her out, and my dad's hadn't been supportive either, insisting he choose between my mom and them. He'd chosen us, and they'd left Kentucky to make their own future.

It was bad luck that had them settling in Dragonfly Lake thirty-five years ago—their car had broken down in Dragonfly as they'd been on their way farther south, and they'd been stuck here. My dad, who was the type of person who could repair just about anything, got a job working at Skeeter's Auto Repair Shop to pay off their repair bill. That was the beginning of a life beholden to multiple jobs between them, and they never seemed to get ahead. But the one thing they had between them was honest-to-God lasting love. That alone had seemed to get them through hard times.

My stomach tightened, because my situation with Holden was the opposite in every way.

I reminded myself that I'd chosen this. To go through with a marriage of convenience, yes, but also, I'd decided long ago to put my energy into my career instead of a long-term relationship. My most important relationship was with my job, intentionally, because I never again wanted to go without lunch or shoes that fit or a furnace that worked. I also was determined to ease my parents' lives as they got older.

I'd long ago set out to help my parents out however they would let me. We had a standing monthly date in Nashville, where I treated them to everything—from a fine dinner to a hotel room, lunch, a show, sometimes even shopping when I could get away with it, though they were proud and didn't like to accept anything they considered "excessive."

My biggest victory had been an SUV when their fifteen-year-old truck had died. Even then, they hadn't let me buy it outright for them, but they'd accepted a big enough down payment from me that they could manage the monthly payments.

After a few minutes of winding, we took another left turn onto a narrow gravel road called Trout Lane, which led to my childhood home. From here, you could see the hill in the distance that overlooked town and made up Dragonfly Heights, the neighborhood that was the exact opposite of where I'd grown up. My childhood home didn't have a neighborhood name, not officially. Though there were no train tracks anywhere nearby, *wrong side of the tracks* pretty much nailed it.

Another turn, and we were on the long, rut-filled gravel driveway that led to my parents' place. They'd put up a sign my dad made years ago that said Bluebird Lane, because my mom loved bluebirds, but there wasn't much idyllic about it in reality.

The driveway was a half-mile long, and the trees were thick on both sides. As we rounded the last bend, my breath caught as a tidal wave of emotions rolled over me. Pulled me under.

"God," I said before I could stop myself.

The exterior paint had been peeling when I still lived here, and it hadn't been touched since. On one end of the trailer was a window box for flowers, and rust was overtaking it. The screen door was missing its screen, and the wood planks of the deck that my dad had built on the front decades ago desperately needed to be replaced.

That was mostly status quo. No matter how handy my dad was and how hard he worked to maintain the place, their funds and his time had never been enough to keep up on the nonessential repairs.

Now though...

I blew out a gust of a breath, taking in the whole scene.

In addition to the trailer where my parents lived, there was a carport, a storage shed, and my dad's shop. He'd constructed all the outbuildings over the years and had taken meticulous care of each of them. As he liked to say, *They aren't much, but they're mine.* Now they were even less, and it made me sick to my stomach to see.

The shop looked okay, but both the storage shed and the carport had been... crushed. That was the only word for it. My parents' SUV was parked close to the front door, away from the carport, seeming undamaged, so that was something. The two buildings looked to be a total loss though.

"Wow," Holden said, and I whipped my gaze to him, wishing I'd insisted on coming here alone. There wasn't anything about this visit that was comfortable.

"Do you want to pick me up later?" I asked and bit down on the inside of my lip. "There's no sense in—"

"What?" He sounded outraged. "Chloe, we're telling them we're getting married. That's not a one-person job… unless you know something I don't, like your dad has it in for me or something."

"My dad doesn't have it in for you. He isn't the type to have it in for anyone," I said quietly.

My dad, bless his heart, was a gentle giant who was capable of so much, could take anything apart, fix it, and put it back together, but life hadn't been kind to him. Had never given him a break. And yet he didn't hold an ounce of bitterness.

"Then let's go tell them our good news." His tone had lightened, and I peered at him, looking for some hint of sarcasm, but I didn't see any.

With another glance toward the damaged buildings, I sucked in a deep breath, opened my car door, and hopped out, my ring catching momentarily on my jacket.

As we walked to the wooden steps, Holden took my hand in his. Part of me couldn't believe I was taking him inside with me for the first time. Another part of me was thankful to have him at my side.

"Watch yourself," he said when we were two steps up, and he held his hand in front of me to stop me. The right half of the third step was bowed on the end, cracked, and looked like it could collapse with five pounds of pressure on it.

I tentatively stepped in front of Holden, to the left side of the step, and tested it slowly with my weight. When it held, Holden followed me up.

"I could fix that for them," he said quietly as we reached the door.

"My dad can do it," I assured him, then I knocked on the door.

As I heard footsteps approaching inside, I forgot about my

dismay about the outward appearance of my childhood home. Anticipation of seeing my parents, of seeing their reaction to me finally visiting them here, bubbled up in my chest and had a genuine smile tugging at my lips.

The inner door with the diamond-shaped window eased open, and my mom stood there, whipping her hands up to cover her mouth in shock, happy shock, I was pretty sure, even though she was silent for a few seconds. Then she squealed and said, "Chloe, you're here. Brian, Chloe's here!"

My mom opened the screenless screen door, which Holden caught, and I rushed into her outstretched arms. The rose scent of her hand lotion engulfed me and took me back to my childhood like nothing else could. That scent alone conveyed caring arms, a light, fairy-like laugh, and a mother's compassion.

My dad appeared over her shoulder, his eyes lit with welcome. "There's our girl."

Tears sprang into the corners of my eyes, and I squeezed them shut, refusing to let a single one spill out. I'd just seen my parents three weeks ago. What was wrong with me?

This house was what was wrong with me. Or rather, the fact that I had avoided it for all these years. I'd convinced myself that bringing them into Nashville each month was a treat for them, a break. I knew they enjoyed their day trips, the fine meals we had, the sightseeing we did, the time we spent together. I did too. And I'd told myself we were as close as ever, but now, as I stood there in the long, narrow living room with the wood paneling on the walls, I suspected I'd been grossly unfair, and I regretted not coming back before.

"Holden Henry," my dad said, then shook his hand.

My mom and I ended our hug, and she took Holden's hand in both of hers, a kind of motherly handshake.

"Come on in and sit. I've got apple pie," she said, and that was all it took for me to register the heavenly aroma of cinnamon and apples.

"Yes, ma'am," Holden said. "My mouth is watering."

Nerves aside, my stomach growled. My mom baked the best pies around.

I sniffed, swallowed, swiped underneath my leaky eyes, and led Holden to the eat-in kitchen at one end of the trailer. The table was rectangular, with ends that folded up and down depending on how big you wanted it to be. It had a laminate top with a boomerang-shaped print that screamed 1960s. On the pink laminate counter, there was a faded yellow drying rack filled with their dinner dishes, as if my mom had just finished washing them. My eyes were drawn to these signs of poverty, and I tried to imagine what Holden must think.

"Wow," he said, his gaze locked on the baker's rack that was crowded with hand-carved bluebirds.

"Look at all your birds," I said, in awe of how many there were now.

"Did you carve those?" Holden asked as he went closer to the shelves.

"He did," my mom answered for my dad. "He knows how much I love bluebirds, and he carves me a new one every few months. This one he gave me last Christmas."

She pointed to the one front and center on the middle shelf, which I hadn't seen before. Many of these I hadn't seen before. This one was a single bird perched on a rock. Its eyes were glossy and realistic, and every feather was carved in detail.

"You've got some talent there, sir," Holden told him.

My dad laughed uncomfortably and said, "Just a hobby to keep my wife happy. Have a seat, kids."

While my mom sliced the pie, my dad went to the coffee maker and started a decaf pot, same as he'd done after dinner every day for as long as I could remember.

"What happened to the outbuildings?" I asked as I sat at the table. "Was there a storm recently?"

"Oh," my mom said and glanced at my dad as she took a half gallon of vanilla ice cream from the freezer. "Not recently. It's been a couple of years."

"Close to four years. Happened before we got the SUV. There were some high winds that took an old tree down and nailed both the shop and the carport. We'll get 'em rebuilt soon."

"What a relief it missed your house," Holden said, but I barely heard him, because my mind was spinning.

Four years ago? And they never said a word?

"Why didn't you guys tell me?" I asked.

"You have plenty on your plate, sweetie. This is our issue to resolve," my dad said simply. "I can do all the repair work myself."

I knew he was waiting till he had the money to pay for materials. He was always waiting till he had the money to pay for whatever was broken, and yet he never complained. This was how my parents existed. It never failed to hurt my heart that everything was such a financial struggle for them.

That right there... *that* was why I was married to my career. *That* was why I thrived on making money.

"You know I can help you with the materials," I said.

"I appreciate that, Chloe, but we've got this. You save your money for you."

I bit my tongue before insisting I had enough for myself and their repairs both. I'd revisit the argument later, when Holden wasn't here.

As if signaling to me to change the subject, Holden put his hand loosely over mine on the table and said to me, "Should we talk about what we came to talk about?"

I nodded as my mom set a plate of pie and ice cream in front of each of us. "What's going on, Chloe?" As she sat down on my other side, she glanced at our hands and gasped, and I realized she'd spotted the ring. Her eyes darted up to mine, then Holden's, then back to mine with a hopeful light in them.

"What's going on?" my dad asked, clearly not seeing what my mom did as he waited by the drip coffeepot.

"Holden and I are getting married," I said in a rush, my heart thundering for too many reasons to count.

My mom gasped again and her hands flew to cover her mouth, just like when she'd answered the door. "Oh! Chloe!"

My dad stood against the counter, his spine slightly hunched from the backbreaking work he'd done all his life, the expression on his face one of puzzling something out. "What did I miss? I didn't know you two were dating."

My mom's head whipped back to us, as if she had the same question.

"It happened fast," Holden said. "Well, fast if you don't count almost thirty years of getting to know each other."

My dad let out an approving chuckle. "Well, I'll be damned."

"I have to admit I didn't see this coming," my mom said, "but I'm thrilled with your choice, Chloe."

My mom rose and pulled me up too and threw her arms around me. The guys shook hands, then we traded, and my dad hugged me, and my mom grabbed Holden's hand, hesitated, then held out her arms as if asking his permission to hug him. She was a hugger through and through, but I knew, in this situation, there was a class difference that held her back.

"Come here, Mrs. A," my fiancé said warmly, which came as no surprise to me. As aware as I'd always been of the differences between us Abramses and the rest of the town, I'd gotten over it with Holden and his family long ago because they'd never seemed to hold our poverty against us. With the exception of letting him into our house, of course.

"We've always thought the world of you and your family," my mom told him.

"I think the same of yours," Holden said, not looking in the least uncomfortable. That's how he was—comfortable with just about everyone. Another way we were opposites, but it was something I admired him for.

Once we'd all sat back down again, my mom said, practically bouncing in her chair, "Have you picked a date yet?"

A date. Yeah. This part likely wasn't going to go over as well. "We've decided to do a private courthouse wedding," I spit out quickly.

I'd lain awake in the middle of the night thinking about logistics, timing, the ridiculousness of spending tens of thousands on a wedding for show. Holden and I had agreed that sooner was better, particularly because who knew how long Angelica would be alive, so simple and cheap made the most sense.

"You know I've never been one to dream of a white dress and a big church," I continued.

"Always my practical girl," my mom said with a half grin that told me she was disappointed, as I'd expected.

Holden had just taken a bite of apple pie, and he set his fork down and took my hand in his, giving me a conspiratorial look. He swallowed his food and said, "We don't want to wait a minute longer than we have to, Mrs. A. If I could've pulled it off, I would've flown her to Vegas last weekend." His eyes lit up, and he pulled off the excited groom to a tee.

As much as it killed me to see the twin looks of disappointment on my parents' faces, I didn't want them at our wedding. They'd read all kinds of things into it that weren't there, like love and forever, for example. And yet I understood, to some extent, that they wanted to be included in what was supposed to be such a milestone event in their daughter's life.

"Maybe we could have a reception or party later on," I offered without really thinking it through. I just wanted to avoid hurting my parents if possible, and that meant giving them something to be included in.

"Oh, I would love that, Chloe," my mom said.

"It's not every day our girl gets married," my dad added.

I dared a glance at Holden to see what he thought of the idea I'd sprung on everyone, myself included. He smiled and nodded. Of course Mr. Social wouldn't mind a party, I thought, smiling back at him, ignoring the uneasiness jabbing at my gut. I could do a party if it would make Holden and my parents happy.

"Maybe we could have it here on the property," my dad said as he forked another bite of pie, and my stomach went from uneasy to dread.

"I-I was thinking at Holden's restaurant, overlooking the lake," I stuttered out, pulling the idea out of thin air. I hadn't thought *anything* before now, of course, but I couldn't *imagine* having it here. "His brother Cash is an incredible chef, and that would make it easier for him to provide food."

When I looked at Holden, his eyes were on my dad, and then he met my gaze, seeming concerned. "We'll talk about it," was all he said.

I glanced at my dad to try to see what had made Holden frown, but my dad had his mouth full and swallowed, then said, "You outdid yourself once again on the pie, my love," to my mom.

We all turned our attention to the pie, which was even better than I'd remembered, and I told them about Angelica and my new role at Marks, admittedly to avoid more discussion of party details. Holden and I would have to tackle that beast together, in private.

After an hour, the pie and ice cream and coffee were gone, and I was more than ready to leave. Nothing against my dear parents, but I was on mental and emotional overload after the whirlwind that had been my weekend and day. Holden had worked all day as well and was probably exhausted.

We said our goodbyes, gave our hugs, received another round of congratulations, and finally, just after eight thirty, we were back in Holden's car.

Before he started the engine, we both just sat there, and I let out a long exhale.

"Thank you," I said, taking in the ruins of the outbuildings in the dim porch light, "for dealing with all that."

"All what? They were happy. They believed us. They love you, Chloe, and seem to think I'm an okay guy. There's nothing to deal with."

"This," I said, gesturing to my parents' property in general, "is a lot. And I'm not making a pun," I added in all seriousness.

"This is your parents' home. It's where you came from. There's nothing to thank me for dealing with, okay?"

He started the engine, as if everything was settled.

In his mind, everything *was* settled, because these weren't his roots. As well intentioned as he was, it was something he'd never understand. *I* was something he'd never truly understand, because unless you'd been here and lived it, you didn't get it. As much as I'd tried to outrun it, remove myself from it, I feared it would always be deep inside of me.

CHAPTER 10

Before I could knock on Kemp's door Thursday evening, there was a cacophony of friendly, excited barking coming from his two Labradors, Baxter and Mack.

I could relate to the dogs completely. I, too, was about to burst out of my skin with excitement and had been ever since last weekend when Chloe had first proposed our deal. Somehow, though, I'd managed not to say a word to Kemp by phone or text.

Kemp had been at a craft brewing conference in South Carolina for the past few days, soaking up info we would use for our brewery. We'd gone to a conference together last year, and before that, we'd hit a couple of home-brew cons when we could. Back then, it'd been just for fun. A few years ago, when Kemp decided to take classes to become a master brewer, we'd both turned serious and started pursuing what it would take to open our own brewery.

More than once over the past week, as Kemp had filled me in on the phone or by text about what he'd learned at this session or that, I'd had to literally bite down on my tongue to keep from blurting out the news of Chloe's offer, but this wasn't something I wanted to share in a text message or celebrate long distance.

"Hey, man," Kemp said as he opened the door, wearing old jeans, a blue tee, and a ball cap. His dogs flanked him on either side.

"About time you get your ass back to town," I said as I entered Kemp's house, roughing up the fur on Baxter, the yellow Lab, while Mack, the chocolate, assaulted my legs with his killer tail wags.

"Somebody has to do all the hard work if we're making this brewery happen," Kemp said happily, and I let him feel superior for a few more minutes, the anticipation of telling him about Chloe's investment making it impossible for me not to smile. "The conference was worth every dime and then some. What'd you bring?" Kemp asked, eyeing the six pack of home brew in my hand.

"Couple of surprises," I told him. Understatement of the day. Kemp was going to shit himself when I told him about Chloe's investment.

I set the cardboard six-pack on the kitchen counter as we entered the room. I was almost as anxious to show off the strawberry-lemonade pale ale as I was to tell him the news.

He got two beer glasses down and I took out two bottles of ale, then put the others in the fridge.

"Where's Natalie tonight?" I asked about his sister. If she was home, she usually surfaced to say hello as soon as she heard me. "I know she's not working."

"Studying at a friend's, and unlike you and me, that girl is actually for real studying."

"No surprise there. She's smarter than both of us put together," I said. "She'll go far, no doubt."

"Maybe I shouldn't say this out loud, but sometimes I wish she'd take time for fun. She acts like she's forty."

Kemp and Natalie's parents had died several years ago when Natalie was only twelve years old. Kemp, then twenty-eight, had stepped up to become her guardian and had never looked back. Natalie had been his priority ever since. Now she was a senior in high school, just about to graduate. She was headed off to college in the fall, and we would feel the loss at the restaurant, where she worked the host stand like a boss.

Kemp poured beer into the glasses, while Baxter and Mack swarmed us, as they usually did, whacking people and things with their tails, soaking up all the pats Kemp and I doled out.

"Come on, mutts," Kemp said. "Outside."

The dogs knew what that meant, and they beat him to the back door. Kemp let them out to the fenced-in yard and closed the door, and the entire house felt less frenzied and a lot calmer.

"They're going to be like that for the next day, trying to make up for when I was gone," Kemp said.

"Those two are a bigger handful than your sister."

Kemp laughed. "Natalie's never been a handful. I've got so much shit to show you from the conference, man," he said. He went over to the breakfast bar, where his carry-on sat. He dug into the main pocket and pulled out folders, pamphlets, pens, and promotional pieces. "The session about start-ups was worth the price of admission alone. We're on the right track in a lot of ways."

I walked around and took a seat on one of the barstools, grabbing some of the papers, eager to look over what he'd collected.

I'd wanted to go with him but hadn't been able to make this one work at the restaurant because one of our assistant managers was out of town. Turned out it was a good thing I'd stayed home, what with the eventful week between Chloe and me.

"It hit on some of the legal and trademark stuff we've been trying to figure out," he continued. "I've got the materials here, plus a notebook full of notes. You can take them home and read them. The marketing sessions got my brain going and I'm not anything close to a marketing guy. That doesn't even touch on the ones about brewing specifics. You know those always get me revved up. I went to a session on water-soluble hops. My head was about to explode."

He wasn't normally a fast talker, but he was going a mile a minute now, like if he didn't spew everything he'd learned in the next five minutes, it would disappear. His excitement was contagious.

He finally paused and took a drink of the beer I'd given him. "This is some damn good stuff. You made improvements." He took another swallow, analyzing. "They worked."

"I'm finally happy with it," I told him. "Still working on the lager."

Kemp was full of energy even though it was nearing nine p.m. and he'd been traveling for most of the day. After another good swig, he said, "We need to talk about more investor targets. I'm ready to do this. Beyond ready, and I know you are too."

This was the part I was waiting for, but I tried to play it cool. "Actually," I said, then I picked up the beer, took a couple of gulps, let the fruity flavor linger on my tongue, thinking that it was one of the best mixes I'd made. "It's been an eventful week."

"Yeah?" Kemp asked, finally seeming to really look at me. "Busy at the restaurant?"

"We're always busy at the restaurant," I said. "What would you say if I told you I got an investment commitment for a quarter mil?"

"I'd tell you to shut the fuck up." Kemp stood straighter, his eyes went wide, and he watched me expectantly as if trying to determine whether I was shitting him or not.

As if I would joke about this. I continued to look back at him, trying to keep my face serious, but my lips couldn't help twitching toward a grin.

"You're serious, aren't you?" he asked in what could only be called an explosion of words and emotion. "What the hell, man? Who'd you find? Where did this come from?"

I couldn't help it—a wide-ass grin broke out on my face. Even though I'd been dying to tell him everything for nearly a week, I drew it out for a few more seconds by taking another long swallow of beer. I hesitated until I was sure he was about to punch me.

"This is all confidential," I said. "I know you know that, but I mean, the deal hinges on that. Nobody can know this or the investment is off."

"Who?" Kemp demanded, but his eyes lit up in spite of him wanting to kick my ass for holding out on him. "Tell me who."

"Sometimes you miss what's right under your nose," I said. "Chloe offered the funds."

He narrowed his eyes, looked more than a little startled, and took a moment, like he was doing long division in his head or something. "Chloe Abrams?"

"How many other Chloes do you know?"

"You're gonna need to fill in some blanks. How does Chloe have a quarter million dollars and why would she give it to us?"

Kemp had never really understood my friendship with Chloe. Probably nobody understood my friendship with Chloe. It had likely always seemed illogical and unlikely to others, but the foundation of our friendship was planted when we were little kids. In fact, I'd been friends with Chloe longer than I'd been friends with Kemp.

My family had moved to Nashville when I was in fourth grade, and I'd lost touch with both of them for a while. I'd never taken to being a big-city boy, never really adjusted. In middle school, I'd gotten in enough trouble that my parents got fed up quickly, and when I'd begged them to let me move back to Dragonfly Lake and live with my grandmother during high school, they'd all agreed.

Maybe Chloe and I wouldn't have reconnected then, as we were so different. She was still an outsider, somewhat by choice by that time, and I, well, I could get along with just about anybody. It was fate that, on my first day back, Chloe and I had a class together and sat next to each other. The puns had started as if we hadn't lost five years.

Kemp and I had been friends throughout high school, had been on some of the same sports teams, hung around the same crowd, but we hadn't become best friends until after we graduated. That was after Chloe had left town.

The only times I'd seen Chloe since had been when I went to Nashville. Kemp was never with me, so the two of them hadn't run into each other for years. In high school, though I'd been friends with both of them, I'd kept them separate.

Back then, Chloe had kept herself separate from most people, and I'd understood that and respected it, even if it was the opposite of how I operated. I knew she'd had a completely different experience than I had growing up, and there were reasons for her aloofness. She was my quiet, bookish friend who spent her spare time studying. Kemp was a jock, a popular guy, the polar opposite of Chloe, and I appreciated both of them for what they were. Always had.

"It's a long story," I told him now. "You probably better sit down."

He finished the last of his beer, then went to the fridge and pulled out a second one for each of us. He took out two clean glasses, as he was a stickler for not mixing different beers so as not to bastardize the flavors, then hurriedly poured us both a stout. After sliding them across the counter, he came around and took the stool next to me.

"Tell me."

"A week and a half ago, Chloe walked into Henry's," I told him.

"I didn't think Chloe ever came back to town."

"Correct. She hadn't been back once since I drove her to college, so you can imagine how stunned I was to see her sitting at the bar."

A skeptical look crossed Kemp's face. "And she just stopped by to give you a quarter of a million dollars to make your dreams come true?" he said, dripping with sarcasm.

"Not quite."

"Why would Chloe Abrams give us 250 big ones? I have never seen evidence that she has a big heart," he said.

I hesitated.

Chloe and I had agreed that I'd be completely honest with Kemp, just as she had been with her friend Presley, and those were the only two people who would know the entire truth behind our marriage.

"I'll tell you everything, but you've got to keep it to yourself."

"Of course," Kemp said with a look of annoyance, like he couldn't understand why I had to say that out loud. I wasn't going to leave anything to chance though. The stakes were too high for Chloe.

I explained to him about Chloe's job and her boss and her reasons for pretending we were in a relationship. Kemp listened intently. When I finished the story, he narrowed his eyes and said, "That is seriously twisted."

"I can't disagree with you on that. There's more. Pretty sure you'll think it's even more twisted."

I told him about the deal Chloe and I had made—that she would invest in our company and I would marry her for a year.

He'd been taking a drink, and he slammed the glass down noisily on the counter. "You have got to be kidding me." He stared at me with his mouth hanging open, like I was the biggest fool alive.

"Not kidding you, man. I couldn't make this shit up if I tried."

Kemp went quiet, sipping his beer distractedly, not giving the flavor the attention he normally would. His mind was obviously churning over everything I'd said. With good reason. I knew it was fucked up on some level. But I also knew it could work.

"I don't know what to say," he finally said.

"You can be honest. We always have been, haven't we?"

He spun his beer glass around on the counter, more than three-quarters of the second beer gone already. "You're sure you have to marry her?

I shrugged. "Seems like a small price to pay. I like Chloe. I know you don't know her very well, but I do, and I don't think it's that big of a deal."

Kemp let out a disbelieving laugh. "Not that big of a deal. Getting married? She's basically paying you to be her husband for a year. And you don't have a problem with that?"

Now I laughed because it did sound questionable when he put it like that. "To me it's worth it. She gets what she wants, and I get what I want. *We* get what we need. What we've been trying to secure for, what, two years? Three?"

He couldn't debate that. It'd been a long road already, and who knew how long it might've taken us to find someone to fund us if Chloe hadn't come along.

"We have to put up with each other for a year, sure," I continued, "but if she gets that job, she'll be traveling for a significant part of the time anyway."

"Yeah, but you've basically thrown away your personal life for twelve months, man. Have you really thought about it?"

"Of course I've thought about it. I haven't thought about

anything else for the past week, and I still can't find a reason not to do it. There's a small sacrifice, sure, but to me it's worth it because I like Chloe. I like spending time with her. I want to help her, and I'm stoked that she's willing to help us. I thought you would be too."

"I think it's a bad idea."

"Are you saying you don't want me to take the two-hundred-fifty-thousand-dollar investment from her? If you're morally opposed, I suppose I can go to her tonight and tell her the deal is off. Seems like that would be insane."

"I think you're fucking insane," he said, "but you're the one making the sacrifice. If you're comfortable with it, then who am I to argue? I'm benefiting without having to live with some woman who likes books more than people."

"You really need to get to know Chloe better. You'll have plenty of opportunity now that she's back in town." I laughed. "Particularly since she's going to be my wife starting tomorrow."

"Tomorrow?" Kemp closed his eyes and ran his hands over his face. "I guess you're a big boy and you can figure out what you're comfortable with. But let it be known that I think it's going to cause problems."

"What problems do you think it's going to cause?" His reaction was so much less enthusiastic, hell, so much graver than I'd expected, I was still trying to understand what he was so worried about.

"Somebody could get hurt. Chloe could get heartbroken. Maybe she has the hots for you, and this is her way of getting what she wants."

He really didn't know her at all. "She's always been married to her career. She doesn't have the hots for me, and her heart isn't going to get broken. If I thought Chloe would get hurt, there's no way I'd do it."

"Hell, you could get hurt in this, bro.

"How am I going to get hurt?"

He studied me intently for more than a few seconds. "You got feelings for her you're not telling me about?"

I swallowed and shoved down the thought of kissing Chloe. Ignored all the tension that sleeping next to her had evoked in the past few days. Attraction was something I could handle, and that's all it was.

"My feelings for Chloe are platonic. She and I go way back. She deserves to have Angelica leave her the reins of Marks International just like you and I deserve to have somebody invest in our business so we can realize our dreams."

Kemp went quiet for a little longer, finished his beer, and said, "So tomorrow? What, a courthouse wedding? You think people are going to fall for this?"

"Chloe and I are giving it everything we've got. We've already told her parents and my family. They all support us. Everybody supports us except you. So tell me... is this going to come between us?"

Kemp got up and walked around the breakfast bar. He rinsed out the empty glasses and put them in the dishwasher. "It's not going to come between us. As long as you have everything wrapped up tight as can be in a contract, something that protects that money, then I'm on board."

"You can read the contract yourself. I'll email it to you right now, but it's tight. Chloe's lawyer drew it up. Ours went through it meticulously."

"Send it," Kemp said.

I took out my phone, accessed the doc, and emailed it to him. I knew he'd read it later, and that was fine with me.

At long fucking last, he grinned like a lunatic and shook his head. "We got ourselves an investor. It's time to do this." Kemp reached out a hand across the breakfast bar. "Sounds like we're in business, partner."

I blew out a relieved breath, still a little uneasy at his disapproval, but he would see. It was going to be fine. "We are in business indeed."

CHAPTER 11

CHLOE

n all my years, I'd never wasted time daydreaming about being a bride or planning a wedding. Why would I? I'd never intended to get married.

So when I stepped out of the handicapped stall in the county seat courthouse ladies' room, the only one big enough for me to change into a wedding dress, modest though it might've been, and caught sight of myself in white, I sucked in a breath and nearly choked as I inadvertently swallowed my minty-fresh gum.

A girl couldn't get married with bad breath, after all.

The image of the bride staring back at me from the mirror slowed me down for a moment, only a moment, but then I took the necklace from my purse and hesitated again.

My mom had loaned it to me. She'd come all the way out to my office at the construction site and, apologizing for taking up my work time, told me she respected Holden's and my decision to have a private wedding ceremony and then presented me with her one request. She wanted me to wear the necklace my dad had given her on their tenth wedding anniversary years ago.

It qualifies as something old, something borrowed, and something blue, all in one tiny little bauble, she'd said with a nervous laugh, as if I would reject her offering. *I know you could buy something much grander and nicer, but this is special to me, and I was hoping you'd wear it for your special day.*

My eyes moistened now just thinking about it.

Of course I wouldn't reject it. It meant the world to me to have this little piece of my parents here with me whether this was a true love match or not. The short silver chain had a charm that was two entwined hearts of sterling silver with a teeny-tiny speck of a deep blue sapphire between them. I wasn't even sure if the sapphire was real, but I didn't care. The symbol of my parents' love was what mattered to me, but I understood why my mom would question that.

I was the one who hadn't gone home for sixteen years.

I was the one who'd inadvertently sent a message that I didn't want them closely involved in my life. And here I was sending that message again by not including them in the ceremony.

I knew my mom and dad supported my career and my goals, and they embraced Holden. They wanted what was best for me and I believed marrying Holden was best.

As I fastened the necklace, I vowed to be a better daughter and actively, regularly—more than once a month—show my parents how much I loved them. To do a better job of including them in my life.

As much as I dreaded having a party, I knew that was the first step. My mom could help me plan it. My parents could celebrate with us and feel included. In the end, I would live through it just fine and everything would work out.

Another twinge of nerves sprung up regarding Angelica, but she was the one who'd set forth ridiculous requirements, and after her phone call this morning, I wondered if she was beginning to realize it.

In a less than robust voice, she'd requested that I take a video call with one of the governmental higher-ups in the Peruvian city we'd be building in early next year. Apparently Angelica had set up the meeting two weeks ago, before her whole life had changed, and it was of the utmost importance that one of us was available for it. Gloria had reminded her she'd be on a family vacation next week and wouldn't be available.

I'd assured her I would take the call and had bitten down on pointing out that this job wasn't always compatible with a family. After all, she'd soon find out I'd made my own family of two official.

I refused to feel guilty for what I was about to do. She was the one who'd changed the rules after twelve years.

Necklace fastened, I gazed at myself in the mirror and finger-combed the waves in my hair one last time. I took out the lip gloss that was a shade bolder than I was used to and applied it. As I pressed my lips together to even out the gloss, I shut down any lingering doubts.

I was doing this. I'd made up my mind days ago. Over the course of the week, I'd decided to go all out.

I'd ordered this dress online, had it express shipped, thanked the heavens when it fit. I'd swallowed my self-consciousness when I'd seen how low the neckline dipped, because a girl only got married once, if that, and if her wedding dress showed a tiny bit of skin to her groom, so be it.

I'd managed to find a photographer who could show up for a half hour and take a few shots of us outside of the court-house, which luckily was somewhat picturesque, with its old columns, tall, imposing doors, and majestic concrete exterior stairs. At least it wasn't an ugly, institutional-looking 1950s building. The historical aspect would make it a fine backdrop for our wedding pictures.

As a bonus, the photographer had agreed to pick up a bouquet of flowers for me to hold. Our wedding photographs would look like it was a real marriage.

And I reminded myself one more time, it *was* a real marriage in the sense that this was a partnership. Holden and I were in this together. Maybe not the traditional way, but maybe that wasn't what was important.

I backed up as far as I could without running into the stalls to see my reflection. I took one more deep breath, shoving down my nerves, glanced at the time on my phone, smiled at my reflection, and said out loud, "Time to get married."

I picked up the bag that had my work clothes in it, shoved everything else in, and walked out of the ladies' room.

There were several people in the main lobby of the court-house, and I felt their eyes follow me across the room as my heels clicked on the tile floor. Since we were one town over from Dragonfly Lake, I was confident no one knew me here, but I wasn't comfortable with their attention. I raised my chin ever so slightly though, strengthened my imaginary armor, and blustered through with determination.

I smiled like a bride would smile on the day she was marrying the love of her life and didn't allow my thoughts to go anywhere close to the word *love* where Holden was concerned.

I heard a feminine voice behind me, to the side, breathe out, "Beautiful," and when I was almost to the big exterior doors, a man who'd just entered caught my eye and said, with a warm smile, "Congratulations."

Without a single waver in my own smile, I replied, "Thank you," and then I pushed open the heavy door to the outside.

The refreshing spring air hit me, and I saw him imme-diately.

Holden was close to the foot of the stairs, peering up at me.

I faltered at the sight of him.

My God, he was such a sight, so sharply dressed in his dress pants and matching vest and silk tie. He was a class act all the way and knew how to dress.

Despite all the determination I had summoned, the hard shell I was hiding behind, I felt my insides go warm and soft at the sight of this man who I'd had a thing for for half of my life—a thing I'd never intended to let him know and never would.

This might've been the dumbest thing I'd ever done, but there was no turning back now. Even if I should have, I couldn't walk away.

Who in her right mind could walk away from a man like Holden Henry?

———

HOLDEN

It was Friday afternoon, my wedding day. It was also April Fool's Day.

Coincidence? Or was I being the biggest, dumbest dumb ass alive?

As I strode along a walkway outside of the county courthouse one town over from Dragonfly, my head was swimming with a general oh-shit feeling.

What the hell was I doing?

Married?

For a year?

Marriage was something I'd always thought I'd get around to someday. Someday later. Sure, I was thirty-four, but some days I barely felt like a grown-up, let alone someone capable of a long-term partnership.

It wasn't like I'd had months of a relationship to get used to the idea, used to Chloe on that level. We'd been sleeping together for almost a week now, and I did mean exactly that —*sleeping*—but I wasn't sure if I'd ever get completely used to having a woman in my bed, fully clothed, who I hadn't ravished six ways to Sunday in the wee hours. I'd woken up rock hard more times than I was comfortable admitting to myself, and you can bet your ass I'd done everything I could to hide it from Chloe. That wasn't part of our deal.

It was nearing our four p.m. appointment. Yes, we had a fifteen-minute slot to be united in holy matrimony—or unholy if you wanted to get technical. Chloe had barely made it out of work in time for us to drive the short distance to the county seat. Now she was inside in the restroom, changing clothes, getting ready for our wedding.

Could you still call it a wedding when it was in a courthouse?

Could you still call it a marriage if it was purely platonic and there was no consummation?

And that circled me right back around to, what the hell was I doing?

I was signing up for an entire year with no dates. No sex.

I wasn't one of those guys who was led around by his dick and had to sleep with somebody every weekend, but I liked sex. I liked having the option. I liked women. I liked dating when I felt like it.

It was true that I hadn't felt like it for a while now, but that was because Kemp and I were so wrapped up in our brewery plans. Between that and working long hours at Henry's, I hadn't made a lot of time for dates, and I guess I hadn't met anyone worth dating lately.

However, having the option taken away made me itchy.

I swallowed that thought because it was a little late for it to crop up.

As I fought to keep my pacing nonchalant and unbothered, I pulled my phone out of my dress pants pocket. Six minutes till four. I pivoted to go back toward the door.

It was a beautiful spring day in Tennessee. The sun was shining in a cloudless sky. The temperature was in the sixties, and spring flowers were popping up everywhere, especially around the courthouse. The building was old, historical, a little majestic, and somewhat imposing. Functional. To me, it said laws and rules and regulations and the legal system. Not romance.

I glanced across the street where there was a picturesque, old-fashioned church—a white one with a steeple out front. The kind of church that populated postcards and jigsaw puzzles and small-town Tennessee.

That looked like the place to get married.

Though I'd never imagined my wedding day, if I would have... I glanced between the two buildings again. Yeah. The courthouse was not what I would have pictured for the day I got hitched.

As I approached the wide stairs that led to the entrance, I started feeling shaky and anxious. Maybe Cash and Kemp were right. Maybe I was crazy. Maybe this was stupid. Maybe we were about to make a giant mistake.

No.

I let out a gust of a breath, willing it to be less shaky.

I was getting the brewery of my dreams. Chloe was going to get the reins of the company she'd always dreamed of moving up in.

You knew this was a business deal going in and you were fine with it. It makes good sense, I coached myself, beginning to feel a little more leveled out.

I took in a breath of the fresh spring air, catching the sweet scent of the flowers in the front bed that lined the walkway. I needed to stop freaking the fuck out. I would be just fi—

Oh, shit.

The tall, dark wood hundred-year-old front door had opened, and Chloe came out from the courthouse.

I stopped in my tracks and stared up at her.

She wore a white dress that reached to her calves. It had an off-the-shoulders neckline that plunged into a deep vee between her breasts and, between that and the way the waist gathered tightly, it had me noticing her chest like I hadn't before.

She turned partway, holding the door open for the guy coming out behind her, and don't think I didn't notice the way he gave her a head-to-toe gaze and a smile.

When she turned, I got half a glimpse of the interesting cut of the back, which gathered in a point below her shoulder blades and exposed the bottom half of her back. Her beige heeled sandals with straps around her ankles made her legs supermodel long. She'd left her wavy hair down, and the breeze picked up several strands around her face as our eyes met.

I swallowed hard and my mouth went dry.

In all the years I'd known Chloe, I'd never seen her look quite like this.

She wasn't overdone in the least, just… stunning. Was it the white? The cut that emphasized her chest?

Her dress was sexy in its attempt to be subtle and *nearly* sweet. It was the *nearly* that had me unable to form words. That and the expanse of soft-looking skin between her shoulders and the neckline.

"Wow," I finally managed. I glanced down at myself and felt outclassed by my bride.

I guess that was how it should be. I sure as hell would be happy to have her on my arm.

"It's time," she said, flashing me a smile.

There was not a hint of vulnerability on her face. She looked calm and confident, as if she'd just signed a billion-dollar contract for her business. That was the side of Chloe that had always blown me away most. Looking at her now, you'd never know she had any insecurities. I knew she hid her self-doubt from just about everyone but me. The real Chloe was somewhere in the middle, with an exterior shell of steel and soft insides.

As I stood looking at the woman who was going to be my wife in name only, it hit me that I wanted more. I was attracted to her. I wasn't having trouble because there was a woman in my bed; I was having trouble because *Chloe* was in my bed.

There was no longer any denying that Chloe Abrams, soon-to-be Henry, got my blood pumping.

The deal between us had nothing to do with blood or anything else pumping. We might not be in love with each other, but I couldn't deny that, as of this moment, I was open to anything.

The next year was either going to be fun in more ways than I had expected or it was going to be the longest, most painful twelve months of my life.

CHAPTER 12

CHLOE

Twelve minutes later, Holden and I were husband and wife.

We'd elected to exchange vows and rings. And when the justice of the peace had asked if he wanted to kiss his bride, Holden's brows had floated up, his grin had widened, and he'd pulled me into him before I could prepare myself and kissed me till my legs went weak, which, I'll be honest, took approximately two-point-two seconds. It didn't matter what the justice of the peace thought, but I felt confident the guy believed we were madly in love, based on the show Holden put on.

The photographer had been waiting on the courthouse steps as promised, and not only had she been organized and efficient but she'd made it easy to forget we weren't a couple madly in love, what with all the gazing into each other's eyes and the traditional "in love" poses. Holden had acted fully into it and made it fun instead of awkward.

If I hadn't loved him before, I probably did now, but I pushed that from my mind with a hard shove.

There'd been onlookers then, as we moved from one scenic photo op to the next, and there were onlookers now, as we walked into a quaint, cozy Italian restaurant Holden had found on his phone. It was easier to ignore all the stares and whispered comments with my hand in Holden's.

Once we were seated at a little table in the corner, Holden said, "All that's left is to eat, drink, and be *married*."

Grinning, feeling a little more at ease with the shift back to our go-to of dorky puns, I shot back, "That and *elope* for the best."

Holden laughed appreciatively, and we crept another degree closer to our normal.

Our server showed up then with a bottle of champagne and two flutes. "On the house for the newlyweds," he said as he poured the bubbly into our glasses. "Congratulations."

We thanked him and he went quickly on his way as if to give us privacy for our first toast as a married couple.

"That was unexpected," I said. "This whole thing is unexpected." I gestured around us. "Cute place and it smells amazing. Thanks for finding it."

Our eyes met, and I couldn't help but be rattled by the impact of those familiar, compassionate green orbs as we sat there so close together, at a table for two, in wedding attire.

Holden held his glass up in a toast and said, so that no one else could hear, "To both of us getting what we dream of. Cheers, darlin'."

I'd been so caught up in the moment, in that look between us, that his mention of business, the very reason for all of this, jolted me back to reality.

Reality was that this *was* a business deal. Reality was that Holden wanted his brewery, not me, and it would do me good to remember my first interest was my career as well.

How could I forget what we were really doing even for a couple of minutes?

I recovered quickly and said, "To beer making and Marks International."

We clinked our glasses and sipped our champagne.

The server appeared to take our drink orders, then hurried off again.

Holden and I spent a few minutes looking over the menu, discussing options, and when our drinks showed up along with a basket of steaming, oven-fresh bread that smelled divine, we placed our orders, Holden going with a swordfish cioppino and me sticking with a chicken fettuccine Alfredo in deference to my white dress.

"So, we did it. Tying the knot was smooth and painless," he said once we were alone again.

I couldn't help but laugh. "Were you expecting torture?"

He held the bread basket out to me. I took a slice, and he did the same, then mixed oil, grated Parmesan, and black pepper on a small dipping plate.

"I had no idea what to expect," he said. "I've never been married before. Almost seems like it shouldn't be that easy."

"I'll be honest," I said, exhaling, "I think the hardest part is going to be the party I promised for my parents' sake."

"You never have been a party girl."

"Social is not my strong point and you know it." I managed to keep from saying out loud, *And now you're stuck with me for a year.* That kind of thinking would serve no purpose. It was more useful to figure out how we'd navigate everything moving forward, our opposite personalities only one aspect of that.

I tore off a piece of bread and dipped it. It was soft and flavorful and promised an amazing meal if the entrees were even half as delicious.

"I'll be right by your side," he said, covering my hand with his.

I let out a little laugh. "Be real. At a party, the last thing you'll do is stick by any one person's side, Mr. Social."

"It'll be a challenge," he said, grinning, "but I'll do my best." His smile disappeared abruptly. "I've been meaning to talk to you about something."

I tensed because he was suddenly super serious. "What's up?"

"When your dad offered to have the party at their place and you turned him down, I saw a look cross his face, just for a flash, when you weren't watching. I suspect his pride might've been hurt."

Oh. Oh, no.

There was an instant sinking feeling in my gut, because I knew without thinking too hard about it that Holden was likely spot on. "That's why you frowned," I said, remembering.

I took another sip of champagne that turned into more of a gulp. The last thing I wanted to do was hurt my dad in any way, but...

"We can't have a party out there, Holden."

His gaze went to our hands, where he was running his finger over the back of mine, back and forth, a gentle caress that I didn't hate. "Why can't we have it out there?"

I looked at his face to see if he was still being serious. He was.

I didn't even know where to start. "It's... depressing. It's overflowing with poverty and struggle."

"It's filled with love, Chloe."

"It's filled with falling-down buildings and in-need-of-repair steps and missing screens," I reminded him.

Holden frowned and retracted his hand to grasp the stem of his glass. "It's got a flower box full of colorful blooms lovingly cared for by, I'm guessing, your mom," he countered. "It's got cheery curtains with ruffles at the window and the scent of home-cooked food wafting throughout. It's got a kitchen filled with an entire flock of bluebirds that your dad lovingly carved for the woman he adores."

"Pretty sure it's more like a dozen flocks," I said lightly.

"That house is chock full of signs of a proud, loving family," he said, not acknowledging my comment, his eyes bursting with intensity.

The server showed up with our meals then, and I barely noticed as he grated fresh Parmesan over Holden's. I was too busy thinking about everything Holden had said.

I was more than a little bowled over to hear his reaction to seeing the trailer up close for the first time. Bowled over and feeling chastised, even though I knew that wasn't his intent.

My mom loved to see the rainbow of flowers out the kitchen window when she was cooking or washing dishes. I had so many memories of her tending them, up on a step ladder, either before or after a shift at her job, sometimes between shifts on a doubled-up day.

The curtains she'd sewn herself, and she took them down each season, gave them a thorough washing, then ironed them and rehung them, so they still looked good after all this time, even if faded from the sun.

And the bluebirds… there was no question each and every feather, beak, and tiny bird foot was carved out of intense love and devotion during the spare time my dad, who'd also worked two jobs for years, had very little of.

Twirling creamy noodles around my fork, I felt ashamed that I'd needed Holden to point it out to me, but he was right. If you could look past the poverty and the damage and the hard times my parents had always endured, their home was well loved. They put their hearts into it.

"Maybe you have a valid point," I allowed. "But of all the places we could have a party to celebrate our marriage, surely that's not where you want to do it." I finally took my first bite and had half a thought that this was the best Alfredo I'd ever eaten.

"I don't want to do anything that makes you uncomfortable," he said. "I'm sure we could have it at the restaurant if you want to. Or any other number of places. You're the bride." He grinned. "That means you get to choose."

"I hate to hurt my parents."

"Your dad *is* a proud man, and I don't mean that in a bad way."

"I don't want to make them feel bad. That's never been my intent."

I couldn't help thinking that was exactly what I'd done by never coming home.

"Would your dad be open to me helping him with his outbuildings and maybe the stairs? That way he wouldn't have so much work hanging over his head and the place would be party ready."

I studied him to see if he really meant it, my insides going warm and mushy at his kindness toward my dad. I couldn't see any signs of insincerity. And didn't that just make him a better person than me? Because I was still struggling.

Holden had always been the most unselfish, caring, protective person I knew.

"We don't have to decide today," I said, but I was still pretty set on the restaurant for the location. I'd have to think long and hard about whether I could embrace a party at the trailer home—the very trailer I'd never let anyone into until a few days ago. I didn't love the idea of allowing all of Holden's friends and family into the humble place where I'd grown up.

"All right," he agreed, "we can talk about it later. Think through our options, but I do wish you'd stop hiding."

"Who me?" I said, putting on an innocent act when I knew full well what he was talking about.

"You had a lot to get through this past week with your new job, but I'm betting you used that as an excuse to hide away in your office."

"I feel seen and not in a good way," I said lightly. "Yes, I was hiding in my office. Half of it was legit. I had a crash course in running Marks International. Half of it was me hiding. It's just, I know how the town can talk…"

"Oh, they're talking," Holden said. "About us, of course. We're big news, but the way to make that go away is to be seen around town together and be open about getting married. That's the whole point of our getting hitched, right? Angelica will realize it's real, and that's what we need to do to get you what you want."

My stomach knotted, and my appetite vanished. "You're right. I know you're right."

"I'm usually right," he said cockily.

I rolled my eyes, but once again he'd made me smile. Holden was good at making me smile.

"In case I didn't mention it, when you came out the door at the courthouse to find me? You looked stunning. Took my breath away, EVP, soon to be just P for president."

A thrill shot through me and, strangely, not from the president part but from the compliment.

"If you knew what was going through my mind at that moment…"

"How good I looked?" he said cheekily, and I laughed.

"Before that." I debated whether I should level with him. "I was scared to death you'd change your mind, that I'd go looking for you and wouldn't be able to find you," I finally said.

"What? Chloe, I wouldn't let you down."

"I know," I said quietly, setting my fork down and ending the charade that I was still eating. "It's just that it's such a sacrifice. I know you're getting a lot out of it, but…" I worked up my nerve to speak of the elephant in the room. "I'm just going to say it. You've basically agreed to give up sex for a year, and that's no small ask."

"Last I knew, you gave up the same," he said.

"I'll be fine. Probably." I grinned and my cheeks heated with a blush. "But you're a guy," I blustered on to get the focus off me. "Isn't it proven by science that a guy can't go longer than a couple of weeks without getting lucky?"

He let out a sort of subdued howl kind of laugh. "Tell me something. When's the last time you were with a guy?"

I didn't have to think for long. It took me a few more seconds to say it out loud, simply because we hadn't traditionally discussed our sex lives. "It was in Switzerland in December."

Holden's eyes popped open a little wider. "Getting a little international lovin', huh?"

I shrugged. "He was the ski instructor and probably five years younger than I was, but it was just for fun and we both knew it. What about you?" I took the last couple sips of my champagne, doing my best to act like I didn't care about his answer, bracing myself to hear what I didn't really want to hear.

"This got personal fast," Holden said. "Married for an hour and already we're to the deep, dark secrets."

"Most couples start it long before they're engaged," I said in a voice just above a whisper, relaxing a little.

"I guess I started it, huh?"

"You absolutely did, so come on, fess up. Has it even been two weeks?"

With a self-deprecating laugh, he said, "Let's just say more than six months and call it good."

Now it was my turn for my eyes to pop wide open.

"You've got me beat," he said and then he dropped the grin from his face and looked down at his nearly empty plate as he scooped up another bite. I sensed he was trying to seem nonchalant but maybe wasn't really, and I held my breath for what he was going to say next. "I don't want to make you uncomfortable, but hell, we're sleeping in the same bed. That itself could be uncomfortable if we let it."

Uncomfortable was putting it mildly. I thought back to that first night with him, when I'd maybe slept for an hour in the end. Over the past week, I'd gotten a little better but not a lot. Twice I'd stayed up late, working on the couch until I fell asleep and lying awake once I went to Holden's room.

"We're both adults," he said, and he suddenly seemed unsure of himself. I wasn't sure I'd ever seen Holden Henry unsure of himself. "We're married. We might have physical needs, and I wouldn't be opposed to crossing that line if you're ever comfortable with it. That said, I'm okay if you're not comfortable with it," he said in a rush, then expelled his breath. He gave me a hesitant smile. "And so much for not making it awkward."

"Where's your strong home brew when we need it?" I asked to distract from the pounding of my heart and the flush of my cheeks.

He poured us both more champagne, and I didn't argue.

"To awkward and uncomfortable," I said, raising my glass, avoiding thinking too hard about what he'd just proposed. Semi-proposed? It wasn't quite the passionate declaration of my dreams, but... Holden had just said he wouldn't mind having sex. With me.

Because I was his wife.

Obviously I was convenient, and in any other situation, I'd probably be open to it. But in this one, the stakes were so sky-high. I was already on shaky ground trying not to let on how deep my feelings ran. It could destroy our friendship if he knew I'd imagined him naked a few hundred times.

Just as big of a risk was that, if we had sex, I'd have an even harder time keeping my heart unscathed. I was already concerned about a year from now, when we walked away from each other. If we dropped the boundaries physically, it would leave me even more vulnerable. I knew without a doubt I'd be the one whose heart got crushed in that breakup. Maybe it would anyway, but I had to do whatever I could to try to prevent that. Keeping my pajamas on would play a key part.

"Forget I said all of that," he said after gulping half his champagne. "I'm thinking we should get a hotel room somewhere for tonight—with two beds if you want. It wouldn't look right for us to show up back in Dragonfly Lake a couple hours after tying the knot."

"Good thinking." Yet another thing I hadn't gotten around to considering. "What time do you work tomorrow?"

"I need to be there by eleven at the latest."

"We can do that. And then"—I drank more champagne, starting to feel the first hints of blessed fuzziness around the edges of my brain—"this week we'll make a point of being seen together. A lot. No more hiding."

"That's my girl." He laughed quietly as he looked into my eyes. "Guess I should say, that's my wife."

Our server showed up and asked about dessert, saving me from having to think too hard about my new role. I'd only finished half my entree and was about to decline.

"Do you have anything resembling wedding cake?" Holden asked.

After a moment of thought, the guy said, "I have a lemon crème layer cake or a triple chocolate bourbon cake."

We ended up going for one of each and sharing them, slipping back into a more comfortable, normal-for-us range of topics. Admittedly, the alcohol might've helped a little.

When we'd done all the damage we could on the two monster-sized slices of cake, Holden excused himself to go to the restroom.

As he stood and walked away, toward the back, I watched him. *My husband.*

His dress pants fit him perfectly. Maybe dress pants weren't supposed to highlight a guy's butt, but I couldn't keep my eyes from checking it out like a newlywed wife would. His ass was rounded, muscular, not one of those guy butts that was flat and uninspiring. Everything female in me kick-started.

The woman at the table closest to ours—she was probably in her fifties and with a salt-and-pepper-haired man who was presumably her husband—leaned toward me, snapping my attention from Holden.

"I'd say you're a very lucky girl," she said conspiratorially with a deep drawl. "Congratulations."

"Thank you," I said, feeling flushed, and though I would've liked to blame it on the bubbly, I was pretty sure it was all Holden's doing, because I couldn't banish the thought of holding those perfect butt cheeks in my hands. And he'd, in essence, just told me he'd be fine with that.

"Enjoy your weddin' night," she said with a wink.

I made the mistake of looking at Holden again just before he disappeared around a corner. "I will."

And in that instant, the truth became clear as day to me. The damage was already done. I was already half in love with this man, and denying myself a physical relationship with him wouldn't keep me from crashing and burning. Nothing would.

Might as well enjoy this man to the fullest for every second I had him. I'd deal with the fallout later.

CHAPTER 13

HOLDEN

Something had changed with Chloe in the last half hour or so. I wasn't sure what was going on, but when I'd come back from the restroom, she was quieter. Almost… nervous.

Which didn't make sense at all, unless…

Hell, I knew exactly what it was.

I never should've brought up sex.

There was already enough awkwardness about our wedding night, and then I'd gone and made everything weirder between us by saying I was open to getting it on. With the girl I'd known since grade school. One of my best, longest-standing friends.

What a fucking idiot I was.

As we walked the couple of blocks back to my car, I held her hand mostly because I thought a groom should hold his bride's hand on the evening of their wedding, and Chloe let me.

"Did you bring extra clothes?" she asked as we rounded

the corner outside of the courthouse, which was lit up dramatically now that the sun had fallen below the horizon.

"I did." As soon as I said it, it hit me that that might sound as if I'd been expecting more than a platonic wedding night, and hell, now that I'd made that one blunder, everything felt wrong. "Just in case we wanted to stay somewhere. We could even get two rooms if you'd prefer—"

"I've got it taken care of," she said as we reached my Mustang. I opened her door and held her hand as she got in, then made sure the white dress that did great things to her figure was tucked away from the door.

I closed her in and got in the driver's side. "What's the plan?"

I knew there were a couple of chain motels in town. Nothing worthy of a wedding night, but maybe I needed to stop calling it our wedding night, because that was misleading. All we needed was a crappy but preferably clean room with a couple of double beds. We could do a king if we had to, but tonight, it felt safer to have that separation. It'd been hard enough not to reach out to her in the middle of the night when I hadn't seen her in a flattering, subtly sexy white dress all day or exchanged vows with her to love, honor, and cherish. It lodged ideas in a guy's head. Ideas I needed to get the hell out if we were going to make this work.

Chloe was messing with something on her phone, pulling up the map app, I realized. "Start heading west."

I started the car and followed her directions, trying one more time to ask her where we were heading, to which she replied, with no lack of mystery, "You'll see."

It didn't take more than five minutes for us to reach the outskirts of the county seat, and then with another blink, we were on a dark country road, per Chloe's directions, with no other traffic in sight. This wasn't the road to Dragonfly Lake nor was it the way to Nashville.

"I see what you're doing. Now that you've got me legally

locked down, you're going to take me deep into the woods and off me for my fortune, right?" I said.

"And I was trying so hard not to let on that I was only marrying you for your money," she said with a quiet laugh.

We could laugh about it, but the reality was that in all the premarital paperwork for our grand marriage deal, there'd been a prenup included—to protect her assets, of course. All I had were my house, an embarrassingly small savings account, my car, and my share of the restaurant, whereas I didn't know exactly what she had. Suffice it to say, she had *more*. A hell of a lot more. We'd agreed that everything needed to be spelled out so we could dissolve the marriage easily and quickly a year from now.

"In half a mile, you're going to take a left," Chloe said, and my brows went up. We were literally in the middle of nowhere.

"Sort of freaking me out for real now."

She laughed. "Don't you trust your wife?"

It'd been nearly three hours since that had become official, and it still rattled me to hear the *W* word in any context relating to me.

"I need to keep saying things like that to get used to them," she said, as if sharing my take on the matter.

"Good idea… *wife*."

We shared a conspiratorial look that gave me hope that maybe I hadn't fucked up our friendship by mentioning sex, and without thought, I reached over and took her hand. I was surprised enough when she didn't take hers back. Downright shocked when she lifted our entwined fingers and pressed a kiss to my knuckles. Then she kept ahold of me and let our hands rest on her thigh.

I glanced across the front seat, lit only by the console and dash lights, and I must've had a questioning look on my face because she said, "You *are* my husband."

"I confess I'm more than a little worried about what you're *grooming* me for."

Instead of volleying a pun back my way, she grinned and said, "You should be. Here's your turn."

I took my hand back to steer as I peered out the windshield at the gravel road. There was nothing but trees and hills and a windy road. And dark. "Are we almost there?"

"Three point seven miles to our destination."

Our destination turned out to be better than anything I'd imagined on the short, dark-as-fuck drive. After a driveway that was more than a half mile long, the headlights hit a cabin, and as we pulled up, a security light came on on the porch.

"Wow."

I killed the engine but not the lights and took in a small but new-looking cabin with a porch that stretched all the way across the front. In the center were three steps up to the door, with a large window to each side. There was no garage, no room for one actually, as the cabin seemed to be perched over a steep drop-off. To the left was a black Weber charcoal grill, looking as if someone had intentionally placed it far enough from the house to be safe.

"It's our wedding night," Chloe said in a rush. "I thought we should have something better than a Motel 6."

"You rented this for us?"

"While you were in the restroom. Spur-of-the-moment. I hope it's okay. I didn't have time to scroll through all the photos before you got back. Barely had time to get my credit card entered."

I held back from asking how many bedrooms. It didn't matter. We'd be okay even if one of us had to sleep on a couch. This definitely was a hundred times better than a fifty-year-old low-budget motel room back in the town where we'd tied the knot.

We both got out, she grabbed her duffel, and I went to the trunk and got mine. It was cooler now but still mild, a beautiful night, with a half-moon in the clear sky. Chloe led the way, and when she got to the door, she referenced her phone and tapped in a code on the door. She went inside and I followed. Before I could see anything, she sucked in a gasp.

"Oh, my flipping God," she said.

I glanced around at the living area we found ourselves in, and my brows shot all the way up my head. "What the actual...?"

Chloe burst out in laughter, laced with *oh my God*s and *you've got to be kidding me*s.

The living room was cozy, with a gas fireplace on one wall, a decent-sized flat-screen above it, a sumptuous-looking gray leather sofa and...

"There are hearts *everywhere*," Chloe said, wiping her eyes, looking as if she was going to lose her composure again. "It... It said... It called it a romantic love nest, but I had no idea..."

The throw pillows were heart-shaped. The armchair was some kind of ultra-modern bright red thing with a heart-shaped back and more heart pillows. The windows to each side of the fireplace had red heart garlands dangling over them like window coverings. On the wall, hearts and sayings with hearts. On the end table, a double heart sculpture.

I couldn't think of what to say, because I was still trying to take it all in.

The living area was open to a small dining table, and as I went closer, I saw it was set with red heart-shaped plates on top of rectangular placemats that had a border of hearts. There was a heart-shaped wooden fruit bowl with apples, bananas, and oranges, and naturally, the salt and pepper shakers were hearts as well.

A glance at the kitchen, and I, too, couldn't help laughing. "Jesus." Heart mugs, heart canisters, a heart cutting board, heart-covered oven mitts, and more of the heart dishes… "Someone vomited hearts."

I looked at Chloe, who was walking toward me to see the small kitchen area herself, her lips pressed together against more laughter, her eyes lit up with amusement.

"I had no idea," she said. "I swear. It's a nightmare of hearts."

"Perfect for a couple of newlyweds," I said, unable to *not* grin.

"I can *heart-ly* believe my eyes." Then she laughed again as her eyes skipped over the overload of hearts in the kitchen.

She took a few steps across the wood floors—if you squinted past the decor, the place was actually very nice, obviously built recently, with high-end finishes and quality furniture. Chloe opened a couple of kitchen cabinets until she found an empty one, then she began loading anything with hearts inside. Piece by piece, she "cleaned" the kitchen of every last hint of hearts, and then the dining room.

Next, she marched into the living area, located the coat closet near the door, opened it, and when she saw there was plenty of room, in went the throw pillows and any decor that wasn't attached. When she was done, we were left with the armchair and the window-covering garlands, but she'd cleansed the place of all the other heart vomit.

With a look at me, she nodded once as if to say, *There.*

"Feel better?" I asked, still grinning.

"Much. This is a great little place when you get rid of the awful decor."

"Not a romantic, huh?"

"If you need hearts to be romantic, there's something wrong with you," she said.

I definitely did not need hearts to be romantic, if *romantic* was the right word, because as I watched Chloe bend over to grab a heart-framed plaque she'd missed on the bottom shelf of the coffee table, I couldn't take my eyes off the curves of her ass outlined in that pure-as-snow dress.

I wrenched myself out of my stupor and strode toward the one bedroom I'd spotted so far, wondering if there were others but suspecting there wasn't room for more.

The bedroom was carpeted and had ship-lap walls and, you bet your ass, a shit ton of heart-shaped pillows on the bed. I was shocked and somewhat relieved that there wasn't some kind of giant heart-shaped headboard.

Before I could follow Chloe's lead and shove the pillows in a closet, she came into the room.

"Ahh, this isn't as bad." She went to the doorway of the bathroom. "Would you believe, a safe zone? There's not a single heart to be found in the bathroom."

"An oversight," I said. "You know there's only one bedroom here?"

I was still standing next to the heart-pillow-covered bed, and she turned and came out of the bathroom.

"I do," she said, crossing the room toward me.

When Chloe reached me, both her hands went to the knot in my tie, and she fidgeted with it, as if to straighten it, but I was pretty sure it was perfectly straight. I'd checked it in the restroom at the restaurant.

"Everything okay?" I asked, gazing down at her. Her lashes were long and lightly mascaraed, and she'd glossed her lips in the car with that bold pink I hadn't seen her wear before today. As she raised her gaze to meet mine, I couldn't help but think how pretty she looked. My body responded as well, my pulse kicking up, blood going hot with her so close.

I thought I must've imagined it when her gaze flicked down to my lips.

As she looked into my eyes again, she moistened her own lips, and when she said, "I was thinking..." her voice was soft, lower than usual, and she sounded unsure of herself.

"What were you thinking?" Hell, my voice went low and

a little rough too. I could swear she had me under some kind of spell.

She averted her eyes and fixed her attention on the top button of my vest, running one finger around and around it. "I was thinking that I wouldn't be opposed to... crossing a line... you know, since we're married and all."

CHAPTER 14

t took half a second for her meaning to sink in, and then my heart skipped a beat and all the blood in my body made a rush for my dick. Clearly it'd been too long since I'd gotten laid.

I realized I hadn't said anything when her gaze darted back up to mine, her pretty eyes steeped in doubt.

"Married with benefits," I said, smiling, because I could get behind this plan one thousand percent.

"It solves a lot of things." She unbuttoned the top vest button, signaling she was ready *now*.

I was *all* on board.

"Very practical," I said, my voice a raspy growl as, damn, it took less than two heartbeats for me to go rock hard.

"We both have physical needs," she said, mimicking my words from the restaurant, when I thought I'd stuck my foot in my mouth and ruined everything. Thank fuck I was wrong.

She had all four of the buttons on my vest undone now, and then she shucked it off my shoulders and let it fall to the floor.

Okay, then.

My wife was no meek girl in the bedroom, it appeared.

I ran my hands over the baby-soft skin of her upper arms, dipped them under the dress at her shoulders, loving the feel of her.

She had my tie undone in two seconds flat, and I thought it probably wasn't the first time she'd done that. I'll be honest, it bugged me a little even though that was the most ridiculous thing in the world.

After removing my tie, she met my gaze, a sexy, flirty look in her eyes, and I couldn't not taste her lips for another second. I pressed my mouth to hers and pulled her body into mine, finally running my hands over the silky white fabric that had been beckoning to me for hours. The fabric and the curves under it.

My hands slid downward, over her narrow waist, to her hips, and around to her ass, and it did not disappoint. I pulled her even closer into my body, pressing my cock into her softness, needing more but determined to take it slowly.

I felt her fingers at my neck, going for my shirt buttons, and if she wanted to be the one to rush things, I sure as hell wouldn't argue.

I kissed her again, running my fingers through her long, silky hair, bowled over by the taste, the scent, the feel of her. This woman I knew so well in some ways was like a playground I'd been allowed to look at from a distance but never explore. Now that I was being given free rein, I realized there was so much more than what had always met my eye. There were layers of femininity and sensuality, in her quiet, sexy moan, her sweet floral scent, the hint-of-sugar taste of her tongue, the boldness of her fingers that now had my shirt unbuttoned to my waist.

Chloe tugged my shirt out of my pants and left it hanging on my shoulders. She pulled back from the kiss to run her gaze over my bared chest appreciatively, hungrily, and then her hands were all over it, as if it was a tactile feast she'd been longing for.

I caught my breath as I watched her. I'd had plenty of eager, enthusiastic lovers, but no woman had made me feel quite like she was making me feel, so… *desirable*, cherished, as if she couldn't get enough of *me* specifically. The way she was eyeing me lit me on fire.

"Chloe," I said in a growl, almost as if I had to reassure myself this was her, the girl I'd known since she was three feet tall and reed thin.

She apparently took that for the approval it was, because her hands trailed down to my pants as her lips returned to mine. Our tongues tangled, and I had the half thought that she kissed like no one I'd ever kissed before—and I'd had some damn good kisses in my life.

Then every thought flew out of my mind as I felt her fingers on my dick. She grasped me, then fingered my tip. My head fell back and I let out a groan as my blood thundered through me like a freight train.

Seconds later, she shoved my pants and boxer briefs down to my thighs. As one of her hands grasped my bare ass, the other stroked my hard-as-steel dick. Her lips hovered over mine, her tongue teased my mouth, and then with a shaky breath, she lowered herself slowly, kissing and licking and nipping my chest and abs as she went down.

When I felt her tongue swirl over my tip, just a teasing taste, I nearly lost my mind. Next thing I knew, she was running her tongue from base to tip in a slow, savoring lick, as if I was her favorite lollipop. It took everything in me to keep my touch on her head gentle and undemanding, but I fought to do just that, letting her have the reins, seeing where she took it, because this woman was blowing my ever-loving mind.

Her mouth closed fully over me, and my eyes rolled back in my head. I bit down on my lip to try to slow down the effect she was having on me. I opened my eyes to take in the sight of Chloe, on her knees in front of me, her hair tousled from my hands. Her white dress draped around her, and that finally got through to my brain—she was fully dressed still, heels and all, and I was a millisecond from going off like a barrel of dynamite.

"Chlo," I managed as I gently tugged at her. "Mmm…"

She did a thing with her tongue that had me fighting hard to remember why I needed to slow this down.

"Com'ere," I gasped, nudging her head again.

She looked up at me with her lips still around me, and swear to God, that scorching-hot image of her, with fire in her eyes and her dark locks cascading over her sexy shoulders, was burned in my mind for eternity.

I took her hand and entwined our fingers and pulled her up. When her mouth slipped off me, I wanted to howl over the loss, but at the same time, I was dying to give her the same pleasure she was giving me.

I pulled her to a stand, drawing her body tight against mine. "You're incredible," I said in a growl. "But fully dressed. Need to remedy that."

"Guess I'm just better at getting you naked," she said with a sexy smug grin that I wanted to kiss off her face. Of course Chloe could bring competition into the bedroom, and damn if I didn't love it. There wasn't much she could do at this moment, short of walking away, that I wouldn't love.

I kissed her lips that had lost the artificial pink gloss to a natural rosiness. As I distracted her with my tongue, I found the two little buttons in the middle of her back and the short zipper at her waist that kept her dress up and undid them all. With our lips still locked, I put some space between our bodies at the same time I slipped the fabric off both of her shoulders. The dress fell partway down, getting hung up on her arms at the elbows.

She broke the contact of our mouths and lowered her

arms. The dress puddled around her feet, leaving her in a white lacy strapless bra and matching panties that I suspected were a thong.

"Is this what you were looking for?" she asked, her voice an irresistible purr.

She stepped out of the dress, still wearing her heels, and I feasted my eyes on her long, gorgeous legs and the innocent-looking lace at the juncture of them.

"Better than I ever could've hoped for," I said as I kicked my own shoes off and rid myself of the rest of my clothes. "Bring that over here."

———

CHLOE

Looking at Holden fully clothed on an average day usually gave me a jolt of attraction. Seeing him stretched out in front of me, naked, hard, motioning me to come to him? It was like my whole universe was knocked off-kilter.

The way he was looking at me, with heavy lids and a sensual hunger, made my breasts heavy with need. The hollow ache deep within me peaked to a needful throb as I stepped toward him, keeping my heels and lingerie on, thankful I'd made the effort to order the bridal set even though I hadn't planned on *this* happening. It gave me added confidence. I knew men, in general, at least the ones I'd slept with, found my body attractive, but this was Holden. There was more to it than physical parts and potential orgasms, regardless of what we told ourselves.

That thought sparked a tiny pulse of doubt, so I blocked it out, focused on his reaction to my physical parts as I closed the two feet between us. I moved between his legs where he sat on the edge of the mattress.

His arms closed around me, and his palms covered my

butt, as if he'd been dying to verify it was a thong I wore. He kneaded my cheeks, his fingers flirting with a spot deep between my thighs. He ran his tongue around my belly button and pressed kisses to my abdomen for long, maddening seconds as I longed for him to touch me where I was throbbing and damp with need for him.

I realized the error in my decision to leave my lingerie-and-heels armor on. No matter how cool I could play it with other men, that all went out the window with Holden. I reached back and unfastened the strapless bra and let it fall to the floor, my breasts bursting free.

Within half a heartbeat, Holden had them in both of his hands, with his tongue swirling its way to one of my nipples. The moment he touched his mouth to the tip, a current of need shot straight to my core, and I arched into him with a gasp.

Within seconds, my legs were shaking, my body crying for him to fill me and make the ache go away.

"Your breasts are incredible," he said as he switched his attention to the other one.

His tongue was incredible, I thought.

My knees were on the mattress now, straddling his thighs, and I reached back to slide the ankle straps of my shoes down over my heels to get them out of the way.

As I was about to press him down on the mattress and climb up his body, it was as if he read my intention. He grasped my body to his, stood, turned, and pressed my back into the mattress, my legs dangling over the edge. Instead of climbing over me as I'd hoped, he peeled the thong down my thighs and swirled his tongue around the pulsing spot that was aching for him most, then nipped my inner thigh and… disappeared.

I popped my eyes open and realized he was digging through his pants pocket for his wallet.

"You came prepared?" I asked, thankful and curious at once.

He tossed one condom to the nightstand and ripped open a second one. "Always," was all he said, and I decided that was good enough.

I held my hand out for the packet, and after a questioning glance, he handed it over. I propped myself up on my elbows and sheathed him, grasping him and squeezing once the condom was on. His moan affected my body like a physical touch, and I opened my legs to him, rubbing one foot up his outer thigh as he stood there for a second, raking his gaze over me.

In an instant, he had me repositioned, my head cushioned by the pillows at the headboard and my body the right way on the bed instead of sideways and hanging off. He crawled up over me, between my knees, and his hardness teased my folds exactly where I was aching for him.

When his face was even with mine, a breath away, he paused for a moment and peered down into my eyes. It was the most intense exchange I'd ever had during sex, no shields between us, and I felt like he saw deep inside of me in that instant. It rattled me more than a little, so instead of letting it continue or thinking too hard about what he'd seen in my eyes, I reached down, found his cock, and guided it to my entrance.

"God," he said on an exhale as he pushed inside of me, stretching me in the most delicious way.

I willed my muscles to relax and adjusted my body to pull him all the way in, closing my eyes and allowing myself one heartbeat to think, *Holden Henry is inside of me, and it's even more magical than I ever could've imagined.*

As he pulled partway out, the hot, wet friction made us moan as one. Holden propped himself up slightly on his forearms, pushed slowly back in, and said, "You're perfect, Chlo."

He was so perfect that I couldn't utter words. All I could do was show him by wrapping my legs around his waist, opening myself up even more to him, grasping his butt, and pulling him into me.

His thrusts were slow and savoring at first, enough to drive a girl out of her mind. I'd had good sex, but I'd never felt so frantic for more, so desperate for him to drive me over the edge that was speeding toward me as he started thrusting faster, unquestionably right there with me.

Our bodies melded as one, moved as one, toward a single goal. Time ceased to exist, only sensation, and all I could do was hold on for dear life as Holden rocked me to my core like I had never been rocked before.

"Come for me, Chloe," he said in a desperate, strained voice in my ear, and I did exactly that, as if he had that much command over my body.

I cried out as I clenched and contracted around him and flashes of light and color exploded behind my lids. The orgasm stretched out and seemed to ricochet off itself into another one as Holden climaxed too.

Spasms and shots of sensation washed through my body, and all I could do was lie there and nearly weep from the pleasure and ride it out, clinging to every second.

I gradually became aware of Holden's weight resting on top of me as we both breathed hard, unable to form words. Eventually I ran my fingers lightly up his side, the only movement I was able to manage. His response was a sensual, satisfied groan that I could feel vibrating through my every cell.

"Mmm," I said in response.

A few seconds later, he shifted slightly and then his lips were on mine. His kiss was gentle, tender, slow, not the heated frenzy from before.

I wilted into the mattress, savoring the weight of him on top of me, the light attention of his mouth on mine. I'd be completely content to never move from this position.

Eventually he ended the kiss and ran his fingers through

my hair at my temple. I knew he was gazing down at me even with my eyes closed. It took more than a little courage for me to open them and meet his gaze as I came back into reality bit by bit.

As soon as I lifted my lashes, I registered his alluring, lazy, satiated smile. I grinned back.

"Happy wedding night," he said, his voice a growl.

The understatement of that blew my mind, as there was no way he could even begin to fathom what that had been like for me. The sex itself was spectacular. Add to it my years of wishing, wanting him, finally realized…

A pink pillow to the side of my head caught my eye, and a laugh escaped me as I took in our surroundings. "We just consummated our marriage in a nest of heart pillows."

Lifting his brows, his lips sliding into a bigger grin, Holden glanced around us and plucked up a red pillow. "A love nest, indeed." With a laugh, he pressed a quick kiss to my lips. "Effective as fuck. No pun intended."

"Marketing win," I added. "I'll never think of hearts the same way."

He kissed me again, then said, "What do you say we take refuge in a heart-free zone and move this to the shower?"

I'd follow him just about anywhere at that moment, and a shower sounded full of possibilities, depending on whether one time was enough for Holden or he was open to more.

"A shower sounds good," I said.

He rolled to the side, severing our intimate connection, then slid to his feet. "Wait here."

The view as he walked to the bathroom was incredible—his ass was incredible—and I watched the muscles in it and his thighs shift with every step and let out a quiet sigh of appreciation.

The water started, and a few seconds later, he emerged, plucked up the second condom from the nightstand, then surprised me by hoisting me off the bed in a cradle hold and carrying me into the bathroom. Turned out, he *was* open to more, and shower sex with Holden did not disappoint. I was reasonably certain *no* sex with Holden could ever disappoint.

It was maybe an hour later, after our memorable shower and a sampling of the, *of course*, heart-shaped chocolates we'd found in a candy dish in the kitchen, that we were tucked back in bed, the throw pillows tossed to the floor, the lights out, and Holden back on his side of the bed and me on the other that it really hit me.

By giving in to my years-long attraction and having sex with Holden, I'd upped the stakes incredibly. I might've told myself I would deal with the fallout later, that I'd somehow be okay, but lying there in the dark on my wedding night, I knew without a doubt… I was so screwed.

My heart was going to be wholly, devastatingly crushed when this was over.

CHAPTER 15

'd been married for two days—and two nights—and I had to admit... I could easily get used to this. I *wouldn't*, because it had an expiration date in 363 days, but for now, "married with benefits" was rocking my world.

It was Sunday morning, and Chloe and I were heading to the Dragonfly Diner for breakfast with my family, instigated by my sister, Hayden. Sometimes the youngest Henry and I butted heads, but since she'd married Zane and become a mom to the cutest little boy in the known universe, she'd mellowed around the edges and we got along better. I had to give her credit for excelling at her mom role, particularly after I'd doubted her when she and Zane had first confessed their oops.

Hayden had insisted we Henrys get together to celebrate my marriage this morning before Cash and I had to head into the restaurant to oversee brunch. It fit Chloe's and my agenda perfectly—our first married public appearance, which we'd both agreed needed to happen sooner rather than later. The bonus was I'd get some prime spoiling time with six-month-old Harrison.

We'd decided to walk, since the diner was two blocks from my house and it was a bright, sunny spring day. As we turned onto Main, I took Chloe's hand in mine. She outclassed me in my jeans and polo by a mile this morning, wearing tailored ankle pants, a tank, and a thigh-length draping wrap thing along with heels—lower than her usual, she'd claimed when I'd reminded her we were walking.

I knew she was uneasy but I wasn't sure why. She looked fantastic. We *had* this. We didn't have to fake the affection between us, and we sure as hell didn't have to fake the sparks.

"You know my family already loves you, right?" I asked as we strolled past several businesses that weren't yet open for the day—Posh Salon, Fat Cat Yarn Shop, Lake Girl Boutique. "Their shock has passed, and they just want to welcome you into the family."

"I know. Your family's awesome. They were warm and welcoming at your dad's wedding, even though I hadn't seen most of them for years." She flashed a smile I almost believed, but there was a slight wobble to it. "I'm still getting used to being back in town in general," she said.

We had to walk by the windowed front of the cafe to get to the door, and the place was crawling with people. As I glanced inside, eager to see who besides my family was there, I felt Chloe tense at my side.

"I'm right here with you," I said as we reached the door. I pulled it open and let her precede me in.

The diner was on the corner, and not only was the front side windowed but the righthand wall was too, and booths lined both of them, back-to-back, their upholstery bright aqua. In the open space were faux-wood tables of four. On the left side of the diner, a single apple-green upholstered bench ran the entire length, from the front window to the back of the place, with four-toppers spaced evenly along it and two chairs per table opposite the bench. Nearly all of the tables were occupied, as was the counter at the very back.

The Henry group took up three of those adjacent tables along the wall on the left, putting them pretty much right smack in the middle of everything. Chloe, I realized, wasn't looking at them but rather was scoping out the place like some kind of fugitive who expected to be blindsided by the law. Her gaze lingered first on a table with Olivia, Anna, Maeve, and Emerson sitting around it, all focused on Olivia as she appeared to be telling a tale. Next, her gaze skipped over to the last table on the window side and paused there, where Magnolia and her fiancé were sitting across from each other.

With my hand at the small of Chloe's back, I gently nudged her toward my family, leaning down and saying into her ear, "Smile, EVP."

The nickname did its job, and by the time we reached the group, she appeared to have forgotten those she considered threats.

"There he is," my dad said. He sat with his back to the wall, next to Faye, the woman he'd married last month, who was smiling warmly as she got to her feet.

"The other newlyweds," Faye said as she held out her arms to Chloe for a hug. "It's so good to see you again. Congratulations, Chloe."

They hugged while my dad slid out to give me an overzealous but quiet back-slap man-hug.

"Hi, Dad."

"Congrats, son," he said, his eyes crinkling at the corners with his approval.

He and my new stepmom traded places, and Faye hesitated for a moment as she searched my face. Her reluctance was understandable since I'd struggled with my dad's remarriage and hadn't really embraced it until their wedding day.

"Come here," I said to her with a welcoming grin and my arms open.

"I'm so happy for you two," Faye said as she eagerly accepted the hug.

Cash had his back to us, seated across from our dad and Faye, and once the older newlyweds were out of his way, he stood and hugged Chloe.

"Welcome to the family officially," he said. He'd given me congrats and skepticism yesterday at work and nodded at me now, saying, "Holden."

Next to Cash was his new BFF, Zane, Hayden's husband. When Hayden had broken her pregnancy news to my brothers and me over a year ago, Cash had put on his badass brother act for all of about five minutes. Then he'd learned Zane was fresh out of the Navy, and the two had bonded over their military ties.

"Congratulations, you two," Zane said.

"Thanks. It's good to see you again," Chloe said. She'd met Zane for the first time at my dad's wedding.

"Who is that?" Hayden asked in the baby voice she used for her beloved son. She sat at the end, on the other side of an empty high chair. Harrison, world's cutest baby, was bouncing on her leg until she hugged him to her and stood. "Do you see Uncle Holden?"

My favorite chubster of all time peered up at me with the corner of a slobbered-up soft purple block in his mouth, unsure blue eyes, and a serious expression on his rosy apple-cheeked face.

I made my eyes go big, smile go exaggerated, and then I leaned in slowly toward him and said, "Hairrrrry baby!"

Hayden pretended to hate my play on *hairy* and *Harry*, but then she'd started calling him Harry as well, despite insisting his name was Harrison—and only Harrison—when he'd been born.

It was my destiny to be the kid's favorite uncle, and little

Harrison finally gave me what I was working for—a big, toothless grin and a near hit of my nose with the purple block. I held my hands out and took the boy from my sister.

"Chloe," Hayden said as she hugged my wife. "I can't tell you how thankful I am to have another female in the family. With you and Faye, we've almost caught up."

"Until you count the North side of the family," Seth said from his spot next to my dad. He'd also congratulated me and tossed me plenty of good-natured shit yesterday at Henry's.

"The North babies are throwing it all off," Hayden said. The family she'd married into consisted of five sons, of whom Faye was the matriarch. Female genes were proving hard to come by even with the newest generation. "Besides Harrison" —she addressed Chloe—"Zane's brother Mason has Jasper and Calvin. Gabe and Lexie have Wyatt. No girl babies to speak of so far."

"I'm considering offering a reward for the first grand-daughter," Faye said with a laugh.

"Harrison's darling," Chloe said, watching the baby in my arms as I lifted him over my head then made motor noises as I lowered him to my face and kissed him. His giggle was infectious, his hesitancy completely gone.

"Holden needs one of his own," Hayden said, and Chloe's eyes popped wider, as if she hadn't even considered the possibility.

Obviously, we hadn't had anything resembling the *do you want kids someday* talk since we knew there was no someday for the two of us.

"Can we just be married first?" I jumped in.

"Of course." Hayden didn't miss a beat. "You just went from friends to engaged to married on fast-forward, so..." She shrugged. "You never know. *These things happen.*"

Everyone at the table laughed, because this chunky, lovable baby in my arms qualified as *these things*, being the unplanned pregnancy that had brought Zane and Hayden together.

"My unsolicited advice," my sister continued, "is to take your time and do exactly what you said. Be married for a good bit first. While I love that little man to pieces, he comes with lots of stress."

As soon as Chloe slid in next to Seth and I sat on her other side, still holding my nephew, Maribella, one of the servers, came by to get Chloe's and my drink orders. Chloe was looking over the menu, as were Faye and Zane, while the rest of us knew the offerings by heart and talked about Sergio Vega's new-to-him Lincoln, which he used to drive Nigel, his Boston terrier, around the square every day like clockwork. After Maribella delivered our drinks, she took our orders and disappeared again.

When everyone else was deep in conversation, Chloe leaned over and, peering back at Magnolia's table, asked in a whisper, "Who's she with?"

"It's her fiancé. Rick something. He's from Nashville."

"I don't understand what someone could possibly see in her. She's pretty on the outside but..."

"Possibly her daddy's company. I believe he works for her old man."

"That makes more sense." She shook her head. "All these years later and she still gets my dander up. I know she's not worth it."

"She has that effect," I said, hating that such an insecure, mean woman affected Chloe after all these years. Magnolia had always been the most heartless mean girl of them all but had kept a foot in the popular crowd by virtue of the lavish parties her parents would throw for her, and later, the parties she'd throw when they were out of town. "You shouldn't worry about her anymore. You're prettier, more successful, kinder, and a decent human to boot."

That drew a smile from Chloe, and she momentarily

leaned her head into my shoulder, squeezed my arm, and affectionately tweaked Harrison's little nose.

A few minutes later, I'd just handed Harrison across the table to Zane to put him in the high chair when I heard Chloe's intake of breath. At first I thought it was because the baby was so damn cute, but when I glanced at her, it was alarm I saw on her face. I followed her gaze to the main door, saw what she saw, or rather who, and I was still confused.

CHLOE

My heart skipped a beat when my parents walked into the diner. Their appearance threw me off for two reasons. First, because my parents had never gone to restaurants much, other than when they came to Nashville and I treated. They'd never had the money for going out. The second reason I was shaken was because I had insta-guilt for not inviting them to this celebration.

"We should've invited them," I said quietly to Holden.

"We're having dinner with them in two days to celebrate," he said. "They're welcome to join us though."

He was right on both counts, and I relaxed slightly—I didn't know if I would ever fully relax when out in the heart of Dragonfly Lake, frankly—and stood, slipping between the two tables to make my way toward my mom and dad.

Before they spotted me, I was taken aback again as my mom beelined for a table along the front window. I slowed down as my dad followed her. They greeted a couple close to their age, my mom hugging the woman and my dad shaking hands with the guy, and then before I could get there, my parents slid into the booth across from the two.

They had a breakfast date with another couple? My parents, who'd had no social lives to speak of for all the years I'd lived with them? It was obvious they were close to these people.

I realized I'd slowed almost to a stop in the middle of the diner and forced myself to head that way.

"Mom? Dad?"

They turned toward me as I reached the table, and my mom swatted my dad's forearm to let her back out of the booth.

"Chloe!" she said as she stood and hugged me. "My beautiful girl. Look at you. You're glowing! Chloe—" She cut her overzealous self off and asked, in a quieter voice, "Can I tell Hank and Shirley your news?"

I nodded as I hugged her back, soaking in the smell of her lotion and feeling less off-kilter.

"Chloe and Holden Henry got married this weekend!" my mom said, loudly enough that multiple heads turned her way.

Chalk up Operation Going Public as a success then.

Sixty seconds later, fully aware of the stares from all corners of the diner, I'd been introduced to Shirley from my mom's knitting group—I didn't even know she had a knitting group—and Hank Moody, friends of my parents, who they apparently had a standing Sunday morning date with.

My parents had friends?

It blew my mind a little, and I was suddenly certain that they fit into this town more than I ever would. I was happy for them but it just showed how disconnected I'd let myself get.

I invited them to join us, and the four of them eventually traded tables with the people next to us. It was a big commotion, but hey, Holden and I were already the center of attention since my mom had told literally half the town about our marriage in a single breath. It made my skin crawl, but hopefully things would die down any second now.

By the time our food was served, my mom and dad had met and oohed and ahhed over little Harrison and been introduced to Zane as well as Faye at the opposite end of the row of tables. I expected things to turn awkward, but my mom became engrossed in a conversation with Hayden about baby food and teething, and my dad, when he found out Zane was a pilot, had a dozen and a half questions for him.

Shirley and Hank had apparently shopped at Hayden's home furnishings store on Hale Street in Nashville. It was close to my apartment—less than a mile away—but I'd never visited it, because I'd had my furnishings since before she'd gone into business, and home décor was not on my radar.

Hayden and I had reconnected at Mr. Henry's wedding three weeks ago, but we'd never been what I'd call close, even when I'd spent so much time at the Henry house as a child. The two-year age difference back then had been a barrier, and I'd always gravitated more to Holden, who was my age and grade in school, than his little sister. It hadn't helped that, back then at least, Holden and Hayden had bickered nonstop, often making me glad I was an only child.

Now, though, I liked my new sister-in-law. She was warm, friendly, funny, and she and her new husband, Zane, were so in love it could make a girl rethink her anti-forever-love policy.

Two servers delivered our food, including the four newcomers to the group, and conversation flowed at both ends of the table, with Holden having no trouble keeping my parents and their friends engaged, while Hayden and I talked business—Holden's little sister was sharp and entertaining, and she asked a lot of questions about the hotel. Work, of course, was my comfort zone for topics—much safer than whether Holden and I were going to pop out any kids.

I ignored the little jump in my pulse at the thought of that, because it wasn't a possibility. I didn't have kids on my radar and never had. They didn't go with demanding careers, at least not for me. A woman could do both if she wanted to, but I'd never wanted to. I didn't want to be the mom who left before her kids were awake to go catch a plane and then Face-

Timed them from another part of the world more than she saw them in person, and that's how it would be if I was at the helm of Marks International.

I was halfway done with my scrambler skillet when Anna Delfico and her friends stood from their table to leave. I'd had one eye on them as well as Magnolia since we'd been seated. I wasn't sure why. I knew Magnolia wouldn't attack me when I was ensconced in the Henry family, and Anna and Olivia and their group, like Holden had said the last time I saw them, had never been mean girls. Still, they intimidated me even now, made me feel like a bumbling idiot even from across the room. It was unwarranted, I thought as I glanced down at my designer cross-body bag and clothing that I knew was on trend. On the outside, I wasn't a bumbling idiot. In business, I wasn't a bumbling idiot. In Nashville, I could don a mantle of confidence with the best of them. I needed to get over this crap even if I had to fake it till I made it.

I needed to do that ASAP, apparently, because instead of heading to the exit, the four of them made their way toward our group, all smiles and calling out greetings to the Henrys and stopping in the center, opposite Holden and me. My heart was racing like a scared rabbit's.

"Congratulations, you two," Anna said with what appeared to be a genuine smile. "Exciting news! And Chloe, it's really good to see you."

Holden and I said thank you at the same time, and then I added, once my brain caught up, "You too. It's been a long time."

"Congrats, guys," Maeve McGinnis said as she came up beside Anna. "Your engagement had everyone buzzing last week, and now this… Heads will be exploding, no doubt." I couldn't detect anything but friendliness in her words, even though I was searching for more.

"They'll get over it," Holden said good-naturedly. "Thanks, Maeve. Hey, Emerson, Olivia."

"Hey, you two. Congratulations," Emerson said.

"Yes, congrats," Olivia added. "And, Chloe, welcome back to town." She moved down the table toward my parents, and I was more than a little stunned when Olivia bent down and hugged Shirley and then reached across my dad to grasp my mom's forearm affectionately. "How are you ladies doing? Patty, are you coming to knitting group this week? I'm dying to see the sweater."

The other three girls kept talking to Holden and Hayden and probably me too, but my attention was stuck at the end of the table. Olivia London was friendly with my mom?

It didn't equate.

I guess a lot really could happen in sixteen years. I never in a thousand years would've thought my mom would be on a first-name basis with one of the most popular girls in my graduating class. Olivia had just said more to my mother than she ever had to me. Of course, now that I thought about it, that was probably by *my* design, as I hadn't left myself open to interactions back then.

"Chloe, we do girls' night on Saturdays," Anna said, jolting my attention back to the conversation at my table. "We'd love to have you join us."

"Oh." My brain froze momentarily as I shifted into fight-or-flight mode. Holden squeezed my thigh under the table, which jolted me out of it enough to realize the three had their eyes on me, waiting for a response. "I, um... This coming Saturday?"

"Yep. It's Maeve's birthday so we'll be celebrating," Anna said.

"The more the merrier," Maeve added.

"I haven't thought—"

"You should go," Holden said, his hand still supportively on my leg. "I'll be working as usual."

Right. Because he worked most Saturday nights. I knew this, but to be honest, whether Holden worked or not hadn't even crossed my mind yet. I was too stuck on the girls' night invitation itself, the mini panic it induced.

With so many eyes on me—not just Anna's, Maeve's, Emerson's and now Olivia's but also Hayden's and Zane's and…

I blew out a shaky breath and hoped no one could hear the shakes over the restaurant din. "Sure," I finally said, hoping I hadn't waited so long to respond that it was obvious I was terrified of a girls' night invite. "I could do that." I took a couple of seconds to swallow down some anxiety and then added, "Thank you," and forced a smile back on my face.

Anna took her phone out and asked for my number and said she'd text me the details toward the end of the week. That gave me a few days to block it out of my mind completely, I thought.

As the four said their goodbyes to the table as a whole, re-congratulated Holden and me, and headed out, I coached myself to take in a deep, steadying breath. What kind of social moron was I?

Most times, I wasn't. I would never, ever be Ms. Social, but I could handle a few hours with four or five people who seemed to be kind and welcoming. I just needed to get out of my head, forget my history, and embrace that my world for the next twelve months was in Dragonfly Lake.

CHAPTER 16

Saturday night, I made it into the Barn Bar thanks to two things. One, Presley came into town to go with me. Two, we had a generous glass of wine at Holden's—*my*—house, so I was feeling warm and buzzy.

The Barn Bar was on the way out of town, past the schools and Tripz. The building was—shockingly—an old barn that'd been converted. I'd been by it a thousand times but never inside. The double doors were centered, as was the main bar when you walked in. The counter formed a central square, with three sides lined by stools, and the back was a tall wall where all the liquor was displayed. There were pool tables and dartboards and plenty of high-top tables, plus what looked like a dance floor to one side, and the decor was rustic and minimal.

When Presley and I walked in, it felt like everyone in the place turned to check us out. I pretended not to notice, tried to steer my brain away from freaking out or feeling the attention in a bad way. Thanks to the wine, I mostly pulled it off.

"Drink first?" Presley asked, well aware of my trepidation

in general and a firm believer that a little alcohol could make most things smoother.

I didn't disagree and nodded, scanning the place for any of the girls we were meeting. It was a big room, and there were already a lot of people there, from twentysomethings to my age and older. I probably knew who a lot of these people were, but since I hadn't seen them for a decade and a half, I didn't readily recognize many.

As soon as we had our drinks—wine for Presley and a hard seltzer for me, I heard someone calling my name from the front corner of the bar. When I turned, I saw Anna, Olivia, Emerson, and Maeve at a high-top table for six. There was a trio of guys gathered around the end where Maeve, the birthday girl, was. Olivia waved us over as she laughed at something someone said.

"Hey," Anna said as we approached. "So glad you made it, Chloe. Hi," she said to Presley.

I introduced Presley to the four women and stole glances at the guys, trying to figure out if they were people I should recognize.

Anna saved me.

"Presley, this is Max Dawson, Anton White, and Alex Costello. You guys remember Chloe Abrams? Or Henry... Are you changing your name, Chloe?"

"I did." Which seemed like a pain to do it just for a year, but I hoped it would work in my favor toward convincing Angelica. "It's good to see you all."

I remembered the guys now, by name, anyway. They all had deep Dragonfly Lake roots and had grown up here, some older than us, some younger. They'd been athletes back in the day, popular guys who everyone knew, and they were still good-looking. Presley seemed to agree as she greeted each one individually and smiled at them all, which didn't go unappreciated, judging by the smiles she got in return.

She and I took the two empty chairs, with me next to

Olivia and Presley on the end. I couldn't help but notice that Alex drifted to stand close to her chair and helped her scoot it in.

"Happy birthday, Maeve," I said to the pretty brunette at the other end of the table.

"Yes, happy birthday," Presley repeated. "I want to buy you a drink. What would you like?"

Maeve settled on a chocolate martini and looked like Presley wasn't the first one to treat her for her big day. She was all grins and her eyes gleamed in a telling way.

"So Holden Henry, huh?" Max said to me, still standing between Maeve and Olivia, and I wondered if I would ever *not* look for doubt and disbelief when it came to Holden being with me. "He's a good guy."

Good enough to marry his friend, I thought, then shook it off, because I needed to just own that I'd married one of the best guys and he knew just about everyone in town.

"I think so," I said with a laugh that I willed to not sound nervous. I took a healthy swallow of my drink.

"I hope he finds an investor for his brewery soon," Anton said. "This town could use that kind of draw."

"We could use some good beer," Max said with a laugh as he raised his bottle of mass-produced brew.

"He's determined," I said vaguely, since we'd all agreed not to breathe a word to anyone but Holden's brothers until the money was in place and all the paperwork finalized. That should happen within the next few days, and then I had a feeling it would take less than a half day for the entire town to hear the news. Maybe less than an hour.

"I heard you're heading up that hotel project south of town," Emerson, sitting across from me, said. She was a dark-haired beauty, with flawless olive skin and green eyes.

"Yeah, we want to hear about that," Olivia said, leaning on the table beside me, totally at ease, totally the opposite of how I felt.

The subject of my job helped though.

I answered their questions, which ranged from what the hotel was like inside to what kind of job opportunities there were to when it would be open. It didn't take long, and only half of my seltzer, for me to begin relaxing.

The guys eventually left for the dartboards, and there was a continuous stream of people to and from our table to say hello to my table mates, who were obviously still as popular as they'd been in school. If I'd wanted to keep the evening low-profile, I'd agreed to do girls' night with the wrong people.

I was surprised to realize I knew almost everyone once I heard their name, and it struck me how many people I'd grown up with had stayed here in Dragonfly Lake—something I'd never considered for even half a heartbeat.

Maybe it wasn't such a bad place if you didn't have my baggage.

I really needed to figure out how to unload that baggage. I guess tonight was a step toward that, particularly if I ordered another drink, which I did when the server, an early-twenties shaggy-haired guy named Stone, came by.

My optimism and determination took a hit when Magnolia James waltzed up to our table and presented Maeve with a small wrapped box. My body went tense and my smile slipped off my face. When Emerson seemed to notice, I forced a grin for her benefit, and I could swear there was a look of understanding in her eyes. Like maybe we shared an opinion of Magnolia.

"I was hoping I'd run into you here, Maeve," Magnolia said in a syrupy-sweet voice, and I watched the faces around the table, trying to discern whether people bought her bullshit or saw through her. "Happy birthday."

"Oh." Maeve looked down at the present as if she couldn't think of what to say, which was entirely possible considering the birthday cocktails she'd been served so far. "Thanks, Magnolia."

"Who are you here with?" Anna asked, and she seemed warm just like she always was to everyone.

Magnolia looked around the table, smiling, her makeup and hair perfect as usual. She said Olivia's name and Emerson's in greeting, nodded at Presley. When her gaze got to me, she said, smile still on her face, "Weird night, huh?"

"Happy night," Olivia said cheerfully, emphatically, making me feel as if she was on my side in this unspoken years-long battle.

I bit down on the inside of my lip and fought to keep my dislike hidden. Thankfully, at that moment, Stone was back with another round, and I busied myself helping him distribute to the table while Magnolia prattled on.

"I convinced Rick to stop by," she was saying. "He's in such a hurry to get home after our dinner in Nashville." Her tone made no secret of *why* he was in a hurry, and I inwardly rolled my eyes.

"Super-cute dress," Olivia said.

It was cute, of course, because apparently trolls didn't walk around in ugly burlap bags but rather thousand-dollar designer dresses. I recognized this one from my favorite high-end store in Nashville.

"Thanks, yours too," Magnolia replied in such a fake voice it nauseated me. "Open it now," she said to Maeve, who'd started to put the box in her purse, obviously with the intention of opening it later.

"Oh. Okay." Maeve laughed, took another sip of her drink, then ripped the paper off and tossed it over her shoulder, making all of us laugh because that was the alcohol, not the usual Maeve. Even I could tell that.

Then I noticed the color of the box in front of her—Tiffany fricking blue. I glanced at Emerson in time to see a flash of WTF in her eyes before she flipped that into a smile like it was perfectly normal to give someone whose birthday girls' night out you hadn't even been invited to something from Tiffany and Company.

"Oooh," Maeve said, and I caught a flash of confusion on her face as well, and then she buried it in a wide grin. She opened the box to find a chunky but simple silver bracelet. "Wow. Thank you." Maeve took it out and had Anna fasten it around her wrist. "It's beautiful, Magnolia."

The others around the table said complimentary things as well. I sat there barely breathing, hoping Magnolia didn't pull up a stool and join us.

"Enjoy your celebration. So sorry I can't join you, but it looks like Rick is ready to go." Magnolia leaned over and hugged Maeve from the side. "Celebrate for me too."

And then she was gone and I let out my breath.

The table was subdued for a few seconds.

"She means well," Olivia finally said.

"I know I'm just a visitor but she seemed like a head case," Presley said perceptively.

Though I'd told her plenty about my childhood and this town and my status as an outsider, I'd never said anything about Magnolia specifically. Never wanted to waste the breath on her.

I pressed my lips together and waited to see how the others reacted. These were Magnolia's friends, as far as I knew.

"Magnolia is difficult," Emerson said quietly, matter-of-factly. "She knows how to cut someone to the bone with barely a blink of an eye."

"I suspect," Anna said, "it sucks to be Magnolia. It doesn't excuse any of it, but I think she's insecure and lonely. I'm not her BFF or anything, but I went to her big, pretty house plenty of times over the years growing up, and her parents..." She shook her head. "Not warm and loving, I don't think."

"They give her money and material things instead of love," Maeve said. "Which is sad but no excuse for being the way she is. Does she think she's going to buy my friendship?" She held her wrist up and inspected the bracelet.

"That's always been her way," Emerson said. "The birthday parties growing up? The high school parties when her parents were out of town?"

None of which I'd been to, of course, but I didn't say anything. It was embarrassing, even if Magnolia seemed to have bigger problems than I had.

"She didn't need to say what she said to you." Olivia directed this to me.

"That was mild," I said with an uneasy attempt at a smile. "We have a history, I guess you could say."

Emerson tilted her head. "Did she bully you?"

I suddenly felt hot, as if they'd cranked the heat by ten degrees. Did I want to answer honestly or blow off the question? I was trying to fit in for the first time in my life, and opening up about this past pain was so personal. I looked around the table and saw nothing but concern and support. If I wanted to get rid of the baggage, maybe I needed to air it out. "You know, I never thought of it as bullying, but I guess it was. I don't know what I did to make her hate me, but it started in grade school."

"I don't think you did anything," Presley said. "I didn't know you then, but what's to hate about this girl?" She gestured to me and turned the question to the others with a broad grin. "Chloe isn't mean."

"She's not," Emerson said. "I don't know you well, but I've never known you to be mean."

"Thanks. I've never been very social," I admitted.

I'd been on the shy side as a kid, and then to have Magnolia embarrass me in front of my class more than once, it'd become easier to try to disappear, stay off her radar. She'd gotten in trouble enough times that she learned to taunt me in private. When Holden and his family had moved to Nashville in fourth grade, I'd basically lost my only friend. I'd seen him a few times between then and high school when he was back in town for the weekend or during the summer, but it wasn't until he'd been sitting in my science class in ninth grade that we really reconnected and I got my friend back.

"I'm sorry she's treated you badly," Anna said, her tone empathetic.

"I personally am glad it's you sitting with us tonight and not her," Olivia said with a shrug to Anna, who I got the impression wasn't mean to anyone ever.

"Thanks," I said again on an exhale, more than ready for a new subject.

"Cheers to our new friends," Maeve said, holding her glass up, looking flushed and just like a birthday girl should. "I'm happy you two joined my birthday night."

We all held up our drinks, stretched to clink them in the middle of the table, and drank to the toast, laughing and, I'd admit it, feeling really good. Not necessarily from the alcohol, although it provided an underlying warmth. Rather, the longer I sat here, the more I understood that these four who'd grown up in Dragonfly Lake, who I'd not trusted just *because* they'd grown up here, were caring, genuine women, in spite of their tolerance of Magnolia. And they seemed to accept me. Maybe it started because I'd married Holden, and they were all friends with him, but in spite of my ingrained insecurities, I didn't feel any ill will from any of them. I'd grown up fearing Magnolia's treatment of me, but now that we were adults, these four—and probably most others—didn't seem to have it in them to be cruel or condescending or snobby because my family was so poor.

"What are we toasting to?"

At the sound of Holden's voice behind me, my happy level climbed. When he wrapped his arms loosely around my neck from behind and leaned over and kissed me right under my ear, my blood went hot and an ache started between my legs. Just like that.

I grabbed his arms with both my hands and held on to him, not ready for him to step away, as the whole table greeted him with obvious affection.

"Kemp's with me," Holden said. "Lost him already."

"He'll come say hi if he knows what's good for him," Olivia said teasingly.

"Hey, happy birthday, Maeve." Holden took his arms from around me and went to Maeve's end of the table, and though I hated losing his touch, I didn't let it show.

I was still learning to balance so many things. I had to make sure Holden and I showed a newlywed level of affection in public, which was probably more than I'd be comfortable with in a normal situation—whatever a normal situation was. At the same time, I had to hold myself back on the inside and remind myself I wasn't the love of his life and this was still a charade, even if we were compatible in bed. And trust me, we were compatible in bed.

"Hey, ladies," Kemp called out as he approached from behind me.

Another round of hellos sounded from all ends of our table as I turned toward him.

It'd been years since I'd seen him, and he was still easy on the eyes. And cut. He had muscles that had muscles, I was pretty sure. Apparently he was a volunteer firefighter in addition to working construction, though he would quit the construction gig as soon as the money for the brewery went through.

"Hey, Kemp," I said.

He surprised me by taking my hand, putting my drink down, and pulling me off my chair. "Come here, Mrs. Henry. I haven't congratulated you for marrying my best friend yet. Or maybe I should offer you sympathy."

I laughed as he pulled me into a hug and swung me

around, a couple of feet away from the group. Before he released me from the hug, he put his mouth close to my ear and said, so no one else could hear, "Thank you, Chloe. For investing. I can't tell you how much it means to us."

I glanced around and, yep, people had their eyes on us, so I kept it light and full of smiles and merely said, "Of course. I believe in you two."

"Get off my wife," Holden bellowed from the table, making everyone laugh.

Kemp and I went back to the group, and as soon as I climbed on my stool again, Holden pulled me down.

"Never got my wedding dance," he said to me as Kemp drew everyone else's attention with birthday wishes and a hug for Maeve. "Come on. Let's give everyone a show." His voice was a low rumble I felt throughout my body.

Both Chloes followed him willingly—the one who loved anything to do with feeling Holden's arms around me and the one who appreciated his dedication to helping me convince everyone that we were devoted... and ultimately Angelica.

The dance floor took up the back quarter of the barn, and though there was a small stage at one end, there was no band tonight, only a DJ. It was surrounded on three sides by high-top tables, so people could sit and watch the dance floor like it was a football game—or a town gossip source.

As we approached, multiple people called out to Holden, hellos, random smart-aleck comments, and even some congrats, which they included me on.

If I'd done an exhaustive search of all the age-appropriate guys in Dragonfly Lake to find the most connected, best-loved guy to be my partner in this giant charade, it still would've ended up being Holden. I was crazy lucky that he was the one person I knew well enough, felt comfortable with, and trusted to marry. His popularity gave us a built-in audience, and while I knew Angelica wasn't connected to this town beyond the hotel, it couldn't hurt to have everyone from Dragonfly Lake in the "know."

As the notes of a slow song started up, Holden led me to the middle of the dance floor and pulled me into his arms, as if he'd known it was coming.

"How'd you do that?" I asked.

He laughed. "Pays to serve the DJ good beer on his night off."

"So you just walk into the biggest bar in town on Saturday night, ask the DJ to play a slow song, and your wish is his command?"

"Pretty much. You married well. Adrian and I go way back." He took one of my hands in his and slid the other down my back and rested it just above my butt, pulling me into him, and that took my mind right off of our conversation.

I yanked my mind back, because while we were putting on a show, this wasn't the place to totally lose myself. The only time that was safe was in the dark, when Holden was inside of me. We kept the light on sometimes, and those times, I had to work harder to keep my feelings buried, just like I did now, so he wouldn't figure out I cared more than I was supposed to.

With my wedge heels, he wasn't that much taller than I was, and while our bodies teased each other, we held eye contact.

"I didn't expect to see you here tonight," I said.

"Didn't want to miss out on a dance with my wife."

"I had no idea you were such a good dancer."

"I used to be addicted to the hokey-pokey," he said, staring into my eyes, "but I finally turned myself around."

"Yeah? Was that a two-step program?"

We shared another private laugh that was genuine, not for show, because this was us. It had always been us. Just not usually with our thighs touching, our chests a whisper apart, breathing in each other's every breath.

As the song played on, he whispered into my ear, "You know what would really seal the deal on our newlywed act tonight?"

"Sneaking into a broom closet?"

Holden laughed and I felt it vibrate in my chest. "That would do it." We swayed from side to side a few times before he continued. "I prefer something a little more private, less rushed. If we left here right now, we'd have tongues wagging for sure."

"What about my girls' night?" I asked, thinking I no longer cared about girls' night or making friends or belonging. Not if this man was offered up as an alternative.

"They'll understand. We'll go say goodbye, tell Maeve happy birthday one more time, thank them for including you, give Presley the key to our place, and make our escape. I'll take your hand and pull you urgently toward the door, rush you home, and, as far as anyone knows, ravish you until sunrise."

"Hmm," I said into his ear, because our bodies were flush now, and I could feel that he was hard. "I'm in, under one condition."

"Which is?"

"You have to actually ravish me once we're home."

The hand on my lower back dipped down to my butt and pulled me into him more firmly. "You drive a *hard* bargain, but okay." He pulled his head back enough to look into my eyes, grinning, and then he kissed me. Thoroughly enough that someone hollered, "Get a room, Henrys!"

When we came up for air, I said, "I can tell you're definitely up for the task."

"Mm-hmm," he growled, "and now I need to think about beer recipes for the rest of the song so I'm able to walk out of here."

As we left the bar five minutes later, my hand in Holden's and multiple people calling out goodbyes, the strangest sensation swept through me. I was Holden Henry's wife, which made me welcome by association like I'd never been before in this town. I was starting to make friends with people who seemed like genuinely good, caring women. For the first time in my life, I was beginning to feel like I belonged.

I had to keep reminding myself, as Holden tugged me toward his Mustang, that this was exactly what he'd said it was… an act.

CHAPTER 17

Holden didn't end up ravishing me until sunrise.

He'd ravished me so thoroughly by about one a.m., though, that I was still warm and sated as I opened my eyes for the day a few hours later.

As I shifted between the sheets to grab my phone and check the time, the high-thread-count fabric glided over my naked skin, and I turned my head to verify that Holden was sound asleep next to me. Though we tangled our bodies plenty before sleeping, we always rolled to our own side of the bed to sleep separately. It was kind of the one line we'd maintained that, in my mind, helped to remind me on a daily basis that this was not quite real.

He was breathing deeply, and I knew he had to work the full day at the restaurant, so I let him sleep for as long as he could. Besides, I needed to make sure Presley was okay. Emerson had said she could give her a ride to my place when they were ready, and I'd stacked blankets and sheets on the couch in the living room. Presley had assured me I didn't need to play Holly Hostess and that she'd be just fine.

After a stop in the master bathroom, I tiptoed out of our bedroom, wondering if she was already awake. It was a little after seven a.m. and Presley was an early riser like me, though maybe not so much after an evening of drinks.

As I walked through the dining area, I could see the stack of blankets intact, and Presley was nowhere. She clearly hadn't been here, because nothing had been moved.

Where are you? I texted her, my heart speeding up with alarm.

I let out a breath when I saw dots signifying that she was responding.

Stayed at Anna's house. Didn't want to bother the lovebirds. She added ridiculous heart emojis in every color, making me laugh.

Told you you were welcome here. Is my couch not good enough for you?

Holden's couch, I amended in my mind.

Stop. I'm on my way there. Where can I pick up some breakfast for us all?

Try Sugar on Main Street. They have to-die-for donuts, I replied.

Wanting to let Holden sleep—and also wanting to talk freely with Presley—I took a quick shower, got dressed to go out in public, and pulled my hair up in a neat bun. I went out on the front porch to wait for her.

Just as I sat on the top step, a car pulled into my driveway and I recognized Anna behind the wheel, her blond hair thrown up in a messy bun, friendly smile on her face. Presley stretched over from the passenger's seat and gave Anna a side hug, then climbed out.

I walked to Anna's side, and she rolled her window down.

"Thank you for taking her in," I said, smiling. "I promise you she could've stayed here."

"Mm-hmm." Anna gave me a knowing grin and shook her head. "We closed the place down, so it was pretty late.

Your house was dark and I have a spare bed. All good! I'm so happy you two joined us. Maeve had a good birthday."

I laughed. "She looked well on her way to a good birthday when I left."

Presley came up to my side with a big donut box in one hand and a drink holder with two coffees in the other. "Thanks, Anna. You sure you won't join us for breakfast?"

"I have a thing, so I need to go get myself pretty. You girls enjoy."

We said our goodbyes and Anna backed out.

"I am *dying* for these," Presley said. "The sugar smell…" Her eyes rolled back into her head. "I didn't know what Holden likes so I got a variety."

"He's still asleep. We can leave a couple for him, and I thought I'd take you to the hotel. We can eat donuts on a balcony overlooking the lake."

"Ooh, yes, please," Presley said. "Let's go."

Her hair was pulled back into a messy ponytail, and she wore cutoff shorts, a plain coral-colored tee, and a gray zip-up hoodie with flip-flops.

"You sure you don't want to change into better clothes?" I asked. This was our long-standing joke.

"You sure you don't want to get comfortable?" she replied, raising her brows at my tailored Capris, rayon V-neck, and wedges.

We both laughed, neither bothering to answer because this was how it usually was—I didn't feel comfortable going out without being fully done up and dressed decently. Presley didn't feel the need for the "armor."

"I'll leave a note for Holden, then we can go." I took a chocolate frosted and a chocolate glazed from the box for my husband, knowing he would roll his eyes at the more sugary ones, like the fruity-cereal topped and the sandwich-cookie topped.

"I'll wait in my car," Presley said and headed toward it, parked in the street.

I went inside, scribbled a note, and put it on the microwave, where I knew he'd see it, then caught sight of my own flip-flops on the mat by the back door. They were simple black and… more comfortable than wedges. After a moment of hesitation, I traded them out and walked out the front door in my comfy, flat-soled flip-flops.

A few minutes later, Presley drove us up to the Marks Hotel at Dragonfly Lake.

"Wow," she said as she pulled to the side I indicated. "It's beautiful."

As I did every time I arrived, I took a second to admire the hotel. It had the overall feel of a mountain lodge, with a mix of traditional stone, modern wood, and distinct southern touches. Marks properties were boutique hotels, and this one had only forty-two rooms. With every location, we aimed to give the guest a luxury lakeside experience.

Just like it did every day, my blood pumped a little harder with excitement and pride. Even though I hadn't been on-site from the beginning the way Angelica had, I loved this property with every fiber of my being. Which was sort of strange since I'd been determined to keep my distance from the time Angelica had announced we would build a property on Dragonfly Lake.

Sometimes it was funny the way life threw things at you that you didn't think could ever work out but then they did.

The hotel was deserted, as I'd expected. I'd only just started interviewing candidates for the general manager position, so there weren't any employees yet, and the construction crew didn't work on Sundays.

I took Presley to a door on the side that was close to the executive offices and let us in. The interior was further from being finished than the outside, but the offices were nearly done, so I'd been able to move from the trailer to these much better digs.

"Would you like a tour?" I asked her. I loved showing this place off even though it wasn't nearly as gorgeous as it would be.

"Of course."

She set the donuts on my desk and pulled out her coffee.

"Floors are brand-new, so don't you dare spill that," I teased her.

Raising a brow, she set her latte back on the desk. "I'm not tempting fate."

I led her out of the offices to the public areas. The lobby was taking shape, with a fireplace that stretched up two stories, rustic wide-planked wood floors, and earth tones on the walls. There were wood features aplenty, including a stunning staircase with contemporary hand-carved railings.

"This is amazing," Presley said.

"The floors look fantastic." When I'd left Friday, they'd had another day of work to finish this large area, which they'd done yesterday. I'd worked from the home office I shared with Holden, where he'd added a desk for me. "I need to take a few shots to send to Angelica. She'll be thrilled with this."

I took my phone out of my pocket and snapped photos from different angles and perspectives, put them in an email, and sent them to her.

"How is she?" Presley asked somberly.

"She never says, but her check-ins were sporadic last week, which speaks volumes."

"I can't help but feel for her. No one deserves to go through that hell."

Like Holden, Presley had never been a fan of my boss, but she was even less a fan of her own boss. Hers was an insecure, pompous ass who'd gotten where he was by performing well, but what the powers that be had failed to consider was that he had zero management or leadership skills. Presley put up with him because their firm was the best in Nashville and, as she said, he'd shoot himself in the foot one of these days and the problem would take care of itself. I wasn't as sure about that, since he'd been in his position for a few years already, but I understood why Presley stuck it out.

We hit the restaurant next, then the spa area and the indoor pool, and I continued to document with photos and send them on to Angelica. After showing Presley one of the guest suites, which she oohed and ahhed over and swore she wanted to move into, we went back to pick up our breakfast, then headed out to the sprawling southern-style covered porch that stretched along half the main building and looked out over the lake.

Presley's reaction was an intake of breath and a hand to her chest. "This is going to be incredible, Chloe."

The furniture wasn't in yet, so we set up folding chairs along the low railing that afforded the best view. The lake was stunning today, with the sunshine sparkling off the calm waters and the sky bright blue over the spring green of the trees all around.

Before we could get settled, my phone rang. I took it out and read the name, raising my brows at Presley as I answered.

"Angelica," I said.

"Chloe *Henry*?" she said without preamble.

"Well, yes—"

"So you've gone further with this farce. You've never been a halfway person." Her voice wasn't especially cold, more conversational, if raspier than usual.

She must have received my email and noticed I'd changed my name there, so it came from Chloe Henry instead of Chloe Abrams.

"Holden and I are married. No farce. What can I do for

you, Angelica?" I dug deep for patience, reminding myself she was in a bad place.

"Thank you for sending new photos. The floors look phenomenal. Sabrina agrees. It's just what we envisioned all those months ago."

"They're perfect," I said easily. "I'm glad you're happy with them. Your vision is really coming to life."

"Yes, well… I don't know what you're doing with your personal life or how you got your friend to marry you, but I do appreciate the job you're doing for Marks International."

I bit down on my tongue to let the personal comments go, then I said, "I love this job, as you know."

"Very well." Her voice had become fatigued over the course of our short conversation. "I'll be in touch soon."

She hung up without saying goodbye, and I blew out an exhale that turned into a laugh.

"What on earth?" Presley asked.

I told her Angelica's comments.

"Wow," Presley said. "Don't hold back, Angelica."

"She never has. Not with me." I shrugged, trying to let the conversation go.

"We need donuts," Presley said.

Once we both had our pastries and had shoved a couple of sinful-icious bites in our mouths, Presley relaxed against the chair back and gazed out at the water. "Last night was kind of awesome. This little town you hate"—she licked frosting off one of her fingers—"I kind of like it, Chloe. The people are… real. I mean, there are some odd ducks, I'm sure, and Magnolia is toxic, but Anna and Maeve and the others… I couldn't see anything toward you except genuine friendliness."

"Yeah," I admitted.

I'd had my guard up for the first half of the evening, expecting an embarrassing moment or to be singled out in a bad way. It'd proven unfounded, with the exception of

Satan's spawn Magnolia, and even when she'd reared her head, the girls hadn't teamed up with her. Now that I was removed from the situation, even thinking about that possibility seemed ludicrous, and all I could come up with in my defense was that the groundwork had been laid so many years ago, when I was so young, that it had obviously stuck. I believed I could overcome it eventually. I was starting to trust the girls' night girls, and that was after just one evening.

"The guys seemed down-to-earth too," Presley continued and I whipped my attention to her.

"Did you hook up—"

"No. I told you I went to Anna's. Max offered to drive us home later since Emerson was ready to go before midnight. What's her story? She seemed really nice but… restrained? Something."

"She was married to Blake Estes," I said, frowning. "Apparently he was in the military and was killed a few years back. He left her with two little kids."

"God."

"I know. Awful."

I'd gone to school with both Emerson and Blake but hadn't known either very well. Holden had filled me in on their history, and now that I knew, her reticence made sense. And the sadness in her eyes.

Presley leaned forward to take a second donut, holding the box out for me. I took a caramel-fudge.

"I have to say, the act you and Holden put on… top-notch, my friend. There wasn't a soul in that bar who didn't believe you were going home to get it on."

I stuffed a bite in my mouth and looked out at the lake to buy a few seconds. Though Presley and I had texted briefly a couple of times last week, I hadn't found the right moment to mention the changes between Holden and me. As much as I was dying to have a girlfriend talk about sleeping with the guy I'd crushed on for years, I was also reluctant because she wouldn't hesitate to tell me I was being reckless.

"Chloe?" she drew out in question, and I could feel her staring at me.

I couldn't quite stifle a smile. "Yeah, um, it wasn't completely an act. I mean, it was exaggerated and deliberate. We wanted people to think that—"

"You went home and did him!"

Even though I knew there was no one else on the property today, I glanced around to make sure no one had heard her outburst.

There was caramel on my finger, so I stuck it in my mouth, still grinning.

"Chloe Abrams… Henry… whatever your name is now, spill it!"

I told her about dinner after the courthouse and Holden's comments about crossing a line and my decision to give in to the attraction.

"Smart," she said.

"What? Not smart. Dumb. Stupid. Foolish. But if this is what stupid is like, sign me up."

Presley laughed and took a sip of her latte. She pulled a leg up under her as if settling in. "I'm so happy for you. I don't even need to ask you how it was, how he is, because you can't get that smug little grin off your face."

That made me laugh. "Smug? This is not smug. Smug implies being right, and you know as well as I do that I would've been much smarter to keep my pj's on."

"From what I know, love doesn't care about smart or right."

"This is not a love match, Pres. It's a business deal between friends. Literally, marriage with benefits."

"You're in love with him." She didn't pose it as a question.

"I don't even know what that means. Do I love him? Yes.

He's been my friend for almost thirty years. In love? Doesn't that take two?"

"Sounds like you have two."

"It's just sex. Part of our deal that will go away in a year."

Presley pierced me with a direct gaze. "Why can't it be more? Why does it have to end in a year?"

"You know why." We'd talked about our goals, our ambitions countless times over the years. She knew my aspirations where Marks International was concerned. "The career I want, running this company, it's not compatible with a family. Gloria might think it is, but she doesn't pull her weight. Her kids would never see her if she took the reins. And I'm pretty sure Holden wants kids. He loves them." Watching him with his nephew, Harrison, was a testament to that. He was a natural with kids, whereas I didn't know what to do with mini-people.

"And you're sure you want the career more than the man?"

"Look at this place, Presley." I gestured to the soon-to-be-gorgeous property surrounding us.

"Look at that man," she countered.

"That man who's my friend. One of the best friends I have. He offered to help me because we go way back. Because we're friends. I'm prepared to lose the marriage, but I can't lose the friendship." My throat thickened at the thought of not having Holden in my life at all.

"And you don't think it would be smart to see if he has feelings too? Because if he doesn't, he has some serious acting skills."

"How would that go, exactly?" I asked. "*I'm not trying to make you uncomfortable, but I'm head over heels in love with you and want to spend the rest of forever with you, and I was just wondering if you feel the same?*"

"Maybe."

"Are you nuts? If his answer is no, and I'm pretty sure his

answer would be no because he could have any girl he wanted, then how awkward would it be between us?"

"Okay," she allowed, "I get that. But what if his answer is yes?"

I couldn't let myself think about the possibility, because even that was enough to knock us, Holden and me, off-kilter.

"It's not a yes. He's just happy to not have to be celibate for a year. As am I. Just let me enjoy this, Presley. It's the perfect setup. Holden gets his brewery. I get my career. We both get sex."

"And then, in a year? What are you going to do then, Chloe?"

I bit down on my lip at the emotion that once again surged into my throat and made it hard to breathe. Willing it back, I forced a grin. "Twizzlers and rosé, baby. Lots of Twizzlers and rosé."

CHAPTER 18

HOLDEN

'd been walking on air for nearly two weeks.

The seed money for Rusty Anchor Brewing Company —the name Kemp and I had finally made official—had come through, and Kemp and I had hit the ground running. Kemp's full-time job was construction, so we'd sat down with his boss, Levi Dawson, even before the money was in our account, to go over the blueprints we'd previously had drawn up by an architect.

Levi's work calendar was pretty full, but since he was a personal friend of ours as well as a big fan of good beer, he, Kemp, and I had planned to work evenings and weekends on the old Bergman building, gutting it and turning it into a state-of-the-art brewery. Then, as if God himself couldn't wait for some good beer, a large home addition on Levi's calendar had been canceled at the last minute, so we were moving into that spot. We had a week to demo the inside before the professionals showed up, and I'd spent a few hours this afternoon ripping out shelves and removing junk.

We'd ordered our brewing equipment, which would take

a few weeks to arrive, and we'd moved ahead with all the other facets of setting up a business—getting the corporation in place, meeting with a branding expert, permits, marketing ideas, plans for personnel.

It was already a full-time job and a half for both Kemp and me, and neither of us had quit our day jobs yet. That was coming soon, and though Henry's was in my blood and always would be, I couldn't wait. I told myself I wasn't exactly quitting Henry's, because Rusty Anchor and Henry's would become intricately entwined and have a symbiotic relationship as a brewpub going forward.

On top of all that, having Chloe in my bed every night didn't suck at all. We were both so busy with our careers that, some days, we didn't see one another much until we collapsed in bed. We spent just as much time talking and catching up as we did burning up the sheets, and I wouldn't trade either of them. The one thing we weren't getting was enough sleep, but we could sleep later.

My life was full right now, and I was loving the shit out of it while things were so good.

Tonight, my brothers and I were meeting after Henry's closed to have a long overdue celebratory toast to Rusty Anchor Brewing. It was a Wednesday, one of our slowest evenings off-season, and Cash and I had worked till close, while Seth, our eight-to-fiver, was coming back in for the occasion. I'd finished totaling the receipts for the night and put the cash bags in the safe in Seth's office, then grabbed a new bottle of Grey Goose from storage since Berwin Jepp had just about emptied the old one this evening.

As I came around the corner from the storeroom, Cash was perched on the center barstool, still wearing his whites, looking like he'd just finished a long shift, which he had. My oldest brother and I might not be best friends, but one thing I could never debate was that he worked his ass off. He had to be persuaded not to work seven days a week, and I couldn't remember the last time he'd worked less than six.

All these years later, with him nearly forty and me at thirty-four, I still thought of him—and Seth too—as tough to measure up to. Probably why I'd screwed around so much in my twenties. Hell, my entire life up to my thirties, really. Cash had been a star athlete growing up, then he'd been the military hero, and I was just a kid rebelling against myself so I wouldn't be compared to either him or our brainy brother, Seth. Classic textbook case, but who could blame me?

Now, I was starting to feel like I was getting somewhere, doing something that mattered. Doing something I excelled at, something beyond making sure there was a body at the host stand and that the servers were busting their asses to keep our customers happy. Something that would bring new value to our family business, which I'd retain my ownership stake in. It remained to be seen whether my brothers would view my contribution that way.

I stepped behind the bar, which was my territory the way the kitchen was Cash's, and went to the fridge under the counter.

"Hey," I said as I pulled out three growlers I'd brought for this purpose. There were four plates on the counter in front of him—one with cornbread, one of blue corn and black bean nachos, one heaped with wings, and the last with a pile of onion rings. "Lots of leftovers tonight."

"The cornbread is leftover. The rest I made special. Thought this was supposed to be a celebration."

"Damn straight." I shoved a cheese-and-bean-covered chip in my mouth, acting nonchalant.

Truth? I wasn't nonchalant. Cash didn't go out of his way if he didn't want to, and the fact that he'd prepped food for the three of us... that had always been his way of saying he cared.

"Kitchen all closed down?" I asked as I popped a chunk of cornbread into my mouth.

"Yep. Where's Seth? You heard from him?"

Seth was our unspoken buffer. He was kind of everyone's unspoken buffer, the stereotypical middle child peacemaker, even though there were four of us Henrys.

"Probably asleep on his couch," I said.

It was after ten o'clock, and Seth kept what he called "reasonable hours," while Cash and I were the late-nighters.

The main door opened, which had to be Seth because I'd locked the doors when Jack and Chelsea, the closing servers, left. Sure enough, he sauntered into the bar.

"What's up?" he asked, eyeing the assortment of appetizers. "Did you start without me?"

"We weren't sure you were going to make it," I said.

"Bullshit," he said as he took the stool next to Cash.

"Hot food waits for no one," Cash said. "What are we drinking?"

"Like you, I brought an assortment. I've got my strawberry-blonde pale ale, which we hope to replicate and market as Beach Babe. Then we have an IPA, soon to be Hoppy Summer Days. And last, I brought a crisp, light lager that I'm calling Smooth Sailing. Where do you want to start?"

"I could use some Smooth Sailing," Cash said.

Seth nodded, so I poured us a round into pint glasses. I was about to raise mine to take a swig when Cash held his glass out for a toast, which surprised me.

Seth and I extended our glasses to his.

"To the guy with a dream. I know I've given you shit about it being pie-in-the-sky, but you've turned into one persistent MF and look where it got you. You're on your way."

We clinked and drank, and I used those seconds to swallow my shock and the emotions my reticent brother's praise elicited.

Seth held up his glass again, and we followed.

"I'm proud of you, Holden. Can't wait to see where you go with Rusty Anchor. Here's to your overall smooth sailing."

"This is some top-notch lager," Cash added.

We clinked again and tipped our glasses back. I tried to figure out what to say, but after all these years of pretending like I didn't care what anyone else thought of me and then changing my ways and telling myself it was for me and me alone, I never could've guessed what the support from my brothers would mean to me.

"Thanks," I said simply, meeting the gaze of each of them. I shook my head a little, laughed, and said it again. "Thanks. Means a lot coming from you two hard-asses. You think you could use the lager in a dish or two?"

Cash took another swig, and I could tell he let the flavors roll over his tongue as he nodded. "I'm thinking some kind of pork with bacon dish with a glaze. Or I could make a mean chili with some heat to it. Brisket… Yeah. I could use the lager in a dish or two."

"I was thinking we could introduce a new menu at the same time the brewery opens, kind of a celebration of the marriage of your cooking and my beer," I said.

Seth picked up the thread right away. "Grand opening for the brewery, new offerings from the restaurant… We need to go all out."

"I can get behind using some high-quality beer in my cooking." Cash growled pensively. "I could do some kind of southern-style beer shrimp and grits…" He narrowed his eyes, as if he was envisioning the ingredients he'd put in it.

"I'd eat some of that," I said enthusiastically.

This was what I'd always dreamed of, this collaboration of sorts, though we hadn't taken time before now to discuss it in detail. Cash was the kind of guy you couldn't order around or try to dictate the specifics of his dishes, so you had to approach it carefully. Make him think it was his idea.

"You guys have a timeframe yet?" Seth asked as he piled onion rings and wings on his plate.

"My goal is to be open by July Fourth."

"Two and a half months," Seth said. "That's ambitious."

"It'll be tight," I said, "but we want to take advantage of the busiest week of the year."

"Smart." Seth looked thoughtful while he chewed an onion ring. "You said you're working with a branding expert?"

"A damn good one from what I saw in our first meeting. He should have some tangibles for us next week."

"I'd love to see them. We'll want to tie them into the restaurant stuff. We should use the beer logos on the menu, for starters. With that and some new dishes from Cash, it's the perfect time for new menus."

We talked business details for a few more minutes, even though that hadn't been the point of the get-together. Don't get me wrong, we also downed some of all three beers, each of which sparked Cash's culinary creative chops, to the extent he started jotting ideas on a napkin.

I couldn't remember the last time the three of us had had such a good time together, with no power struggles, no put-downs, no pissing each other off. Sure, we talked business, but it was a laid-back discussion, planning for the near future instead of focusing on the restaurant's day-to-day. Pretty sure the beer helped—and the fact that both my brothers seemed to genuinely love what I'd created. Maybe this was the screwed-up shit in my head, but for the first time, they treated me like a peer more than the dipshit youngest brother who perpetually rode their coattails.

Somehow we got to talking about our childhoods, laughing about the ways I used to get into trouble, even in grade school, and the time Seth had acted like the world was ending because he'd gotten a B on a chemistry test in high school and how Cash had had two girls get in a fistfight over him in ninth grade. The plates of food were empty, and still we lingered as it crept close to midnight.

"You're going to turn into a pumpkin, man," Cash eventually said to Seth as we wound down from another gut-busting laugh over the past. "And you have a wife at home waiting for you." He directed that comment and a still-can't-believe-that-shit look my way.

Before I could respond, a siren sounded outside.

"Sounds like fire and rescue," Seth said as he stacked our appetizer plates.

My thoughts went to Kemp, who was a volunteer fire-fighter, and I wondered if he was on the truck and where they were going.

"Coming this way, sounds like," Cash said. He tipped his glass back to drink the last of his IPA, which he'd declared as his favorite of the three.

I was putting lids back on the empty growlers when the sirens sounded like they were right outside. They must be turning toward the residential area just west of us. I knew a lot of people who lived in that neighborhood and I hoped like hell everyone was okay.

"What the fuck?" Seth said as he went over to the open doorway to the host vestibule to look out the window.

As soon as he said it, I realized the truck wasn't turning to the residential area. It was in the Henry's parking lot. The three of us were out the front door in a split second.

It was in that split second that I knew in my gut, before my brain could even form the thoughts, that something was catastrophically wrong and about to get personal.

The fire truck pulled over to the Bergman building, and the rate at which four firefighters disembarked told me this was not a drill.

I approached, trying to discern whether Kemp was among them, but with them fully turned out, I couldn't tell much of anything.

"What's going on?" I yelled, trying to be heard over the sounds of the truck and the shouts between the firefighters.

I didn't need them to answer, though, as in the next second, I picked up the smell of smoke and then I noticed flames coming from the loading dock side of the Bergman roof. Nausea surged, the taste of bile combining with the acrid smell of smoke, as the realization hit me.

"Fuck," I bit out as Cash and Seth came up alongside me.

"What the fuck?" Cash said.

I'd forgotten to unplug the battery charger.

This was all my fault.

I pulled the collar of my shirt over my nose and mouth as the three of us stood and helplessly watched the firefighters do their thing. One of them seemed to be talking to dispatch. One went to the hydrant near the road and hooked up the hose, then waited there while the guy who'd been driving manned the truck.

The fire chief's truck pulled up, and Chief Thomas climbed down. Yet another siren sounded in the distance as the chief went to confer with the firefighter who seemed to be in charge. The fourth guy, who I was pretty sure was Kemp, went to the door on the opposite side of the building and, along with the first guy, broke the door down. The two of them went in, charged hose in tow, and I swore out loud and hoped everyone would be okay. I wouldn't be able to stand it if someone got hurt because of my mistake.

With my heart racing, I went toward the chief and called out to him by name. I didn't want to interfere with their work, but I needed to know what was happening to my building.

The chief nodded at the firefighter a couple of times, barked something to the guy, then turned toward me as a second truck approached from Main.

"Hey, Holden. You call this in?"

I shook my head. "First I knew was when the truck pulled up. What's happening?"

"Passerby reported smoke coming from the southeast corner. Looks like it's not spread yet. With any luck, we should have it out pretty quickly."

I didn't ask if they knew the cause. I didn't need to. Of course, I'd give them the info I had, the suspicions I harbored, when they took time to ask after the fire was out, but right now they needed to concentrate on the job.

My eyes were watering like crazy, and I could try to tell myself it was from the smoke, but that would be a lie. The truth was, I'd fucked up big-time, and my pride and joy was literally going up in smoke before my eyes.

CHAPTER 19

Two hours and an estimated hundred thousand dollars of damage later, I trudged home from the restaurant, my shoulders sagging, feet feeling like they weighed a ton each.

To think that, just hours ago, I'd been on top of the world… The higher you went, the farther you had to fall, I guess, and I felt like I'd plummeted down the steep side of a dark canyon.

It was well after one a.m. as I walked up the driveway, so I was half-surprised to see a light on in the office. Only *half-*surprised because Chloe was putting in a lot of long hours at her job. I'd hoped she was asleep, not only because she needed the rest but because I didn't want to talk about what had happened tonight. To anyone.

I let myself in the front door, and Chloe came out of the office at the same time, as if she'd heard me.

"Hey, I was starting to worry about— Holden, what's wrong?" She came closer and took my hand in hers, searching my face. "Are you okay?" She wrinkled her nose. "What do I smell?"

I sucked in a breath and heard the shakiness of it. "The brewery… There was a fire…"

"Oh, God. Is everyone okay?"

"Everyone's okay. No one was there when it happened."

"And the damage?" She stood directly in front of me and took hold of both my hands now.

I was having trouble looking directly at her. I felt so fucking stupid. "It's… significant. Going to set us back a couple of months." I dropped her hands and went toward the kitchen, mostly because she was looking at me so intently. "Beer?" I asked her as I pulled out the IPA.

"Yeah. Beach Babe please."

I loved how she'd embraced the beer names. Chloe had sat in with us on the branding meeting, and from time to time, she'd have a thought about something concerning Rusty Anchor and voice it, as if she was getting into the planning too.

I poured a glass for each of us and swigged down half of mine, knowing I needed to tell her everything. The whole town would know by morning anyway.

"I fucked up," I said, leaning my butt against the counter, studying the head on the beer.

"What do you mean?"

"The fire was my fault. Chet Hogan was helping us haul away a bunch of debris earlier in his old truck. He has problems with the battery in that beater, I don't know exactly why, but he brought in a charger and his "spare" battery and plugged it in inside the brewery. He took a load away, then couldn't make it back because his wife needed him for something, so he reminded me to unplug the charger in another half hour or so. I rushed off to Henry's for the dinner shift and forgot about the charger. They're pretty sure it overheated that 1950s wiring and exploded."

"Damn," she said. "The wiring was all going to be replaced in the remodel, wasn't it?"

"Yep," I said, trying to sound flippant. "I should've known better. I *did* know better, but I intended to unplug it when I left." I let off another stream of silent swear words in my head, berating myself good.

"Hey," Chloe said. She set her beer down, walked around the island, and pressed her body into mine, her hands on my chest. "It was an accident. It could've happened to anyone."

I rested my hands on her hips, not hating the comfort she offered. "All these years of dreaming about a brewery, and when we finally get funds, I go and do this."

"Insurance will cover it."

I nodded, not voicing that I was sure it would take forever and a year. I was already sick of hearing myself complain.

"You won't make your goal for opening though," she said, frowning.

"No way in hell. Even if insurance processes in record time. Most of the building is intact, but the loading dock area will need to be rebuilt. Right now, the place reeks of smoke, and there's water everywhere."

She stretched up and kissed me. "I hate that it happened, but it could've been a lot worse, Holden. No one was hurt, and it happened when you were gutting the inside anyway. Think how much worse it would have been two months from now."

I inwardly shuddered because she was right. That would've been a disaster.

"Hey." She ran her finger over my lip, still so close I could smell her floral scent, and I breathed it in, let it soothe me. "It's okay to be upset it happened, but you need to stop beating yourself up." She kissed me again, and it was getting harder to be upset.

"You need sleep," I said to her between kisses.

"You need a shower."

I couldn't argue with that.

"Go get clean and I'll meet you in bed," Chloe said, then pressed one more lingering kiss on my lips, which had me going half hard, in spite of my bone-deep weariness and the despair that'd been hanging on me like a heavy overcoat when I came inside.

She slipped away and padded toward the front of the house, I assumed to turn off the lights and check the locks. I watched her walk away, my eyes on her shapely ass in yoga pants that showed every shift and every sway of muscle and curve. That was the kick of motivation I needed.

I pulled my shirt off and stripped down to nothing as I headed for the master bath, ready to wash the stench of the evening away and even more ready to curl up with Chloe between the sheets.

Six minutes later, I smelled better, felt better, at least physically, and came out of the bathroom to find the bedroom light off and Chloe tucked in on her side, facing the wall. She didn't stir, and my hard-on sagged a little at the thought that she might've fallen asleep. I brushed my teeth, turned out the bathroom light, didn't bother to put pajamas on, and climbed into my side of the bed.

I stretched out on my back, reminding myself Chloe's alarm went off at six a.m. I let my mind go back to the fire because, if anything could kill my need for sex, that was it.

Kemp and the rest of the crew had kicked ass and had the fire completely out within about twenty minutes. Based on what he'd said about where the fire was exactly, it was nearly a sure thing the charger was the cause. He'd pointed out how much worse it could've been if we hadn't already hauled away a bunch of the crap from the inside—ancient wood shelves and counters, bins, boxes of papers, plus a bunch of paint remnants. Just thinking about it sent a chill down my spine because that could've ignited a fire in a different league altogether, something big enough that the restaurant could've been in danger.

Chloe rolled toward me, sidled up against me, traced a finger up my chest. "Mmm. Naked."

I smiled in the dark, but letting my mind go back to the fire had put a damper on my physical needs just as I'd intended. I put my arm around her and squeezed her to my side, glad to have her there but not wanting her to feel like she had to do anything but get some sleep.

"You're doing it again, aren't you?" she said quietly. "Beating yourself up?"

"Not exactly. Just trying to process it all. Not three hours ago, I was on top of the world, soaking up some really good moments with my brothers."

"Tell me about that part. The good moments."

"They've always been mostly supportive, with the exception of a few dick moments from Cash, but tonight..." I shook my head, looking for a way to express it without sounding like a goober. "Promise you won't laugh?"

"Of course."

I hesitated, considering whether I could admit some things out loud that I'd never told another soul, not even Kemp. It wasn't anything earth-shattering, just personal.

But this was Chloe. One of my best friends. My wife. It didn't matter that the married part was short-term; I knew I could trust her. She'd opened up to me about her greatest insecurities, and I'd listened and weighed in but never done the same in return.

"I've always felt like the brother who didn't pull my weight at the restaurant," I began.

"I don't think that's true at all," she said before I could get anything else out.

"Just like I don't think it's true that you have any reason to feel insecure in this town."

I heard her suck in a breath. "Okay. Fair enough. Go on."

"Henry's is what it is because of two things. Cash's cooking and Seth's ability to run a business."

"They're both really talented, but so are you. And you can't say I'm biased, because I'm only your *temporary* wife."

The sound of the grin in her voice had my own lips tugging upward in spite of myself. It slipped away fast though.

"This is going to take a while if you're going to argue with every sentence." I tried to keep my tone light.

"Okay, okay. It's just hard to hear you be down on yourself."

"Mm-hmm," I said meaningfully. "Trust me, I know how it feels."

Chloe growled and then said, "Continue."

"Part of the reason I'm so determined to make the brewery work is because it would make me feel like an equal contributor. Tonight, when we drank our toast, my brothers seemed genuinely proud of me. Excited for me. And excited for the partnership between Rusty Anchor and Henry's. Between our beer and Cash's food."

"That must've felt really good."

"Cash was coming up with new beer-based dishes left and right. Seth wants to use the beer logos on the menus and do a big grand opening thing." My enthusiasm dimmed. "Which was going to include a joint Henry's and Rusty Anchor entry in the Fourth of July Boat Parade. There's no way we'll be open by then now."

"You could do the float anyway. Build the hype."

"Maybe." My first reaction was that it wouldn't be the same, but within five seconds, I started to think it could still be a good idea. "At any rate, we were discussing all these plans for the future when we heard the sirens. Boom. I feel like the screw-off brother once again."

"Holden."

"Chloe."

She was silent for a few seconds and rolled to her back. I could practically hear the gears in her brain turning, and it took some willpower on my part not to preemptively argue with whatever she was going to say.

"You know how you tell me no one thinks of me as the poor girl or the loser loner from our childhood?" she asked.

"Yes," I said with no hesitation.

"I'm absolutely certain no one thinks of you as the screw-off Henry brother or a screw-off of any kind. Everybody loves you. You get along with all ages, all types of people, those who grew up here and those who've transplanted from elsewhere. You manage the best restaurant in town without blinking. People like working for you, like drinking beer with you, and some of us like doing other things with you."

That made me laugh and, not going to lie, perked up my Johnson more than a little.

"Like exchanging puns," she said, and I laughed again. "What I'm trying to say is that maybe your view of yourself is as off-base as you say mine is. And maybe we're both too hard on ourselves."

In that moment, I realized the two of us really were similar at the core, though I'd never seen it before. Maybe that explained why we'd gravitated to each other as friends so long ago.

"You could be on to something," I said as a wave of mental exhaustion rolled over me, and I was unwilling to think about any of it anymore tonight.

I turned to my side to face her, ran my palm over her middle, discovered she was naked too. My fingers homed in on her nipple as if they had a mind of their own, and I trailed circles over it, feeling it pucker at my touch. "Maybe we should switch to doing other things now."

"Yeah?" Her tone had a flirty, seductive edge to it. "Puns?"

A laugh rumbled out of me as, for the first time in my life, I could barely remember what a pun was, let alone come up

with one. "There's not enough blood going to my brain to come up with one."

Next thing I knew, she wrapped her fingers around my cock and stroked me, saying, "Surely you can *come up* with something."

I could, but it wasn't a pun.

I whipped the blankets off and flipped over to hover just above her, propping myself on my forearms, then I kissed her. My tongue dipped into her mouth, and a groan escaped me at the sweet taste of her that I'd come to know so well.

Her hands were everywhere—in my hair, on my back, yanking my body closer still as she arched up into me. I kissed a path from her lips to her tempting nipple and took it into my mouth as I teased the other with my fingers. I could've buried myself in her breasts alone and been happy as a kid in a candy store, but the way she was squirming and letting out the sexiest whimpers and moans had me trailing my tongue down to her belly button and lower, to where she was damp and pulsing for attention.

When I flicked my tongue over her center, she jolted and gasped and clasped her legs around me. Her female scent made my blood pound harder, but I shoved my own needs aside, aching to give her the most incredible orgasm of her life with my mouth.

As I swirled my tongue over her, in her, around her, she clung to me, arched into me, let me know with the sounds she made that she was climbing closer, almost there. I was torn between getting her to the peak she was begging for and wanting to draw out her pleasure for another six hours—or forever.

As caught up in her body, her flavor, her reactions as I was, there was just enough rational power left in my head, the big one, to remember that her alarm would go off in mere hours before she'd likely work another twelve-hour day. This woman was incredible and would pull it off with or without sleep—God knows we'd tested that theory since our wedding. There were nights we were doing well to sleep for three hours before she headed in for a long day of work. Tonight, as she gave me so much free rein with her body and her passion, I had the urge to take care of her in every way possible, my own physical needs aside.

I doubled down on my devotion to driving her out of her coherent mind. With my fingers and my mouth, I worshiped the sexiest, most responsive, most entrancing woman in the world. When she cried out and stiffened and her body clasped to my fingers, I drew more passion out of her until she begged me to stop.

"I can't..." she managed between gasps and full-body contractions.

I lightened my touch, gave her oversensitive spots a moment to recover as I nipped some less sensitive areas. Chloe's gasping became a little more like regular breaths, and I gave her a few seconds before I swirled my tongue over her again, lightly, teasingly at first, until a switch seemed to flip and she went from allowing me to lave and suckle at her to *needing* me to yet again.

It didn't take long for her to climax again, clutching to me, calling out my name, making me feel like the king of the universe. As she gradually went limp beneath me, I kissed another path up her body, a slow, worshipful trail. When my mouth reached hers, I asked, "You okay?"

Her response was more of a moan than a word, but it was unmistakably affirmative and accompanied by a lazy, satisfied grin.

I shifted to the side of her, draping my arm across her chest, kissing her shoulder as I curled up against her.

"It's your turn," she whispered, her words nearly slurred with fatigue and the ultimate relaxation.

"Another time, darlin'," I said. "Tonight's about you. Go to sleep now."

Was I still hard? Oh, hell yes. But oddly, my urge to please Chloe, to do what she needed most instead of what I wanted, overrode everything.

She was incredible. She kept me leveled. She's what had calmed me tonight and helped me believe everything with the brewery would be okay in the end. That I'd opened up to her about my longstanding insecurities spoke to how much I trusted her, maybe even how much I needed her. I'd never felt this close to another person.

There was a little voice in my head warning that was going to be a problem in less than a year, when we were no longer married, but for now I told myself we'd always be close friends.

Burying my nose in her hair, breathing in the scent of her, I let go of all the thoughts tugging at my brain and lost myself in the woman in my arms.

CHAPTER 20

CHLOE

t was the last Saturday night in April, and Holden and I were on the way to a bonfire on the beach.

Our one-month anniversary was only a couple of days away. Not that we had anniversary plans. It didn't really count when your marriage had an end date. Instead of the one-month mark feeling like an accomplishment or something to celebrate, it felt more like a countdown.

Since the fire at the brewery, it had become more difficult to remember our marriage wasn't real. The way Holden had opened up that night, confessing his insecurities concerning his brothers, changed things. Brought us closer. Before that, I'd seen Holden as carefree and confident—and he was—but now I understood another dimension of him. A hidden layer only I'd been allowed to see. One that resonated deeply with me.

In addition to that new understanding, I'd been waking up with his arms around me every morning. That had started the night of the fire as well. I'd never been a cuddler, had rarely stayed a whole night with a man, and if you'd told me before that I would love being held all night, I would've rolled my eyes. But I did love it. At least when it was Holden.

We were blurring the lines further, but I couldn't make myself be smarter now. Didn't want him *not* to hold me while we slept.

We passed Henry's and then the marina, and that led to the residential area.

Dragonfly Lake had several beaches. There were two on the north side—the public one, known as Dragonfly Beach, and a private one in the middle of the residential lakefront neighborhood where we were heading. It was just down the way from Henry's Restaurant and reserved for people who lived on Honeysuckle Road and their guests.

The sun was nearly gone from the sky as we walked along the shoulder hand in hand, Holden carrying a mini cooler with our drinks. The closer we got, the easier it was to hear the din of the gathering, and it was obvious there were more than a few people there. I sucked in a breath, trying to talk myself through the nerves.

"You okay?" Holden asked.

"Yeah," I said on an exhale. I *would* be okay once we'd been there for a while. I hoped.

Bonfires were a regular occurrence in Dragonfly. There was an annual one on Memorial Day Weekend, the official start of the summer season. There were all-ages ones, where families were welcome and young and old and everyone in between turned out. There were smaller ones, usually thrown together last minute and consisting of the twentysomething and thirtysomething crowd. That's what tonight's was. Memorial Day was still a month away, but the weather had been gorgeous all week, and people were in a celebrating mood.

I'd heard about countless parties on the beach over the years, but this was the first bonfire I'd ever attended.

"Will Seth be there?" I asked as we walked past his house,

the third from the marina, which had been Holden's family's house growing up, including their grandmother. She'd kept the place when the rest of the Henrys had moved to Nashville. When Holden had convinced everyone to let him move back to Dragonfly Lake for high school, that's where he'd lived again with his grandmother. I'd spent countless hours there in grade school and knew it as well as I knew my own home.

Holden was studying the house, where there was a light on in the back, on the lakeside. "I'd be surprised if he didn't at least make an appearance," he said.

Three more houses on the left and we'd hit the beach. As we came around the copse of trees that lined the beach, my mouth went dry with anxiety as my brain shot back to being the out-of-place, out-of-her-element kid.

I glanced down at myself and regretted letting Holden convince me that the tailored cropped pants, silk camisole, cloud-soft open cardigan, and my favorite wedge sandals were too much for the beach. Those clothes were my comfort zone. The clothes I'd finally settled on—denim cutoffs, black V-neck tee, zip-up hoodie, and plain sneakers—were comfortable around the house, but I wasn't used to being in public in less than my best.

"You look damn good," Holden said when he caught my glance downward. He pulled me closer and wrapped his arm around my middle, his big hand resting at my waist.

A couple dozen people were there, gathered in clusters, with drinks in their hands, some with food, most of them smiling or laughing. In the middle of everything was a fire, already burning strongly.

Before I could register who anyone was, I heard my name being called.

"There's Anna," Holden said, pointing to a group on multicolored beach chairs closer to the shore, facing the fire.

It was all the girls from girls' night, plus a couple others.

They were each waving, and Olivia gestured for us to join them, pointing at two empty chairs.

"We saved you a seat," Olivia said warmly. "I love your shoes. Wish I'd worn something warmer now that the sun's down."

"Thanks," I said. "Yours are definitely cuter." She wore Bohemian-looking sandals with multiple straps in various colors and textures.

"Hey, Holden. You can join us too," Anna said, and I was beginning to understand that making sure everyone felt welcome, wherever she was, was her superpower.

Holden greeted the seated group as a whole, all smiles and friendliness and ease, like he always was, joking with them for a couple of minutes before he glanced around and said hello to a handful—or a couple of handfuls—of others.

"Get your ass over here, Henry," one of the guys called from the other side of the fire.

"How can I resist when you ask so nicely?" Holden shot back. He leaned down to me and said so only I could hear, "You okay here? Want to come with me to talk to Finn and Cade McNamara?"

"I'm good," I said, determined to mean it.

Holden took out a hard seltzer from our mini cooler, cracked open the can for me, and handed it over. Then he angled in for a quick kiss before heading toward a trio of guys.

I turned back to the row of friendly faces. The welcome from these girls had me forgetting my unease in an instant, fast-forwarding to a more realistic current-day Chloe than the isolated one from the past. I went to the low-to-the-ground Adirondack-style chair between Anna and Emerson and lowered myself into it, acknowledging Emerson, Maeve, and the two on Maeve's other side.

"Shawna Jenkins and Isabel Ballantine," Emerson said, gesturing to them one at a time. As soon as she said their names, I vaguely recognized them as being a couple of years younger than we were. "Y'all remember Chloe Abrams, right?"

"Of course," Isabel said. Her family was a mainstay of town and wasn't one you could forget easily, particularly since Isabel was one of five blond sisters. They'd always turned heads wherever they went. "Or is it Henry?"

"It is," I said. "Good to see you. Hi, Shawna."

"Hey, Chloe." Shawna leaned forward as she spoke, her curly black locks falling across her face. She brushed them back with long, ring-covered fingers. "You look fantastic and I heard you're in charge of that new hotel. Local girl doing us proud."

"Thanks. My company is the developer, so I'm overseeing the construction and opening. I have a general manager who will be in charge of the property going forward."

"The place looks gorgeous from the outside," Isabel said. "I can't wait to see the inside."

"The back porch is incredible," I told them all, as everyone seemed tuned in to hear more about the hotel.

"We should plan a fall girls' weekend there," Olivia said. She and Anna had angled their chairs to make it more of a semicircle than a row.

"I love that idea," Maeve said. "Some spa time, cocktail time—"

"Back porch time," Shawna said.

"To go with cocktail time," Isabel added.

"We'd want you there as one of the girls, not as the badass who built the place," Anna said. "Would that be possible?"

I was at once thrilled to be included and flustered to think that, by fall, I hoped to be the president of Marks International. If all went well, I'd likely be in Switzerland for months on end, overseeing the next project. The thought sent a spark of excitement through my veins, but I tamped down on it. It was easier just to say, "Totally possible, depending on work, of course."

They all pulled out their phones and started discussing dates, and I went along for the ride, not wanting to jinx anything with my promotion.

By the time talk turned to other topics—the preseason sale at Lake Girl, Sergio Vega's fender bender on the square in front of half the town, the best streaming shows right now— the bonfire crowd was even bigger, closer to forty or fifty people. Seth had showed up and was tending the fire with Nick Carlisle, who apparently volunteered for the fire department, and Levi Dawson. There was a constant shifting of people from one group to the next and an overall friendly, happy vibe, as if everyone had officially come out of their winter hibernation, relieved by the mild temperatures.

I'd nearly finished my drink when I realized how relaxed I'd become with the people around me. Others came up to us to say hello, many of whom I knew, whether it was from the past in a distant way or people I'd more recently become acquainted with either through Holden or simply by being back in town. My husband caught my eye several times, as if he was checking to make sure I was doing okay, and honest to God, I was. And I was a little stunned by that.

Even when I saw Magnolia James arrive with her fiancé trailing a step behind her, I didn't feel as threatened as usual. I kept one eye on her, though, as she inserted herself into various conversations and groups.

"Don't let her get to you," Emerson said quietly. "She's not worth it."

I nodded but still kept track of her so as not to get blindsided. I felt like Emerson had my back though, and that just added to my contentment. As I listened to Anna and Olivia discuss concerts they hoped to see in Nashville and half tuned in to Isabel bantering with one of the McNamaras, the truth hit me like a sledgehammer.

For the first time ever, I was kind of, sort of, maybe starting to feel like I was a part of this town. More relaxed than stressed as I sat here among so many people I'd grown up with. None of them seemed to be judging me. Magnolia was present, but even if she came over and shot a barb my way, I felt like I could handle it. I knew the people I was sitting with wouldn't jump on her wagon, and I didn't really think anyone here would.

Over the course of a few hours, it only got better, more comfortable. We eventually abandoned our chairs to *circulate*, as Anna called it. I was introduced and reintroduced to so many people I'd never remember them all. Holden and I got lots of laughs when we described our heart-infested honeymoon love den. Rusty Anchor Brewing was a hot topic for Holden and Kemp, as the hotel was for me. Quincy Yates, who'd apparently just broken up with her longtime boyfriend, over-served herself, threw up in the trees near the road, and had to be helped home.

As a group, we went through multiple bags of jumbo marshmallows, roasting them over the fire. Some of the guys brought hot dogs and buns as well but forgot all the condiments. They devoured them anyway. Dakota Dawson showed up after her shift at Henry's with a carryout container of Cash's mac and cheese for herself and had to fight beggars off.

People had come and gone all night, and even Hayden and Zane had driven in from the city. Apparently Zane's mom, Faye, and Mr. Henry were having Harrison over for his very first sleep-over. After a romantic dinner out, Hayden had insisted on introducing her husband to bonfires Dragonfly style.

It was a little after midnight when the crowd started to thin out a little. When Holden asked if I was holding up okay, I was stunned to discover that I was having a legitimately good time and wasn't ready to go home yet. I'd had a second hard seltzer, but it had been over the course of hours, so I couldn't even blame the alcohol for my enjoyment.

I was alone in the ladies' room, a small building with only two stalls but running water, washing my hands when I heard an alarming sound that seemed to come from outside. Sort of… a sick animal noise, maybe? I shut the water off and listened. Sure enough, it came again, but I could swear a human was making it.

Frowning, I dried my hands, still on high alert, and there it was again, almost a gasping sound, like someone in distress. It sounded as though it was coming from the side of the building away from the beach. As I left the restroom, I headed right instead of left. The building butted up against a grove of trees. The light that illuminated the beach was on the opposite side, so it was fairly dark, but I couldn't miss someone sitting there in the dirt, leaning back against the wall, gasping. Possibly hyperventilating.

I was halfway to her when I realized it was Magnolia.

I wanted to walk away.

I wanted to jog back to the beach as if I hadn't heard anything.

The sounds she made were alarming though, and I didn't have time to be petty or vengeful. I hurried to her and crouched down next to her.

"Put your finger over one nostril," I said. "Hold your breath while I count to five."

She didn't do any of it, and I wondered if she'd heard me.

"Magnolia," I said, then repeated my instructions.

Her hand trembling, she eventually covered one nostril. It took me repeating myself several times before she seemed to make sense of everything. I counted to five for her and she held her breath for several rounds. Eventually, her breaths came more evenly, but her level of upset was still alarming.

"I'm going… to lose everything," she said into her hands,

and the words were muffled enough I questioned if I'd heard her right. "Eve… ry… thing."

"What are you talking about? What did you lose?" I glanced around the dirt and gravel surrounding us, thinking maybe she was missing an earring or something.

"I broke up with that asshole," she said between gasps.

"Slow down or you're going to hyperventilate again."

She sucked in a slow breath with a finger over one nostril, nodding, tears streaming. Magnolia was a wreck, and that in itself was alarming because I'd never seen her anything but in total control and on the attack.

"You broke up with your fiancé?"

Nodding, she managed, "He never wanted to be with me anyway."

"That's not true," I said logically. "He asked you to marry him. He must've wanted to be with you."

"It's… not like that." The sobs got more intense again.

"Hold your breath, Magnolia."

She sputtered and then did as I said while I counted aloud.

"You don't understand."

Ah, there was the scornful, condescending tone I expected. And I thought *my* social skills were lacking.

I fought down the urge to walk away and leave her there by her miserable self.

"Why don't you explain then. What is it like?"

Her shoulders heaved, she covered her face with both hands again, and after holding her breath without my urging this time, she managed, "He only proposed because my father made him. It was just a business deal."

I sucked in my breath, shocked, which was ridiculous, because look at my own marriage. However, that had been my choice.

"Are you sure?" I asked.

She let out a bitter semi-hysterical chuckle. "Nothing left

to question. My dad's company can only be run by family members, either by blood or marriage. Since I have no interest in it, that leaves whoever marries me."

"And Rick wanted the job," I guessed.

"And my dad wanted Rick. As far as I'm concerned, they can marry each other."

"Why can it only be run by family?"

"My grandfather set it up that way. It's in the bylaws." Her tone told me what she thought of the bylaws, and I couldn't disagree.

"Did your grandfather do that to protect you? So you would inherit it?"

Another caustic laugh amid gasps. "No." She shook her head and didn't say more.

"Did you love Rick?"

She shook her head.

"It sounds like you're better off losing this guy then," I said, trying to imagine a father who would try to force a marriage that was doomed from the start on his only child.

Her breath hitched. "If I don't marry him, my father disowns me and cuts me off from everything."

My eyes got huge as I let that sink in. Her father must be a piece of work. "Maybe it was a bluff?"

"He doesn't bluff."

"Wow. But you dumped him anyway?"

"He's a cheating bastard," she said, her voice stronger, ringing with anger instead of despair now. "I caught him texting some ho tonight while he was here with me."

"You're sure it wasn't just a friend?"

"He was texting about her *nipples*," Magnolia bit out.

I never, ever thought I would have sympathy for Magnolia James or be on her side in anything, but that was pretty shitty of him. And her dad… Yeah. Try as I might, I just couldn't fathom—

"I bet you love this," she said quietly, weakly.

"Love *what*?"

"All of this. My stupid, pathetic life."

"Don't be ridiculous."

"Why are you even being nice to me?"

"You looked like you needed help."

She nodded somberly. "I've never had that happen before." We were both quiet for a long stretch before she said, "Once you got me breathing right, you didn't have to stay and talk."

I shrugged. "I know what it's like to be all alone, I guess."

"Things seem to have worked out okay for you."

"I'm in a pretty good place right now," I acknowledged, not letting myself think about where I'd be in, oh, say a year from now.

"Opposite of me," she said almost flippantly, but there was a waver in her voice that gave away her distress. She sucked in a deep, loud breath, her eyes closed. "I don't even know where I'm going to live."

"Where have you been living?"

"In a house owned by my father."

"Oh. Well, I'm sure you'll find something."

"Yeah," she said but I could tell she wasn't optimistic. "I have a lot to figure out."

"I'm sure," I said, unable to really grasp what her life must be like at all. Even if my dad was wealthy, I didn't think I'd be living in a house he bought for me at thirty-four years old.

My phone buzzed with a text message. I took it out, guessing it was Holden before I even saw his name.

Where are you?

How should I answer that briefly without him jumping to the conclusion that I was being held hostage by my longtime nemesis?

Long story. Talking to Magnolia. Everything's okay. Be back soon.

Yeah, I'm going to need to hear that to believe it. Watch your back.

Pressing my lips together against a grin, I sent him a thumbs-up emoji, then stuffed my phone back in my pocket.

"Holden?" Magnolia asked.

"Yep."

"Are you going to tell everyone?"

"About?" I asked.

"Everything I told you."

I scowled because her tone said she completely believed I would. "No. Why would I?"

"Some people would," she said. "I wouldn't blame you if you did. I… haven't been nice to you, like, ever."

"No, you haven't," I said with conviction. "Lucky for you, I guess I'm not that vengeful. I'll tell Holden a little bit, because he already is probably minutes away from sending out a search party, but he'll keep it private."

She blew out a long, shaky breath. "I guess I'll go home and face the shit storm."

"Do you have a way to get there?"

"My car is here, parked up the street."

"How did Rick leave?"

She sat up a little straighter. "Don't know. Don't care. Maybe I'll see him walking alongside the road and I can flatten him."

"Highly don't recommend. It sounds like you have enough to handle without jail time."

"It would solve where I'll live," she said dryly.

We both got to our feet, dusting off our butts and hands.

"Are you okay to drive?" I asked her.

"Fine. I haven't been drinking. Chloe…" She faced me but didn't meet my eyes, instead gazing out toward the water. "Thank you for listening. And not telling the whole world about my screwed-up life."

"Sure."

While I never would've believed I'd be in the position to help Magnolia—or especially that I'd *do* it—I was glad I had. Because in listening to her screwed-up life, I could kind of, almost see what made her tick. From the little bit she'd told me, it sounded like her dad was an epic douchebag who treated her like shit. I wasn't sure why she let him, but that was neither here nor there. Even if he was, it didn't excuse her for being a raging bitch to me over the years. But it seemed like Anna had been right when she'd said it sucked to be Magnolia.

"Um…" Magnolia cleared her throat. I could barely see her in the darkness, but from what I could tell, she looked like crap. Her hair was messed up, her cheeks were splotchy, and her eyes were swollen. "Thank you, Chloe. I'll… see you around."

She pivoted and walked through the trees toward the road. I stood there and watched her, dumbfounded on so many levels, not the least of which was that her thanks had sounded genuine. Uncomfortable and embarrassed, but genuine.

Shaking my head at how weird my life had become lately, I walked back past the restroom doors and to the beach to find my husband.

CHAPTER 21

As I put my phone in my pocket, confused as fuck-all about Chloe's texts—talking to Magnolia? Really?—I glanced around to see if I could spot them in the shadows somewhere, near the water, on the dock, or up by the road. There was no sign of them.

I was half listening to Kemp, Levi, and Carter Costello talk about the brewery. It said a lot about my distraction level that I wasn't leading that discussion, because I could talk beer and brewing till I was blue in the face... and normally I'd probably keep going even then.

Everyone wanted to know when we were opening, what we'd be serving, whether we needed any tasters. The whole town of Dragonfly Lake seemed to be almost as stoked as Kemp and I were.

Kemp was currently getting downright scientific about different types of hops because Carter had asked. While I knew a little about the subject, this was Kemp's sweet spot. He was the one who'd gone through the master brewing classes. His expertise and experience at a microbrewery in

Nashville were one reason I had no doubts we'd make damn good beer and do well. Between his knowledge of the science of brewing and my experience with running a bar and restaurant, we had the perfect combination. Add Chloe's behind-the-scenes business acumen, as well as a few financial tips from Presley, and I was determined we'd beat the odds and make Rusty Anchor Brewing a raging success.

"Hey, you," Hayden said, bumping my hip as she came up alongside me.

"Hey yourself."

My sister had been flitting around for a couple of hours, reconnecting with people she hadn't seen since last summer. Though she'd said hello when she and Zane arrived, we hadn't talked in any detail.

"You guys are really doing this, huh?" she said, obviously tuning in to what Kemp was saying.

"We're really doing it. Finally. Later than planned. Not going to make our July Fourth goal, but we're shooting for late July."

"Some things you can't rush. You know, Sierra's brother-in-law Hunter was a brand manager at a brewery in Chicago for several years until he moved back to Nashville to run his family's bar."

Kemp apparently heard her because he asked, "Which one?"

Hayden tilted her head as she appeared to search her memory. "No idea. One that makes beer," she said oh so helpfully.

"That narrows it down." I tugged a strand of her hair.

"I can find out tomorrow. Sierra might know but she goes to bed early, and I'm sure Kennedy's asleep too, between having a thirteen-month-old and being pregnant again. Hunter owns Clayborne's on the Corner, down the street from my store. I've taken you there several times."

"Close to downtown?" Kemp asked. "On Hale Street?"

My sister nodded. "Right across from Sugar Babies Sweet Shop." Because Hayden related everything to where she could get her next sugar fix.

"I saw Midnight Moonshine play there," Kemp said. "Great little venue. We should drive in and meet this Hunter guy. See if he has any advice."

"You could take me to lunch while you're at it," Hayden said.

It sounded like Hunter could have invaluable experience, and maybe he'd be willing to share info with us. "If you hook us up with Hunter, I'll treat. Lunch *and* dessert."

"You're on." Hayden set her phone to remind her to get in touch with Kennedy tomorrow.

I hooked my arm around her neck and pulled her closer in an affectionate but rough-housing side hug. "Some days you're not too bad, Hay."

Her husband, Zane, had been on the other side of the dwindling fire talking to Cash, who'd showed up just a few minutes ago after finishing at Henry's. Zane strode up to Hayden's side and slid his arm around her middle as I let her go.

"You can have her, man," I said, grinning.

Zane, who I liked a lot—liked him on his own merits, liked the way he treated my sister, respected the hell out of him as both a pilot and a father—was a quiet guy. He just grinned at me and nodded.

"Are you ready to go?" Hayden asked him.

"I am. It's been fun, but we have an hour-long drive, and Harrison will be home before we know it in the morning."

He was classy enough not to say it out loud—thank God because I did not want to know about my sister's sex life—but I got the distinct impression Zane didn't want to let their baby-less night go without some private husband-and-wife time.

"Yes, Lieutenant," my sister quipped, and I was pretty

sure the reference to Zane's military past made him uncomfortable, but Hayden could get away with just about anything with him.

They said their goodbyes to our group as well as to the couple dozen people who remained, and I couldn't help peering around for my wife again. I was starting to get worried.

"I need to take off as well," Levi said. "It's been a great night but I'm beat."

"I'll probably head out in a few too," Carter said. "Got some unfinished business to take care of." He made his way toward Shawna, Isabel, Anna, and Olivia, who were back to holding court in the Adirondack chairs, where they'd been when Chloe and I first arrived.

I checked again to make sure Chloe wasn't with them, but there were only the four of them, seemingly entrenched in a world-changing serious conversation. I glanced around, looking for Rick, Magnolia's sucker, er, fiancé, but he seemed to be MIA as well.

"You've got it bad," Kemp said, then took a long drink of his beer.

Now that it was just the two of us, I lowered my voice and said, "She texted that she's talking to Magnolia."

"That's never a good idea."

"Especially for Chloe. Magnolia's never once been pleasant to her." I couldn't help myself. I glanced around yet again.

Kemp was staring at me.

"What?" I growled.

He took another swig, still eyeing me. Then he shook his head. "Trying to figure out if you've admitted it to yourself yet."

"Admitted what?"

Another group took off, and the gathering was down to

less than twenty. It was time to head home, but I couldn't do that without Chloe.

"You're in love with her." He kept his voice quiet, and everyone else appeared to be wrapped up in their clusters of people, but I glared at him.

"Chloe and I have always been close. You know this."

"Uh-huh. And now you're closer."

With a laugh I wasn't feeling, I said, "Of course we are. We're married."

"You've been seeking her out with your eyes all night, whether you're on opposite sides of the beach or one group away from each other. *Not* like a friend."

"If you've had time to keep track of who I'm looking at tonight, you could stand to get a life yourself."

"Don't need to bite my head off. It's not like you can control the *L* word. Just wondered if you'd acknowledged it or not. Seems I have my answer."

"With all the love in my heart, fuck off."

Kemp laughed, and for a second I wanted to punch him. Then I *realized* I wanted to punch him and questioned why. Olivia called him over to ask a question, and instead of going with him, I decided to search for Chloe.

I went toward the shore, focusing on the docks in both directions, checking the benches. They were all deserted, so I wandered toward the restrooms, allowing Kemp's accusation to bounce around in my head.

I knocked on the ladies' room door and said, "Anyone in there?"

The door whooshed open, and Trinity Parsons came out alone. She sent me a confused look, and I glanced in behind her.

"Just me, Holden. You okay?"

"Looking for Chloe."

Trinity shrugged. "Sorry. I haven't seen her for a bit."

"Thanks."

Trinity headed back toward the stragglers, where Cade and Trey Lancaster were extinguishing the bonfire, and my concern notched up even further.

I was about to look in back of the building when Chloe came around the corner, saw me, and smiled. "Hey, husband of mine."

I'd never experienced such relief before. It was like all the tension rushed out of me, along with a gusty breath. I pulled her into my arms.

It was in that instant that I knew. Kemp, the son of a bitch, was most likely right.

I'd fallen in love with my temporary wife.

CHAPTER 22

The Marks Hotel at Dragonfly Lake was three weeks from its first overnight guests.

Monday, the marketing campaign had begun in earnest, targeting regional cities like Nashville, Louisville, Atlanta, Huntsville, and Memphis. The reservation portal was live on the Marks International website, radio and online ads had begun, and we'd already secured a handful of other media mentions, including a segment on Nashville's CBS affiliate.

On Tuesday, shortly after noon, we'd gotten our first reservation, and I'd shared a champagne toast with Sebastian Dumay, who I'd hired as general manager, and the other executive management team members who were already in place.

Reservations had continued to filter in since then, and it looked like we were on our way to our first official summer season. I couldn't begin to describe how rewarding it was to be involved at this level, to be directly responsible for the birth of a new Marks property, to look ahead to future projects with optimism and excitement and strong hope that I would be living out my dream and guiding the company to success after success.

Our next project was in Hallstatt, Switzerland, and Gloria had been onsite there for the past month, but normally Angelica, as the president who insisted on being intimately involved in each and every property, would split her time between the two during the overlap. Once she had the GM in place at one hotel, she'd move on to the next location, where construction was just getting started.

Her involvement was one of the things that made our properties special—she always said if her name was going on the place, she would ensure that every detail was perfect and that branding was on point as well. It was a philosophy I bought into, and one I would strive to continue for years to come if Angelica made me the president.

It was Friday afternoon, and Sebastian and I had just finished an extra-long working lunch, where we'd selected our first choice for the Security and Housekeeping managers. The next two weeks would continue to be an intensive hiring period, where each manager would fill the remaining spots in their department. Construction was wrapping up, down to landscaping and interior fine-tuning, and we'd had our training department from corporate here for the past few weeks. It was starting to feel like a working boutique hotel, and from what I'd seen, the people we'd hired so far were thrilled to be a part of it.

I'd never had doubts about my career choice, and now I felt totally in my element. This was what I'd been made to do. I loved the job and the company, and when I lay down to go to sleep at night, sometimes I was so exhilarated from the day's work and accomplishments that I couldn't sleep.

I was walking back from the restaurant, where Sebastian and I had met—and been treated to a fantastic meal prepared by Nola Simms, the head chef—checking my calendar to make sure I wasn't forgetting any meetings this afternoon. I had a lot to do and half a chance of getting it all done if I didn't get interrupted. I entered the executive offices and went down the hall to my short-term smaller office just before the GM's. When I walked in, I gasped and stopped short.

Angelica was sitting in front of the floor-to-ceiling window, gazing outside. Sitting on the seat of a walker, I realized as I went closer and walked behind my desk. I swallowed down on my shock.

"Angelica," I said, hoping my voice sounded warm and not semi-horrified at her appearance.

Make no mistake—it was semi-horrifying. Had it really only been a few weeks since I'd last seen her, at the company dinner?

"The docks and the boathouse are exactly as I always pictured them," she said.

Even her voice sounded different than before. Not as strong. A little lower. Like she was depleted of energy.

"I can't decide which is my favorite," I said, striving for casual and unbothered, "those or the sprawling porch."

The office was not big, barely big enough for her to have wheeled her walker behind the visitor chairs on the opposite side of the desk. Her back was facing me, which was awkward, but if I walked closer to her, there was nowhere for me to sit, and I would tower over her. That would only serve to emphasize her weaker vantage point, and that was the last thing I wanted to do.

"The porch is the crowning glory," she declared. "The trademark of our Tennessee property."

"As it should be," I agreed, still standing by my desk chair.

Angelica turned from the window to face me, never leaving the walker seat, using her legs to pivot. I fought to keep my expression neutral as I took in her face. It was thinner, more angled, harder. Her skin was a pale gray, and her eyes… It was as if they'd sunken into her head, deepening the shadows beneath them. Almost like looking at a live skeleton.

"It's good to see you," I managed to get out in a steady voice. "I didn't know you were coming by this afternoon."

"I couldn't stay away once I heard the back landscaping was in and the lakeside terrace was finished." Her frail body rose slightly with a slow inhale. "I don't know how much longer I'll be able to handle a visit."

"I'm so glad you made it," I said, knowing sympathy wouldn't go over well. I also fought not to ask her how her health was or how her fight was progressing. Not only could I see quite plainly that it wasn't going well but when I'd asked her the first couple of weeks she'd been out of the office, she'd snapped at me every time.

"Is Sabrina with you?"

"She's doing our own inspection of everything, inside and out. Taking more photos for me."

Because Angelica would never make it without a wheelchair or a golf cart, I realized, which we didn't yet have onsite. Not that I could see her allowing either if we did.

"Would you like to go out to the porch? Those couches are the most sumptuous, comfortable things I've ever sat on."

She shook her head efficiently. "I came to talk to you privately." Her tone was sharp, stronger than two minutes ago, and it caught my attention.

"Sure," I said with a professional smile. My heart sped up as I wondered whether she'd made her decision and was here to give me news. "Would you like something to drink or eat?"

"I'm fine." She slowly stood and stepped to the closest visitor chair, one hand on my desk for support, then lowered herself into it. I'd just sat down myself when she said, "I know about your little marriage deal with Holden."

My eyes darted toward her, and as soon as I saw her gaze glued to me, assessing me, I realized that was a mistake. It was a knee-jerk reaction, and it'd been revealing.

"What marriage deal?" I asked, tilting my head slightly, trying to act nonchalant.

She crossed her arms over her chest and peered at me. "Holden marries you and you invest in his brewery. You get a husband, which as far as you know will lock you in as my successor. He gets to start the business of his dreams. Win-win."

How the hell had she found out about my investment? Nobody knew that except Holden, me, Kemp, and Presley, and I trusted all of them implicitly.

"Holden and I have a real marriage," I said. Real in that it was legal. Real in that we were living together and sleeping together.

"I'm well aware that you're legally wed. But you have a business deal as the foundation. You've missed the point completely, Chloe. It wasn't to get sly and concoct a bargain that would propel you forward. It was for your own good. I wanted you to find what I never had. Balance. Love. A life outside of work. This scheme to make me think you have that when you, in fact, do not is insulting and conniving."

I could tell Angelica that I loved Holden. That the marriage was at least fifty percent real if you judged it by that and as real as anything I personally would ever find. But she didn't deserve to know that, especially since Holden didn't.

"What did you expect me to do, Angelica?" I said, my tone going hard while I kept my volume down. "You want to talk about insulting and conniving… I've busted my ass for you and this company for twelve years. I've sacrificed a personal life, been your workhorse, as you yourself said, worked long hours and seven-day weeks. I've played by your rules this whole time, and then you *changed the rules.*"

"That is my prerogative."

"And it's my prerogative to marry my good friend to meet your ridiculous demands. What else could I do? It's been mere weeks since you decided it was more important for me to have a love life than to give every fiber of my being to this company. How is that fair? How could that be possible?"

"I never said you had to marry," she said condescendingly, as if I was the idiot who'd misinterpreted.

"You told me to date. Meet a guy. Well, I did one better. I married a guy. I live with him. I have a partnership with him. I have a deep friendship with him that's probably more than most marriages start with. Was the marriage to appease you? Initially, yes. Because in the end, not only do I want this job more than anything in my life but I'm also exactly the person you need at the helm. You know this. You admitted as much back when you threw out this whimsical new requirement."

"Gloria will do just fine at the helm. I'm having the paperwork drawn up as we speak to make her the president of Marks International Hotels."

I felt her words like a punch to the throat. Oxygen stopped flowing, and my brain went offline for a moment, as if my system was hit by a bolt of lightning. As I reeled, I had to will myself to suck in air… in, out, in again. I did my best to tamp down the panic exploding in my chest and rationalize with her.

"Don't do that, Angelica," I said quietly, earnestly. "You know that's not a smart long-term move for the business you've spent your entire adult life building up."

"What wouldn't be smart is to reward someone who has tried to deceive me." Her voice was icier than I'd ever heard it, even when she'd sat across a conference table from the most cutthroat adversary. "How long did you and your husband agree to keep up the charade? Until after my funeral? Then an easy divorce and you own my company, your husband has his business, and I'm left looking like the biggest fool in history?" She shook her head, her jaw locked. "That is not how it's going to go."

"You'd rather leave your legacy in the hands of the second-best person and put your decades of hard work at risk than have the best, most capable candidate ensure that your vision is fulfilled?"

"The only thing more important than my company is my reputation. Once I'm dead, I won't be able to protect it. I can't have you and your marriage of convenience shatter it."

"What would you have had me do, Angelica? What choice did you give me with your unfair, half-baked decree?"

She let out an acerbic laugh. "I only suggested you go on dates, meet people, work on your social life. It's just like you to go all out and do more than asked of you. And it might have worked had you put yourself into a more plausible situation. You aren't the type to have a relationship, but if you did, Holden Henry would not be the match for you. I might have only talked to him for a few minutes, but I could tell he's outgoing, likable, Mr. Social, a friend to all. You… are not. The two of you as a couple makes no sense, Chloe, and everyone can see that."

I opened my mouth to respond, but nothing came out, because she'd hit me *there*. Exactly in my Achilles' heel.

"My trust in you has been broken," Angelica said. "You have thirty minutes to gather your belongings. You're fired."

CHAPTER 23

CHLOE

t only took me four minutes to box up my belongings, as I hadn't brought much of anything personal in. I wasn't the type to keep nonessential things in my work area.

I gasped when the thought struck me: For the first time in my adult life, I didn't have a work area.

I didn't have a job.

Without saying goodbye to anyone—I knew Angelica was still lurking about somewhere and wouldn't allow it even if I did feel like I could show my face—I left via the least-used door and crumpled into the relative safety of my car.

I'd managed to hold it together so far, but the instant my door closed, I let out a shaky exhale that turned into a pained moan as I flung my hands over my face.

My house of cards had collapsed.

All the work I'd done the past twelve years, actually more than that—my college years, high school—had culminated in exactly nothing.

My fake marriage to Holden was a waste.

The life I'd tried to build in my hometown the past few weeks was a mirage.

Holding in sobs, because anyone could walk by me there in the Marks parking lot, I shut out the world by turning my phone off. Then I started my car, backed out, and hightailed it away, wiping tears out of my eyes so I could see enough to drive.

I headed toward home—

No. Not home. What a joke. It wasn't *my* home. It was Holden's. It was where I'd tried to act like I belonged for the past few weeks. But it wasn't where I belonged.

I wasn't sure where I belonged, frankly.

My life had always been centered around my career. My apartment in Nashville had been a place to go in between workdays. Holden's house, as well, had been a nearby place to rest my head when I wasn't working. Without a career, what was left?

I'd gone from a top-tier manager of an international company to nothing in two seconds flat. For a dozen years, I'd garnered my confidence from my career. Gained my self-worth from it. I'd been proud to work for a globally known and respected hospitality company. That's *who I was*.

I'd lost it all in the blink of an eye, and now… I no longer had a clue who or what I was. Where I was going. It was like I'd lost my entire identity.

An awful wail escaped me as I came upon Henry's and took a left on Main. When I got to Holden's street a block later, I couldn't make myself turn down it. Instead, I kept driving, again trying to hold back the racking sobs as my mind raced with a tempest of thoughts and emotions.

You failed.

You tried to believe you were all that, but you weren't.

You turned Holden's life upside down for nothing.

I drove all the way to the city, noticing none of the drive, arriving at my apartment building's parking garage without thinking about it. Pulling into my assigned parking spot as if it hadn't been more than a month since I'd been there.

After looking around to ascertain no one was in the vicinity, I climbed out, feeling ninety years old, my body heavy and sore as if I'd been dragged behind the car instead of in the driver's seat, then hurried to the elevator with my head down.

When I let myself into my apartment, an odd feeling washed through me. The place was familiar but different, even though everything looked the same. It didn't quite feel like home either. I'd taken my clothes and food and some other personal effects to Holden's, but the furniture was all here, the wall hangings still in their places.

Letting my purse fall to the floor, I went to the couch and sagged into it. I picked up one of the pillows and hugged it to my chest, as if that could stem the physical pain. It couldn't. Nothing could.

Pulling my feet up, I reclined and curled onto my side, resting my head on another pillow and letting the sobs come until they ran out, a long, indefinable chunk of time later, leaving me depleted and limp. At some point the sun went down and the room turned dark. My stomach growled but I didn't care. I wasn't sure I would ever move off this couch.

I must've fallen into the deep sleep of complete, utter failure. I had no idea what time it was when I awoke to pounding on my door. Incoherent, unsure at first where I was, I pushed myself up to a sitting position and shoved my messy hair out of my face. In that instant, a dark, suffocating heaviness akin to grief overcame me, and then I remembered everything that had happened. I wilted against the back cushion.

"Chloe! Let me in."

At the sound of Holden's voice, I jolted to the edge of the couch, momentarily panicked.

I didn't want to see him now. I didn't want to see anyone. Maybe ever.

"I know you're in there, Chlo. I'm not leaving, so you might as well let me in."

I believed him, so I worked up the energy to stand, trudged to the door in the darkness, unlocked it, opened it, and made my way back to the couch without a word.

Behind me, I heard Holden come in, heard the door close, and then the kitchen light turned on and I squinted against the brightness.

"What happened?" Holden asked, taking long strides until he stood in front of me, then crouched down and put his hands on my knees. "I went to find you at the hotel and Sebastian said you no longer worked there. I looked all over for you and finally texted Presley. She said she saw your car in its spot when she was leaving and figured we were in the city for a specific reason."

I squeezed my eyes shut because I couldn't handle looking at him. Couldn't stand to let him see *me*.

With my chin to my chest, I eventually found the voice to say, "It's over."

"What's over?"

With a scoff, I said, "Angelica fired me today."

"What?" The outrage in his tone, obviously on my behalf, was sweet and typical. And misplaced. "Why did she fire you?"

I fought to get to a matter-of-fact place so I could explain it to him and send him on his way.

"Somehow she found out I was your investor. She put two and two together, came up with an accurate picture of our 'little marriage deal,' and didn't take nicely to my 'deception.' Didn't listen to my arguments about how absurd her requirements were in the first place. Told me she was having paperwork drawn up to make Gloria the president and owner of

Marks International. Then she told me to pack my things and get out because her trust in me was broken."

"Son of a bitch," he bit out. He planted his forearms on either side of my thighs and leaned his forehead against mine. "I'm so sorry, Chloe."

For once, his closeness wasn't comforting. It made me feel like I couldn't breathe.

"I need up," I managed, and Holden eased away from me enough that I could stand and put some distance between us. I walked to the window that looked out over the city, keeping my back to him. "It's over. I'm eternally grateful for everything you've done for me, but we can end the marriage now. I'm so sorry to have put you through it for nothing."

"Wha— Chloe, what are you talking about? *We are married*. I'm here for you."

"We're *fake* married. There's no point in pretending anymore. We can both have our lives back." Well, he could. I'd have to figure out what my life *was*. Where I would work. What I would do.

He laughed, and it rang with disbelief. "You're a big part of my life. You've been a big part of my life since we were little kids. You think I'm going to leave you now?"

Of course he thought he wasn't. That was Holden. He was the most steadfast, reliable person I'd ever known, and it gave me hope that we could come out of this, out of our marriage with our friendship intact.

I pivoted to face him, though I still didn't make eye contact. I knew I looked a wreck, but even more, I was sure he would see the devastation in my eyes if I let him. Something in me said I needed to protect that. Though Holden had been at my side, so to speak, for the past six weeks, I needed to remember how to forge my way ahead alone once again. I'd let myself depend on him for long enough.

"I know you'd stay here and be supportive for as long as I want you to," I said, "but I really need to be alone."

"That's not what you need, Chloe. We're supposed to stick together even when things go south. *Especially* when things go south."

"Holden," I said sharply, needing to get through to him. "Our marriage is over. We can dissolve it now." I tried hard to smile, to reassure him that I would be okay. "You're free. We're both free. We'll sign the papers early."

"No."

God, give me strength. This man was so determined to "help," so determined to do the right thing… It was part of what I loved about him. It was also why I would absolutely insist on setting him free.

"You can blame it all on me. Say I took a job out of the country or… I don't know." Maybe I *would* take a job out of the country.

He was directly in front of me before I realized he'd moved, his hands on my upper arms, face in front of mine. "Chloe, listen to me. I don't want to end our marriage. I love you."

My chest constricted with longing. I reached out and touched his cheek, my heart pulsing in my throat. "You're such a good man. Such an unselfish friend."

Of course he'd say that. I believed he did love me as a friend. *Love* love though? It was just as Angelica had said, just as I had always known. Holden and I made no sense as more than friends. Truly, we barely made sense as friends, but there were years of history behind that. However, the longer we put off getting back to being strictly friends, the more we were endangering that friendship.

"I don't mean I love you like a friend," he said. "I'm *in love* with you—"

"No. You don't *love* love me. You might've thought you loved the Chloe of the past few weeks, the one who was running an international business and masquerading as a confident small-town girl, but that's not really who I am. I can't live up to what you need. Especially now—" My throat swelled up and cut off my ability to say more.

"Stop it." He ran his fingers through his hair, clenched his jaw, and paced a couple of steps away as if he needed to put space between us to keep his cool. He turned back to me. "I understand your confidence was shaken today. The dictator did a number on you. But that's her issue. Not yours. She fucked up, and we both know it."

"Whether she did or not, I'm the one with no job. She wins. As she said, you and I being a married couple makes no sense."

He was rubbing the back of his neck, but he stopped and whipped his head toward me. "What? She said that?"

"Verbatim," I said firmly.

"And you fucking believed her?"

"She's not the only one who thinks that."

He stepped closer, practically in my face. "It doesn't matter what anyone thinks but us, Chloe."

"I think you'd be better off with someone else." Someone on secure footing, minimum. No question, I was a hot mess, and that wasn't going to be fixed anytime soon.

He stared at me silently, and there was fire in his eyes. I nearly backed away, but I ached for him to leave so I could lick my wounds in private. I held strong.

"You're not doing this, Chloe. You're not slipping back into that little-girl insecure version of yourself. You're my wife—"

"But not really."

He bit down on whatever else he was going to say, then inhaled slowly, deeply, as if I required the patience of Job. I most likely did. "I'm sorry for what happened to you today, Chlo. So fucking sorry. I want to be here for you—"

"There's nothing you can do. You can't save me this time, Holden." I firmed up my voice. "Please..." I went to the door and opened it, feeling like I could collapse at any second.

He strode over to the door and faced me. Studied me intently. I wanted to squirm, but I lifted my chin.

Holden grabbed the edge of the door and I stepped back a bit so he could leave.

"This isn't over, Chloe. We aren't over. But I can only do so much. If you figure out you're not that little girl anymore and want to move forward with me, I'll be waiting."

He walked out, and the door slammed shut behind him.

I leaned my back against it and withered to the floor, and though I'd thought I was all cried out, the tears ran down my face unchecked.

CHAPTER 24

HOLDEN.

By Saturday night, I was going out of my mind. I'd barely slept last night, worrying about Chloe. Missing Chloe.

I'd broken down and texted her a handful of times, asking her to please let me know she was okay. She hadn't replied, so I'd been in contact with Presley, who lived upstairs from her. She assured me that she was keeping a close eye on Chloe, making sure she ate, letting her know she was there to listen when Chloe wanted to talk. She hadn't so far, apparently, and that just made me hurt more for her.

I'd thought for sure I'd hear from my wife on Saturday. I understood she was in an ugly, dark place. Anyone would be after getting fired, but with Chloe it went so much deeper. There were layers and years of insecurity there, a semi-healed wound that that bitch-ass boss of hers had reopened and then poured acid on. If that woman wasn't dying already, I'd gladly help her along.

Though we'd only been married a few weeks, her absence in the bed affected me like I'd never known was possible.

What sleep I'd gotten was fitful, and every time I rolled toward her side, the emptiness kicked me in the gut. It made me wonder how I'd gone for so many years without seeing what she meant to me. I wanted to punch myself for all the time we'd missed out on.

By dawn on Sunday, I awoke from an hour or two of fitful sleep with the sudden fear that maybe Chloe wasn't coming back. Call me dense as a rainforest, but until now, I'd assumed Chloe would take some time to wrestle with losing her job, time to grieve, and then she'd be ready to let me in. Not healed by any means but wanting me by her side.

As the sun peeked through the windows in our bedroom, fear pulsed through me, along with a kind of desperation to convince her to come home. If she wouldn't answer texts or phone calls and wouldn't let me in her apartment, there was no way to convince her of anything or even just hold her. I didn't need her to be recovered from the devastating blow Angelica Marks had dealt her. I needed to be able to help her recover if she needed it. But what if Chloe never let me back in?

What if I'd lost one of my best friends as well as my wife?

Had I waited too long to tell her I loved her? Not long enough? It seemed she didn't believe me regardless, but was that just because of what had happened on Friday? If I had told her sometime before she'd lost her job, would it have had time to settle in and take root in her mind? Or would it have scared her off?

I sat up on the edge of the bed, leaning over my knees, trying not to throw up. I ran my hands through my hair like a desperate man as I took in some deep breaths, willing the nausea away.

When I felt like I could put my head up without vomiting, I grabbed my phone from the nightstand, my hope dim but present that there would be something from Chloe. There wasn't.

With my eyes burning and my chest aching and my body feeling like I was a few decades older than thirty-four, I slowly stood and headed to the shower.

Today I was continuing to train Riley O'Brien to take over managing Henry's front of house so I could transition my full-time focus to the brewery. Prior to this weekend, I'd been exhilarated by the task because it meant I was one step closer to my dream. With Chloe gone and the possibility of not having a future with her weighing so heavily on me, I had a hard time giving half a fuck about the brewery. The thing that had lit me up with motivation and passion and hope for the past few years... it paled in comparison to Chloe. If I could walk away from Rusty Anchor Brewing to ensure Chloe came back and became my for-real wife, I'd do it in a heartbeat.

I'd never felt so impotent in my life.

CHLOE

By Sunday, I was sick of my miserable self. I wasn't ready to move mountains or even get dressed in something other than leggings and a T-shirt, but I'd never been good at wallowing or sitting around, doing nothing.

I'd spent Saturday doing exactly that—lying in bed, alternating between bingeing a mindless show on a streaming service I'd forgotten I subscribed to, crying my eyes out, and being forced by Presley to sit up and eat.

Sleep had been elusive until I'd broken down and taken the supplements Presley, the patron saint of patience, left for me around four this morning. I'd passed out until after eleven a.m., showered, and dressed. Now I was starving. I was about to go track down my phone to text Presley when there was a knock on my door that had my heart racing irrationally.

I knew it wasn't Holden. Why would it be Holden? I'd basically rejected his declaration of love and made him leave.

"Chloe? Open up," Presley called as I made my slow, sluggish way to the door.

"Hold your horses," I muttered, not loudly enough for her to hear. That would take more energy than I had. Funny how fucking up your entire life sucked up every last bit of energy.

When I opened the door, there stood Presley, patron saint of patience *and* nourishment, holding a carryout bag from Clayborne's on the Corner, which had the most delicious fried mushrooms I'd ever eaten.

"You're my favorite person," I said, taking the hot bag from her.

"Mm-hmm." Presley's smile was wide as she came inside. "If you eat all of your lunch, you can have a treat." She held up an unopened package of Twizzlers, presumably for me, and a teal-blue bakery box from Sugar Babies, the bakery across from Clayborne's, likely for her. I could eat a cupcake in a pinch, but Twizzlers comforted me like a pacifier did a baby. "You're dressed," she said, her surprise obvious.

"I got some sleep and a shower."

"Thank God. You were pretty ripe by last night."

"Thanks, friend," I said dryly as we went to the couch. I emptied the Clayborne's bag, spreading two fried chicken sandwiches, a large order of mushrooms, and a large order of pretzel bites with cheese dip on the coffee table.

"How are you doing?" she asked as she unwrapped her sandwich. "The fact that you opened the door and didn't force me to use my key again seems like an improvement."

I bit into a fried mushroom and savored the crisp saltiness of the breading, preferring to focus on food instead of the shambles otherwise known as my life.

"I did a precursory search for jobs in the hotel industry for you," she continued. "There's a lot out there. Everywhere."

That was my cue to shove in another mushroom.

"Maybe the first decision is whether you want to stay in Tennessee or open up your options to other places."

"Here," I said around the bite of food.

I didn't know much, but I was sure I didn't want to move away from my parents and Presley. I wasn't sure whether I could put Holden on that list. He might not even want to talk to me after the way I acted on Friday.

"What are you thinking? Something in a corporate office? Something at a hotel property? You have so many directions you could go…"

I moaned. I was having trouble stomaching the idea of starting over in a new company. I knew I'd had it really good in a lot of ways. I was lucky to have moved up within Marks over the years instead of needing to jump companies to grow.

"Too soon?" Presley said.

I nodded and unwrapped my sandwich. Too soon. Too commitment-ish. Too future-ish. Too everything.

"You have the luxury of not needing to work right away," she said. "You can take your time. I have no doubt you'll have your choice of corporate hotel positions. C-suite, even."

"Honestly?" I said after swallowing. "The thought makes me want to puke."

"Which thought?"

"All of it. I loved what I was doing, and now that feels… soured."

"That's understandable. We don't have to figure it out today."

"Thank God. Can I just be your house bitch and clean the apartment and cook for you and wash your clothes?"

"You don't know how tempting that is," Presley said. "But I happen to know you suck at bathrooms."

That coaxed a reluctant laugh out of me because it was true. My bathroom was the worst room in the place, with all my products strewn about on the counters and towels thrown on the floor for days at a time until I got around to doing laundry. Holden had given me all kinds of hell about it, jokingly, ever since I'd moved in.

Just the thought of him made my grin disappear in an instant.

I missed him.

So damn much.

"Have you talked to Holden yet?" Presley asked, as if she could read my mind—or the look on my face.

My chest constricted. I hadn't told Presley anything that happened with him Friday night except that I'd asked him to leave. Popping a whole mushroom into my mouth, I shook my head.

"Have you at least replied to his texts?"

Again, I shook my head. I'd only turned my phone back on when Presley made me so she could check on me. If I hadn't, she'd threatened to camp out on my couch.

Yes, there were texts. A bunch of them. I hadn't read them. Not because I didn't care but because the very thought of Holden made me literally hurt with anxiety.

"I screwed up so badly," I managed to say even though my throat swelled up painfully.

Presley had her sandwich halfway to her mouth, but she froze and looked at me, assessing. Then she set the sandwich back on the wrapper on the table and scooted closer to me. "You ready to tell me what happened?"

I handed off the container of mushrooms, still half full, because food suddenly made me feel sick. Food or, let's be honest, the way I'd treated Holden.

I sat there with my face scrunched up, eyes closed, soul full of regret. "He… told me he loves me."

Presley put her hand on my leg right above my knee and squeezed supportively. "Wow. This is big." Though she kept her voice calm, I could hear her smile. "Except you said you screwed up. What did you do, Chloe?"

Hanging my head, I drew in a deep breath, eyes still

closed, then I admitted, "Told him he couldn't or shouldn't. Told him we needed to end our marriage. Then I told him to leave."

"Ouch." Presley wove her arm with mine and leaned her head into my head. "I'm trying to be the supportive friend here, but why the actual fuck?"

Why the actual fuck indeed.

"I think, at the time, I didn't believe him. I thought he was saying it to make me feel better."

"I don't know Holden well, but I don't think he'd say *that* to make you feel better. Not unless he meant it."

Her words were a lot like what I'd been thinking for the past however many hours, though I'd waffled between agreeing with her and accusing myself of wishful thinking. "Do you really think that?"

"Of course I really think that. I always tell you what I really think."

My inhale this time was shaky. I don't think I'd quite let myself believe that Holden could love me, even though I wanted that more than anything in this world.

"I sort of get it," she continued. "You were at your lowest point. Probably afraid to believe?"

"Definitely afraid to believe."

Presley nodded. "The man I've been texting with all weekend seems like a man in love and crazy worried about you."

"You've been texting with him?" I scowled.

"A couple dozen times. He's trying hard to give you space but wanted to make sure you're okay."

I let out a hollow laugh. "I'm not okay."

"No. But you will be. And you haven't OD-ed on Twizzlers or anything worse." She sat up straight. "He's a good guy, Chloe. I wholeheartedly approve of you making your marriage real and permanent."

"And you just jumped ahead about twenty-two steps," I

said, my voice wavering at the thought of how I would ever apologize to him. Whether I could ever get him to forgive me.

"I'm feeling confident about your chances." She smiled and sounded upbeat.

I wasn't feeling it.

"How…" Tears burned at my eyes as the possibility sank in that I might've hurt Holden too much to come back from it.

"How do you make up with him?" Presley guessed, and I nodded. "Move back in with him, for starters."

"What if he doesn't want me there?"

"Right. You need to apologize first."

"I feel like I need a grand gesture or something."

"Grand gesture, like what?"

"I could buy him a boat or something," I said in a monotone. "Except he doesn't really want a boat."

"Girl, you bought him a damn brewery. I don't think buying him something is necessary."

"Probably right. What then?"

"Strip for him? I don't know. I get the impression that all that boy needs is you."

If that was true, then we were set, because all I needed was him. Well, plus a job. Whatever. That could come later. One thing at a time.

I needed to plan out a visit to my husband.

CHAPTER 25

HOLDEN

The dinner crowd had thinned out to almost nothing. I'd never been so relieved it was Sunday and that we slowed down and closed earlier than other nights. I felt like I'd worked a forty-eight-hour shift.

Riley was coming along well, learning fast. Another couple of shifts together and I'd feel confident she could handle it on her own. I'd left her in Seth's office fighting with the server schedule for the next week, glad to have that task off my hands. I'd let Dakota, the bartender, go home early tonight since there was no one seated at the bar and I could handle any last-minute orders that came in. She'd stocked the bar but had been in the middle of cleaning when I told her to take off, so I hunkered down to wipe everything clean and do the rest of the closing duties.

I was bent down, scrubbing the inside of the under-the-counter fridge, not paying much attention, when someone walked through the bar toward the dining area. It was forty minutes till closing. We could still seat people for another ten minutes and serve them. My eyes felt like sunken hollows in my head thanks to very little sleep in the past two nights, so when I stood up and saw a familiar brunette following Natalie, the host on duty tonight, out the door to the deck, I squeezed my eyes shut to clear them and did a double take.

The woman didn't quite dress like Chloe, but I could swear that was her.

My heart raced as if someone had floored the gas pedal, and I craned to the side to see around the vertical deck heater between her and me. Though her hair was thrown up in a messy bun and I'd rarely seen her wear it like that to leave the house, I was certain it was my wife.

Riley came around the corner from the office then to confirm how many openers we needed on Saturday mornings.

With my eyes darting outside, I answered and then looked over the tablet screen where she'd been finalizing the schedule. "Looks like you've got it," I said. "Any other questions for me?"

"Yeah. Who's out on the deck?"

I shot a look toward Chloe. Even though I had no idea whether I had anything to smile about, I couldn't help a half grin when I said, "My wife."

"Why don't you let me finish up tonight. Go sit with your wife. You look like you've been through some kind of war zone."

I laughed because that was an apt description of how I'd felt all weekend.

"You comfortable with everything?" I asked.

"I am. You comfortable with me doing it?"

"Hundred percent." I pointed out the last couple of cleaning tasks behind the bar to her. "Thanks, Riley."

At the glass door to the giant deck that doubled our dining capacity for more than half the year, I paused, my eyes locking on Chloe. She was in profile, her hair thrown up as haphazardly as I'd seen it. She wore cutoff shorts that allowed me to feast my eyes on those sexy slender legs of hers, an old, stretched out T-shirt that I could swear had Mickey Mouse on it, and old rubber flip-flops. My insides went liquid at the sight of this gorgeous woman. I couldn't deny that I had equal parts fear and hope taking root. Surely if she meant to end things officially, she wouldn't do it here in public.

As I pushed out the door, the movement must have caught her eye. She turned and met my gaze. I studied her face, trying to ascertain whether this conversation would be happy or devastating, but she gave nothing away. Not so much as a smile until I pulled out the chair next to her and nodded to it in question. Then the corners of her lips tipped upward in a faint polite smile that could've been for any random server or stranger. Not so much for her husband.

My uneasiness increased as I sat down.

"Hi," I said.

"Hi," she replied on an exhale. She averted her eyes as I drank in her features, noticing they were makeup free—and so pretty.

"Did you order something?"

"Just this." She held up her water. "I told them I was waiting for you to get off work. Can we walk toward the water?"

"Of course."

The tension between us was not the good kind. We were acting like two people on a blind date instead of a married couple, and it had my concern level ratcheting up sky-high.

When we got to the end of the walkway, just before the dock, we went to the bench there and sat down together without saying anything. At least we were in sync in one way.

"You look good," I told her, unable to take the quiet another second.

She glanced down at herself. "This was the best non-winter shirt left at my apartment." She shrugged. "Mickey never goes out of style, right?" She laughed, seeming nervous.

She grabbed the bottom hem of her shirt and held on to it, resting her hand on her thigh. I had to fight off the need to run my fingers over hers. It was killing me not to touch her, not to pull her close, but as badly as I wanted to make contact, I wasn't sure I could handle a physical rebuff.

"Holden, I'm sorry about Friday night. I was a disaster."

Her word choice made me smile a little. "I wouldn't call it a disaster. You don't need to apologize. I know what losing your job did to you. It would've been less damaging if the dictator had just cut out your heart."

She was looking at me thoughtfully, nodding. "You know me well."

"Better than anyone knows you. Except maybe Presley, but if you give me more time, I can beat her out."

Her brows shot up and she took in a deep breath. "About that…"

My heart thundered hard as I locked my gaze on her, not breathing.

"You said you love me…"

"Yes, I did," I said without hesitation. I didn't know if she was counting that as a good thing or a bad thing, but it was a fact. "I do."

Chloe blew out that breath she'd taken and turned sideways to face me on the bench. "I love you too, Holden."

I cradled her beautiful face in my hand, looked into her brown eyes, and leaned in to kiss her at last. I kissed her until neither of us could breathe, and then I kissed her some more, and Chloe kissed me right back, wrapping her arms around my neck, climbing closer, until she straddled my lap.

"I need to say more," she eventually said, resting her forehead against mine, our breaths a little choppy, mingling in the air between us. "I have a confession. I've loved you for a long time. Years. I don't even know when exactly I fell, but fall I did, Holden. You've always been the only guy for me, but I never thought I'd be the girl for you."

I was stunned silent momentarily by that reveal, then I said, "Sometimes I'm not the quickest guy in the room. It might've taken me a while, but now that I've figured out you're the girl for me, you're not getting rid of me in ten months."

She laughed and leaned in for another kiss, then pulled back before I had my fill of her.

"A funny thing happened to me on my drive here," she said.

"Yeah? Like what?"

"I got a phone call from Angelica. She apologized and said she'd thought about what I said about her one-eighty being unfair and that I was right."

"No shit, Madame Dictator."

"She asked me to come back to Marks. Because she admitted I was also right that I was the best person for the job. She wants me to lead her company into the future."

"Wow, Chloe. Congratulations. You deserve every bit of that."

"Thank you," she said with a humble smile. "I told her no."

I reared my head back enough to get a good look at her expression. She didn't appear to be shitting me. "Why did you do that?"

"Because I figured out what I really want to do with my life." She laced our fingers together, palm to palm, between us. "I have a proposal for you."

"O-kay." I drew out the word. "That's interesting since we're already married."

She laughed quietly. "Thankful for that. What would you say if I came on as an assistant manager at the brewery? Or an operations chick or… whatever you need me to do. I believe in what you and Kemp are doing, Holden. I love what you're doing. What you said a while back about our careers being similar, that we both give the customer a quality experience... that resonates with something deep inside of me. I loved what I did for Marks, but the new position would require me to travel a lot. I don't want to be away from you. I want to help you build your dream... if you'll have me."

My heart had never been so full. "I'll have you. Hell yes, I'll have you. At the brewery and in my bed. You unravel me, Chloe Henry. Your business sense is sexy as hell and exactly what we need at Rusty Anchor. And these luscious thighs are just what I need in my bed," I said as I ran my hand up her leg and dipped my fingers under the fringed hem of her shorts.

"You dirty, tempting man," she said on an exhale. "One of the many reasons I love you. So it's a yes? Do you need to talk to Kemp?"

"It's a yes. I want to talk to Kemp about making you an equal partner—"

"No. You can pay me a salary, and it doesn't need to be a high one, but my investment was a gift. Because I believe in you, Holden. I've always believed in you. You deserve to have your dreams come true."

"My dream is coming true this very second. It's sitting on my lap."

We kissed, a hungry, urgent kiss born of all the desperation of being without her for two days and the sheer bliss of having her in my arms once again.

She broke the contact way too soon, gazed into my eyes with love and lust in hers, and said, "You, my love, are my very own *hoppy* ever after."

EPILOGUE

ONE MONTH LATER

CHLOE

What a difference a couple of months could make. I'd gone from *thinking* I was happy with my life to experiencing a daily over-the-top sort of bliss that I'd never known was possible.

My husband was everything I'd ever wanted, quite literally. I'd just never believed it was possible for him to love *me*. He did, though. He showed me every day, in so many ways, from the expensive Jamaican coffee he brewed for me before work to the way he worshipped my body every night—and sometimes in the middle of the day and in the morning and… You get the picture. Our sex life was not lacking in the least, and all those fantasies I'd had over the years that starred him? They didn't come close to doing us justice.

Holden's love made me feel beautiful and sexy and confident even without my armor. The designer label wardrobe? I'd given some pieces away, still had a few in my closet, but they were mostly untouched. I wore jeans and tees—most of them with the Rusty Anchor Brewing logo—to work every day, plus sneakers or flip-flops.

And working with my husband? It stimulated me in a whole different way. Learning the brewing business was challenging and fascinating. Applying my hospitality and management skills to our start-up invigorated me, and helping Holden realize his dreams fulfilled me and added yet another dimension to our relationship. We were partners in everything, and while that might not be for everyone, to me, it was incredibly fulfilling.

It was the second Saturday night in June, and our wedding celebration party was in full swing. More than a hundred people had shown up and were currently meandering between the food tables and the bar and the dance floor, all set up for the evening on my parents' property.

I'd been so reluctant to have it here at first, but from the moment we told my parents I'd reconsidered and wanted to hold it behind the trailer on their partially wooded two-acre property, they'd come to life with so much excitement and joy that I hadn't regretted the decision.

They'd finally agreed to let me help pay for some repairs and sprucing up, allowing that, since this was my reception, it would be similar to a rental fee if we'd had it anywhere else. Semantics. I didn't care what they called it. I was happy to have their home painted, stairs fixed, and outbuildings rebuilt, and if using this party as an excuse made it acceptable in their minds, so much the better.

I stood momentarily by myself, taking in the scene, after Kemp had convinced Anna to dance to an eighties song with him, leaving me a rare moment to breathe.

"This was the right choice," Holden said as he came up behind me and wound his arms around my waist. "It looks fantastic."

"I agree. Anna, Hayden, and the rest of them outdid themselves with the planning."

There were white twinkle lights everywhere and lanterns on tables and hanging from trees. The food stations and bar were made of wine barrels on end. There were remnants of an old chimney in the yard that had been there since long before my time, from a previous house, and the girls had put a balloon display in front of it to make it into a backdrop of glitz and brick.

Magnolia, of all people, had asked if she could help with the planning and had come up with the concept for the whole design. I couldn't deny she had some serious party-planning skills. Maybe she could use those somehow. It turned out her dad had, indeed, followed through on his threat and cut her off and kicked her to the curb, almost literally.

Instead of being sad, she'd taken the mad route, and that, in my opinion, had helped drive her to take some major steps in her life. She had her first job ever, working at the paper and stationery store. The owner, Dotty Jaworski, was nearing seventy and had some health issues, so she was glad to have the help. She'd also let Magnolia move into the vacant apartment on the second floor for cheap while Magnolia found her way. She and I weren't close friends by any means, but we'd come to a sort of peace after the bonfire night. I had a lot more tolerance for her now that I had an idea of what her life was like.

Cash and his staff had catered all the food except dessert, which had been supplied by Sugar, the bakery on Main Street. Though I hadn't had a lot of time to eat, everything I'd tried was fantastic, and multiple guests had raved about it, particularly the mini masala sausage rolls and the chicken teriyaki skewers. And of course, the specialty donuts were to die for. They'd even made a Twizzler-topped donut just for me—most likely requested by Holden if I had to guess.

See? He was perfect for me.

Still holding me from behind, he tilted my head to the side and kissed me, turning me inside out in two seconds flat.

"You two are still wearing that newlywed glow, I see. Thank heavens!"

Loretta Lawson, our next-door neighbor, approached along with Kona Powers, the school librarian I'd always adored.

"Hello," I said as Holden stepped up beside me. "I'm so happy you both could make it."

"Hi, ladies," Holden said. "I'm planning to wear that newlywed glow for another decade or so. Hope that's okay."

Loretta let out an "aww" and tapped her chest as if he'd gotten to her heart. He'd definitely gotten to mine.

"Kona, we need to do lunch while you're on summer vacation," I said as she hugged me.

"Absolutely, my dear. You're the one with the busy schedule. How's the brewery going?" Kona asked. The librarian was short and pretty, her dark hair pulled back with a beautiful comb that had coral and turquoise stones inset, to match her coral-colored dress.

"Yes," Loretta piped up. "We're all dying for updates on the Rusty Anchor. I heard you'll be adding a beer garden patio?"

"That's the plan," Holden said. "The brainchild of my wife."

"It's fantastic that you two are working together," Kona said. "The hotel development must have been rewarding, but to work with your husband on a brand-new business"—she inhaled, her shoulders lifting in enthusiasm—"it's romantic. I hope the switch is fulfilling for you, Chloe."

"I'm loving it," I said, and I meant every word. Just tonight, I'd decided the beer patio would have strings of lights for summer evenings, inspired by the scene in front of me.

Kemp joined us then, his dance with Anna having ended, and he threw his arm around me.

"Ms. What's-Her-Name from the hotel did us a solid when she set Chloe free," Kemp said.

"Hey, let's not give the dictator too much credit," Holden said. "I like to think Chloe would've come to her senses and joined us eventually anyway."

I laughed. "I like to think I would too, but she forced me to think about what I really wanted for my life."

"Me," Holden said, overflowing with cockiness.

"You," I acknowledged. "And the brewery."

"And me," Kemp said from my other side, daring Holden to react. It worked, as Holden playfully shoved him away. "Hey, I come with the brewery," Kemp insisted.

"I deal with these two all day long," I said to Kona and Loretta with a teasing eye roll.

"You got it rough, honey," Loretta said.

"Tell me about it." I laughed.

Angelica had done me a favor in the end. I'd been so shattered professionally and hurt personally. When she'd called to apologize and offer me the job after all, it'd been gratifying, and it had helped to soothe my feelings toward her. Last week, I'd taken lunch to her at her home and spent some time with her and Sabrina, who was acting more like a nurse than a business assistant these days.

For the first time ever, we'd not discussed business, since it was no longer my business and Angelica was barely involved anymore. I'd questioned her about one thing that still bothered me—how she'd found out I was Holden's investor. Though she hadn't admitted it outright, I was pretty sure she'd had someone hack financial records somehow. It didn't matter anymore.

Angelica's health was failing fast; it was obvious upon seeing her. She had a hospital bed in her house because she was too weak to sit up on her own at times, and she didn't have energy to do much but lie around and watch streaming shows with Sabrina. The old Angelica had barely known what streaming TV service was, and now it was just about all she had. I couldn't help but feel sympathy for her. Sabrina had told me in private that she'd be surprised if Angelica was still alive in two months. I was glad I'd gone to see her, because it had helped me put my remaining bad feelings toward her to bed.

Nick Carlisle sauntered up to our group then, with Seth lagging behind him, preoccupied with something on his phone. "When are you guys getting that brewery open for business? It's gotta be close. The outside's looking good," Nick asked.

"We're working on the beer and the inside," Kemp said. "Shooting for late-July for a soft opening. We'll be looking to hire a beer boy soon if you're interested."

Nick snorted. "I'm interested in the brewski, not the job."

"We're working as fast as we can," Holden said. "Trust me, I want to open even more than you want us to open."

"Good beer takes time," I said smugly, as if I had all the beer knowledge in the world. I didn't, of course, but I'd learned a bunch.

"So does construction," Kemp said. "Trust me, you'll know when we're close to opening."

"I'll make sure of it," Loretta said, apparently well aware of her reputation as a gossip hound, and we all laughed. "Dotty's sitting all by herself over there. Why don't we go keep her company?" She directed the question to Kona.

"Of course. I could stand to rest my feet," Kona said, and they headed in Dotty's direction.

"What's up, Mr. Antisocial?" Holden said to Seth, who was still hanging back, texting away.

His only reply was a grunt.

Holden, Nick, and I shared a raised-brow look because that was more of a Cash response than a Seth one.

"You know you're at a party, right?" Nick asked. He and Seth had been friends since school, so it wasn't unusual for them to give each other a hard time.

Seth was silent for another few seconds as he typed something in, then he flashed a scowl at Nick. "Busy, in case you couldn't tell."

"Testy too," Nick said. "What's so important that you need to be a dick at your brother's reception?"

I was glad he asked. It wasn't like Seth to be grumpy or unsocial.

It took him another few seconds to answer, as he typed another something into his phone. "I've got some woman inquiring about renting the garage apartment." He'd been remodeling it for the past few weeks so he could rent it out.

"At nearly eleven p.m. on a Saturday?" Holden asked. "Haven't you had it listed for a couple of weeks without a single inquiry?"

Seth nodded, looking perplexed. "She wants to know if it's available tonight."

"Does she know it's a monthly rental and not a hotel?" Nick questioned.

"That was my first question. She said she'll pay for a month up-front. Didn't mention whether she planned to stay that whole time."

"That's pretty weird," Nick said. "Like run-a-background-check weird."

Seth shrugged. "If she needs a place to stay, she can have it as long as she follows the rules."

"Gotta admit I'm curious as hell," Nick said. "Woman on the run?"

"Maybe she robbed a bank," I said, grinning.

Holden laughed and said, "Maybe it's some hot chick who saw your photo on the restaurant website and needs a little lovin'."

"Fuck off," Seth said distractedly as he tapped in another

message. His frown deepened. "I'm going to have to take off. She's meeting me there in an hour and I need to make sure everything's in order."

"No nailing the renters," Nick said as Seth hugged me hurriedly.

"Thanks, Chloe. Great party. Sorry to run." He smacked Holden on the arm in a sign of brotherly love, then flipped Nick off before heading toward the front of the house, where the cars were parked.

Before we could think more of it, Adrian Cormier, the DJ, announced that he was playing the last slow song set of the evening, and that's all it took for butterflies to take off in my gut. It was time to carry out my plan.

"Dance with me?" I said to my husband.

"You know it." Holden took my hand and led me to the dance floor.

As we walked onto the wood platform, everyone made way for us to get to the middle, and all eyes were on us. Being the center of attention in this town no longer made me twitchy. In fact, every single set of eyes I spotted belonged to someone I felt comfortable with. Faye and Simon were there as well as all of the North guys and their wives. My parents were swaying together near the DJ's stand. Presley was dancing yet another song—she'd had no shortage of dance partners tonight—this time with Levi Dawson. A half-dozen other couples swayed to the slow beat, most of them grinning at us as if we were going to bust out in some awesome moves, but they'd be waiting multiple decades for that to happen.

Holden pulled me flush up against him, and like always, my whole body reacted. I wrapped my arms around his neck as his wound around my waist, and our lips met in a kiss. I kept it short, because I actually didn't want to draw attention to us at the moment. A private moment would've been better, but the party for our marriage just seemed like the appropriate place...

"I have the hottest dance partner here," he said so only I could hear.

I smiled. "No, I do."

He glanced around. "I'd cop to hottest of the males."

I laughed, even though I agreed with him completely. "If I told you a secret right now, could you avoid reacting to it, so no one else would notice?"

"A secret, huh? I might be able to."

I looked at the couples nearby. Loretta was dancing with Marty Grimstead not far away.

Shrugging, acting nonchalant, I said, "It's okay. It can wait if you're not up for it."

"I can avoid reacting," he said quickly, as I'd known he would. He was little-boy impatient about surprises, so naturally I loved to drag them out.

I let several lines of the song pass before I said anything.

"Chlo, you're being cruel. Don't make me tickle it out of you."

That was one threat I'd respond to every time, because I hated being tickled.

"Okay, okay." I made a show of glancing at the people around us again, then stood on my toes and said directly in his ear, "I told Presley she could move in with us."

I watched him closely for an obvious reaction. His steps slowed slightly, but only for about two beats, and then he caught himself. He opened his mouth. Closed it. Narrowed his eyes and peered into mine. "Into our house?" His brows dipped.

I pressed my lips together and nodded.

"I didn't know she needed a place to live," he said, looking as if he could be discussing the weather with me.

I had to give him props for the lack of reaction to news that I knew he didn't love. Then I laughed. "I'm kidding. Presley's not moving in with us."

His grin returned as he shook his head and tweaked the

spot on my side that he knew was incredibly ticklish. Just for an instant. Enough to pay me back without causing me to go into convulsions to avoid more tickling.

"You had me there for a second," Holden said.

Before he was over that, I stood on my toes again and said quietly, "The real secret is that we're having a baby."

His head whipped toward me and he stopped dancing. As I lowered from my toes, I met his wide-eyed, raised-brow gaze.

"You're not supposed to react," I whispered, urging him to move side to side. "It's *our* secret." I had to fight hard to stifle a grin.

"Hold up," he said, and he managed some dance-like motion, enough that maybe people wouldn't notice. "Are you kidding me?"

There was no sign of joy on his face; he'd gone dead serious. For the first time, I worried that maybe he wouldn't be happy about having a baby so soon. We'd only been married for two months. He was absorbed with getting the brewery off the ground. Parenthood would absolutely be a challenge on top of everything we had going on.

"I wouldn't kid about that," I said, my heart now racing for an altogether different reason—fear. I took in a shaky breath. "Are you..." I swallowed, thinking I had to be the densest girl on the planet to not have considered for a second that maybe my husband wouldn't be ecstatic. I closed my eyes, trying to grasp that possibility.

A hearty laugh from Holden had me opening them and peering up at him.

He threw his head back and let out a longer, fuller laugh.

"Are you... okay with that?" I asked stupidly, my heart starting to lighten before my brain could fully catch up.

Holden wrapped both his arms around me even tighter, then lifted me off the ground and whirled me around, and my relief burst out of me in the form of laughter.

I held on to him, fully aware that all eyes were on us. "You weren't supposed to react," I insisted, but I couldn't keep a straight face.

I'd had no illusions that our baby news would remain our secret—as long as Holden was happy about it. Keeping good news to himself was almost impossible for him. He'd nearly burst from waiting to tell Kemp about my investment when Kemp was out of town. The one thing that had kept him from spilling it in that case was that he wanted to celebrate with his partner in person. So I'd been certain, if I told Holden our baby news on the dance floor, that anyone who was still at the party would leave knowing it too. I'd gone into this completely okay with it, even though it was early—around six weeks.

He reined himself in for a moment, sobered up, lowered me to the ground, and looked into my eyes as if to verify that I meant it about keeping it private.

Which made me laugh. I loved this man with all of my heart, and I couldn't wait to watch him share the news. Could *not* wait to watch him be a dad.

Ignoring all the attention from our guests, he inhaled, looking as if he was going to try to play it off, as I'd requested. Which only made me love him more.

"You're serious though?" he asked, as if it was still sinking in. Without waiting for me to answer, he asked, "When are we due?"

Though he was holding me closer than before, he was almost—*almost*—managing to pull of the nonchalance I'd asked for now, swaying to the slow beat, nuzzling his nose into my hair.

"Early January, based on an online calculator. We'll know more when we go to a doctor."

"Are… are you okay with this? You've always been all about work."

"And then I married you," I said, "and I found out there's

so much more to life. I love our work, but I love our life together even more. I can't wait to have your baby, Holden Henry."

He pressed a kiss to my forehead. "But we can't tell anyone?"

I pulled back just enough to meet his eyes again. "Do you want to tell someone?"

"Chloe, darlin', I want to tell the whole fucking world." He leaned down and kissed my lips, and he put every bit of his excitement and love and over-the-top joy into that kiss. I liked to think I gave him the same.

He ended the kiss abruptly and said, "I love you like crazy, Chlo."

"I love you like crazy right back. And I knew—well, I hoped—that you'd be bursting with the news. I knew you'd want to let it out. So"—smiling, I nodded, my eyes damp— "let's tell everyone our news."

He picked me up again, whirled me around, and let out several howls and whoops, causing a complete, utter ruckus throughout our guests. Then he slid me down his body to the floor, grabbed my hand, and rushed to the DJ stand. He said something to Adrian, who nodded and handed him the mic. The music stopped mid-song.

"Hey, everyone," Holden said into the microphone as he pulled me against his side. "I wanted you all to be the first to know… Chloe and I are having a baby!"

Cheers went up all around, but I barely noticed, because Holden handed off the mic, turned to face me, took my face in both of his big, talented hands, and planted the sweetest, most passionate kiss on my lips.

All I could think at that moment was that, in this little town, in the arms of this gorgeous, loving man, with his baby growing in my womb, was exactly where I was meant to be.

NOTE FROM THE AUTHOR

Thanks for reading Unraveled! I hope you loved Holden and Chloe. Want to learn who Seth's mysterious renter is and what secrets she might be hiding? Find out in Unsung!

If you missed the North Brothers series, you can dive into book one, True North, in ebook format for free! Find out what happens when Mr. Socially Awkward spontaneously volunteers to be his beautiful boss's fake date.

Visit my direct author store at amyknuppbooks.com for details!

––––––––

If you liked *Unraveled*, I hope you'll consider leaving a review for it. Reviews help other readers find books and can be as short (or long) as you feel comfortable with. Just a couple sentences is all it takes. I appreciate all honest reviews.

––––––––

Unraveled is part of the Henry Brothers series, which includes:

- Untold (prequel)
- Unraveled
- Unsung
- Undone

The Henry Brothers series is a spin-off of the North Brothers series, which includes these stand-alone stories:

- True North
- True Colors
- True Blue
- True Harmony
- True Hero

ACKNOWLEDGMENTS

Many thanks to:

Jim Davies, my "fire guy," who helped with firefighting details and answered random, vague questions when I didn't know enough to ask more directly.

Sean Downey, my "beer guy" who was also patient with weird, vague questions about brewing and breweries and brewski.

Kay, Rachel, Meshanna, Kathy, Heather, and Lisa, my alpha and beta readers who are gracious in dealing with my last-minute scrambling and books missing epilogues and edits. I value every bit of your input and your enthusiasm.

Shayla, Sierra, and Jenna, heartfelt thanks for the hive-mind, the inspiration, and the sisterhood.

Natasha and Emily, who are the sisters I never had—and also brainstorm story details, help with blurbs, remind me I've got this when I'm sure I don't, cry with me, laugh with me, and save my soul with girl-time respites a few times a year.

My family: my mom, my boys, and my husband, who are my biggest supporters, who remind me I can do this on days when I don't think I can and celebrate with me on days that I do.